ALEX UNCHAINED
The Steak and Bourbon Series
Book 3

LAURA PRESLAN

Published by Advoture, Inc

Published by Advoture, Inc.
Cover design by Mila Book Covers

ISBN: 979-8-9915747-7-8

The Fondation Opportunité highlighted at the end of this book is a real organization and an excellent cause. Donations can be made at https://fondop.org/

Books by Laura Preslan

STEAK AND BOURBON SERIES

Julia Unleashed

Kate Released

Alex Unchained

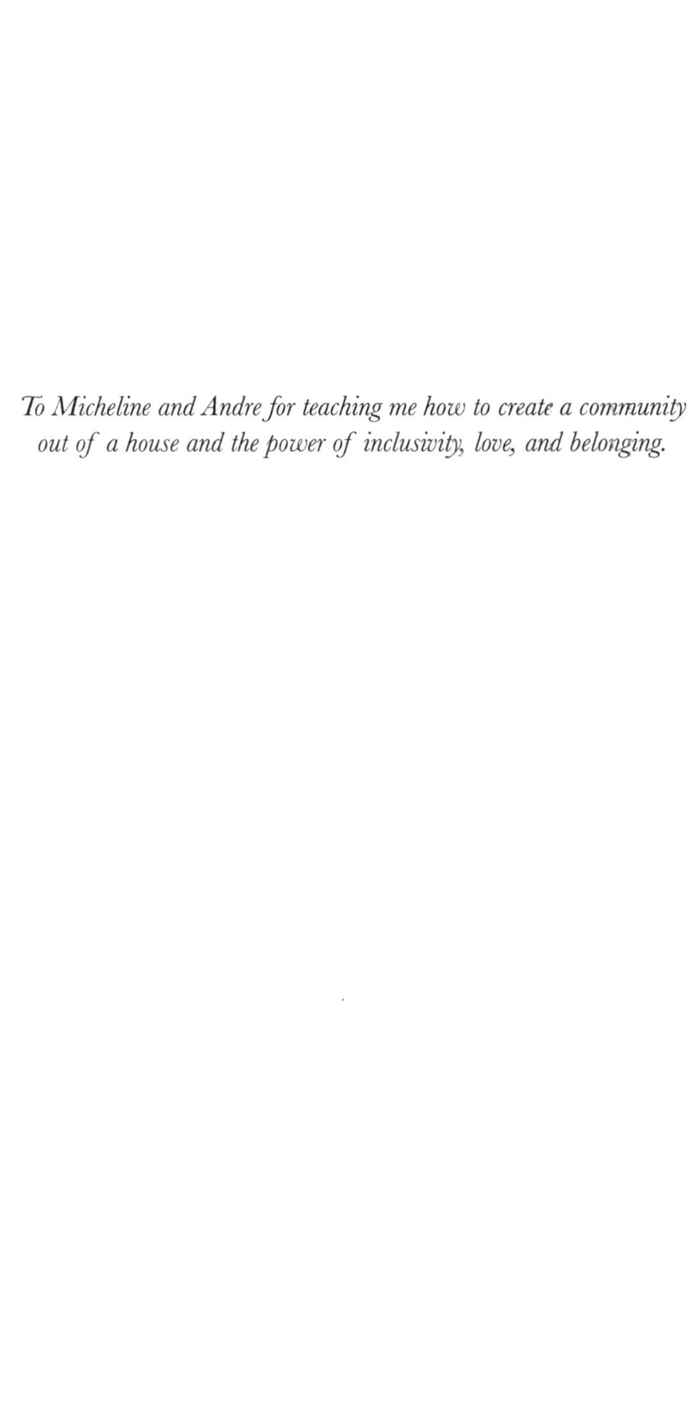

To Micheline and Andre for teaching me how to create a community out of a house and the power of inclusivity, love, and belonging.

Chapter 1

The vibrant chords of the fourth movement of Brahms' First Symphony enveloped Alex on stage as she delighted in adding her part to the rest of the string section. She let the warmth of the music fill her from head to toe, fully immersed in the moment.

This was her happy place. On stage, playing music from the Romantic period. She embraced the joy of the performance, knowing it might be a long time before she would play again.

She had followed her dream, attended music school, honed her craft, and shared her musical gifts with the world. Okay, maybe not the world, but the musical groups she could get into. She was a talented and musical bass player, but she was not the very best.

Alex was well known for being reliable and consistent, always nailing her part and following the conductor. You wouldn't think that was rare, but sadly for bass players, it was. She had made okay money doing studio sessions and leading the bass section in a few tier-two orchestras around

Seattle. She had gigged or rehearsed every day with maybe a day a month off. She loved it.

But then the pandemic hit. Live music dried up and there were absolutely no paying gigs. It had been a terrible time for the music industry and the performers already barely scraping by even before it happened. Many of her musical friends fared much worse than she did.

Four years later, she snuck gigs in at the last minute when an extra bass player was needed. She couldn't do her demanding corporate day job and commit to weekly rehearsals. She wished she could. But she needed the paycheck. And the benefits. She shuddered at the memory of being unemployed during the beginning of the pandemic, worrying that she wouldn't be able to pay for care if she contracted the initially scary disease.

Performances like this refilled her tank. She reveled in the soaring sound of the oboe solo in the second movement. She played her entrance with sensitivity, not covering the soloist but using a rich vibrato to add to the shimmery sound of the string section.

She was far away from her daily grind at LampLight. Not that she was sorry to have a corporate job – quite the opposite. If her friend and additional member of the bass section Julia hadn't gotten her a project coordinator role at LampLight four years ago, she never would have survived the pandemic.

Living in Seattle was expensive. She and her husband Tom had moved to the Pacific Northwest from New York City right after they got married in 2014. Tom had an amazing opportunity at an aerospace company. They hadn't really discussed marriage a lot – things were working for them in the big city. But then he got the job and asked her to come with him to Seattle. Tom's company paid for moves for employees and their *spouses*. Not employees and their *partners*. She and Tom went for it and got married in a small ceremony before heading to Seattle. That's how she rolled then. Her life philosophy had been more of a go-for-it than the wait-and-see approach she followed now.

They found a Craftsman-style house in a hilly neighborhood northwest of downtown. They were so happy. Alex had quickly made a name for herself in the local music scene and Tom had started moving up the ranks at his company. It had been the best time of her life.

And then Tom was killed in a car accident coming home late one night from work in January of 2019. The drunk driver fled the scene, but a witness had come forward and they caught the guy. The driver was so drunk he didn't even remember how he bashed in the front of his car.

It had been a dark time for Alex. She listened to the Mozart Requiem and *Good Morning, Heartache* over and over and cried herself to sleep for weeks.

Then she had to face reality.

Tom's salary had paid the mortgage. And for their health benefits. And for the cars. And for their lives.

She had received a small wrongful death insurance settlement and Tom's company had paid out his life insurance of six month's salary. They only had basic coverage. He was thirty-five when it happened. They hadn't thought much about insurance and a back-up plan.

Now she was all about what-ifs, planning, and monetary security.

Not able to work for six months due to her massive depression from losing her best friend and partner, Alex used up a good chunk of the cushion during her break from playing. Even when she started playing again, the money was short, and she didn't make enough to cover her expensive mortgage. She lived modestly and didn't have many expenses beyond her mortgage, her car, and groceries. But it still wasn't enough.

She was down to her last few thousand dollars when the pandemic hit. Her gigs dried up over the course of two weeks. And then that became six months. She had been talking to her friend Julia about potentially moving back to Boston and in with her grandmother when Julia jumped in to help. After an introduction to a hiring manager from Julia and several coaching sessions with members of her brunch group to help her translate her background managing orchestras into project management, Alex landed a project coordinator job at LampLight.

That's when Alexandra was born. Alex was a fun-loving musician. Alexandra was a hard-working no-nonsense employee. Using different versions of her name helped her remember that she was just playing a tempo-rary role in corporate life. *Or was she?*

Chapter 2

"Go go go!" Alex called after her dog. Sibby ran ahead to catch the ball Alex threw at the dog park near her little house. Alex adopted a pandemic puppy from the shelter and named her Sibelius after the composer of her favorite symphony. Of course, she was rarely called that. Instead it was Sibby, NoodleDog because she was long and thin, Puppins, or even Cuddle Muffin. Alex wasn't even sure her dog knew her actual name.

Sibby had helped Alex cope with the pandemic and gave her something to live for after her loss. Sibelius was supposedly a golden retriever and chow chow mix. She looked like a big Pomeranian. Her tongue was half pink and half purple, a clear indication she had one of the Chinese breeds in her.

It was raining, of course, since it was January in Seattle, so Alex took a moment to bundle her long black hair into a messy bun. She was used to the rain now and wore her contact lenses to avoid water drops on her favorite tortoise shell glasses.

Alex was not looking forward to her workday and was

happy to start at the park instead. It would be filled with calling people to ask about the status of their action items. She should be doing more. She should be back in the music scene. She should express herself more at work. This quiet, background, action-item-tracking mousy person was not her.

Alex knew exactly when she changed from a nervous little girl into a confident leader. She was on stage at age fifteen at a rehearsal of a youth orchestra. They were working on the Mozart Oboe Concerto. Alex sat first chair in the bass section – one of her very first leadership positions. There was an important bass part coming, loud and fast.

Unfortunately, Alex came in two measures early, right over an intricate run that the oboist was playing. The mistake was so bad that several members of the orchestra started laughing. The conductor, the famous Gôan Tjong, cut off the group. As the silence grew deafening, Alex shrunk, the heat of her embarrassment creating a blaze of red on her face. She was horrified by her mistake. Tears started leaking from the corners of her eyes.

In hindsight, she knew it was a complete overreaction. But in real time, she just wanted to melt into the stage and disappear. She prepared for a lecture, her head bowed.

"She's right," the maestro said to the tittering orchestra. Alex looked up to see the conductor looking right at her. Then he turned to the orchestra. "I would rather have you come in with confidence at the wrong place than miss your entrance because you lacked conviction. Thanks for being a leader, Alexandra."

Boom. Her moment of embarrassment turned into a triumph. And Dr. Tjong knew her name! Her shoulders went back up and she held her head high.

That sentiment became one of her most important

lessons and helped her lean in when others leaned back. It drove her to try new things and take risks. She would forever be grateful for that inspiration from Dr. Tjong.

He became a mentor to her. She looked up to him and learned a lot about leadership from watching him on the podium and seeing how he encouraged the orchestra. Because the youth orchestra was affiliated with one of the greatest professional orchestras in the world, many famous musicians and conductors visited rehearsals.

Alex remembered when another famous conductor and teacher of Dr. Tjong at Julliard came to visit and conduct the orchestra in a rehearsal.

Dr. Tjong was beside himself with excitement and treated his mentor with the utmost respect – even though Dr. Tjong had surpassed his teacher in fame and glory. Seeing such an amazing leader bow down to his own mentor was another great lesson for Alex. Always appreciate those who helped get you where you were. Stay humble and thankful.

She had performed this exact piece with that youth orchestra. Memories of Dr. Tjong and that group flooded her as the music swelled around her.

At the conclusion of concerts, the conductor often shakes the hands of the principals sitting in front of them – concertmaster, second violin, viola, and cello. Bass players are usually left out. But not with Dr. Tjong. He shook hands according to custom and then gave Alex a big wave from the podium. She always waved back, perhaps a bit unprofessionally, but she loved his proud smile when he congratulated her.

Thoughts of Dr. Tjong created conflicting and complicated emotions for Alex. When she was in college, she had gone to hear the New York Philharmonic when Dr. Tjong was the guest conductor. She was thrilled to see him again and loved watching him conduct the concert. He got a great sound out of the fabulous orchestra.

Long accustomed to walking backstage, Alex went in the stage door of Avery Fisher Hall to congratulate him and say hello after the concert. He was delighted to see her and asked her to have a late dinner with him after the performance.

A whole meal with Dr. Tjong's brilliance sounded amazing. They went to a Thai restaurant near Avery Fisher and had a wonderful conversation about his life and many achievements after being born on a small island in southeast Asia and becoming a famous pianist.

Alex had the chance to tell Dr. Tjong just how influential he had been for her when she was in high school.

They walked back to the hotel where Dr. Tjong was staying on the West Side. When Alex extended her hand for a handshake goodbye, Dr. Tjong grabbed her face in both hands and said, "I'm so glad we can do this now that you're old enough," and kissed her soundly on the mouth.

She tried to pull away, shocked at his action. "Dr. Tjong. No!" She didn't get very far because he was holding her face.

"Come up to my hotel room with me."

"Dr. Tjong, no." She spoke more gently, but the shock and horror were still alive inside her. She disentangled herself and all but ran away. She didn't look back to see his reaction. And she never saw him again after that.

It was amazing how someone could be so important in her life and also create such a painful, heart-breaking memory.

She tried to keep the two memories separate and distinct. She still valued him as a mentor and kept that separate from worries that he was a sexual predator.

She never talked about what happened because she

didn't want to tarnish his reputation or cause an issue for herself. Music was highly political and one famous conductor talking trash about a musician could end a career before it even started.

Of course, she blamed herself for giving him the wrong idea.

Alex wondered how many other young women had been victims of his. And also how many didn't fight him off.

The music world was such a political industry. And a sexist one.

Alex returned her full attention to the music. As she played a particularly difficult sixteenth note run that she loved, she reflected on Brahms and his imposter syndrome. Some say eleven years, and some say twenty, but it took him a long time to write and complete this symphony, often referred to as Beethoven's Tenth Symphony. Brahms was highly self-critical, like Alex, and had reworked and rewritten the symphony, concerned about not living up to the huge shadow Beethoven cast over him and other composers of the Romantic period.

No one could escape their demons.

Being a woman playing what had been a typically male instrument when she was a kid had given her a pretty big chip on her shoulder. In addition to the Dr. Tjong situation, Alex always did better in blind auditions when the musicians played behind a screen and the judges couldn't see them. She noticed it her sophomore year of high school at her first blind audition for all-state orchestra.

She was just glad to have been invited after being selected as principal in her regional orchestra. The judge had flown in to adjudicate the auditions and he used the blind approach. She got third chair, an amazing feat for a sophomore.

The following year, there was no sheet – it was a regular audition. She only got fifth chair against the same group of bass players minus two really great musicians who had graduated. It happened too many times for it to be random.

Sexism was rampant, especially for bass players and other instruments typically played by men. That's when she started going by Alex instead of Alexandra. They wouldn't know she was female until she showed up.

She had always fantasized that the business world was better. Fewer creative, emotional types. Advancement based on capability and not sexual favors. No blatant sexism.

She'd been pretty shocked when she found out that people were the same everywhere. But at least she was making money while dealing with it, unlike when she was a musician.

Four years had passed quickly. She couldn't believe it was 2024. She was in the thick of several gnarly projects, worked seventy hours a week, and didn't have much time for music.

It made her sad – until she got her paycheck every two weeks.

She'd been able to keep her house and her car. She even had enough money to share with other musician friends during the pandemic who didn't have fallback plans. Since Alex had lived in Boston and New York, she had a vast network of studio musicians, music teachers, and performers. She felt compelled to help them.

At LampLight, she could work half the hours she did as a musician and make five times more money. It wasn't all about the money, but it certainly helped.

She was too tired after work to pull her shit together and go to regular rehearsals. With Sibby to worry about, she couldn't just go from work to rehearsal. And there just wasn't enough time. She had a demanding boss, Michelle, who expected her to drop what she was doing in the evenings and deal with whatever request she had.

She didn't get the same feeling of accomplishment from creating a great action tracking dashboard. But she was building a nice monetary cushion.

Her grandmother, the woman who raised her, was getting older and her nursing pension was not quite enough to make ends meet. Alex sent money to her grandmother when she could. She had to keep working to be able to help Gram.

Her grandmother asked her not to, but Alex felt duty-bound to help her surrogate mother. Gram was too proud to ask for the help, but Alex knew she appreciated it.

Alex had to keep plugging away at LampLight to stash away enough money to protect herself from whatever happened in the future. Gram might need long-term healthcare. Alex might lose her job.

She didn't want to rely on her partner for financial support again, not that she had one. She had to do it all on her own. She was alone.

Chapter 3

"Did you catch that, Alexandra?" Michelle sounded impatient.

"Yes. Action item number twelve." Alex nodded her head and read it back for her boss. The meeting continued.

Michelle didn't mean to be so disrespectful. She just didn't understand how she came across.

Or at least that's what Alex told herself.

Alex knew her type. Michelle was a former ballerina. She liked precision in all things. She wanted everything done her way. Exactly her way.

Alex liked the way Julia explained Michelle to her. Julia knew Michelle wasn't a fabulous boss, but the position was open during the pandemic and Alex needed the money. She remembered Julia's description. "Michelle will ask you to make something that equals ten. When you show up with a solution that shows that three plus seven equals ten, Michelle will tell you she wants it to be five plus five because that's the best way to reach ten. You'll have to do it until it's five plus five. Even though she didn't tell you that from the start, and your solution was perfectly acceptable. To other people."

It was an apt description.

Alex had jumped on the opportunity anyway and would always be grateful to Michelle, even with all of her persnickety characteristics, for giving her the chance. It was the reason why Alex worked so many hours. She wouldn't have been given the opportunity without Julia and Michelle making it happen. She owed a lot to LampLight for saving her from the pandemic and she would work hard to prove they were right to do it.

Alex learned to ask Michelle exactly what she wanted rather than showing any creativity of her own.

While she was called a program manager, Alex's job felt more like checking other people's action items. She spent several hours a day reviewing various spreadsheets for updates on progress and another several hours sending reminder emails to people who had deadlines coming up or had missed one.

Shouldn't there be software to do this? she often wondered. Alex didn't understand why a global company like LampLight paid people to check boxes, but she loved her paycheck.

She made it through another long day of action item checking and drove home before traffic got too bad. The pandemic had certainly given her more freedom to work at home, but they had been called back into the office at least two days a week.

Working at home had been amazing, but it also meant that Alex had created pretty poor boundaries. It was like she lived at work rather than worked at home. It seemed normal for her team, and it had been her first corporate gig, so she went with the flow.

. . .

ALEX PULLED down the tiny driveway next to her cozy house. She was lucky enough to have a single car detached garage. She and Tom had added a small studio onto it, just big enough for her to teach bass lessons in and connected it to the house with a breezeway. Alex didn't have to deal with the near-constant Seattle rain from October to June when loading and unloading her bass and she had a place to teach and practice.

Tom. She missed him so much. Her friend. Her partner. They had been really good together. Sure, they had their arguments, but they agreed on just about everything.

They had a practice of never going to bed angry. They used to joke that you never knew what would happen, and if one of them died in their sleep, their last words shouldn't be said in anger.

Alex remembered the day she got the call. She had been at a rehearsal of Bruckner's Fourth Symphony. She had never cared for Bruckner, and she didn't really know why. She chalked it up to the bombastic – and at least to her – overly-dramatic flourishes that he favored. When she checked her messages during the break, there was a call from the hospital where Tom had been taken.

He had still been alive when the message had been left twenty minutes earlier. She quickly packed up her bass and raced to the hospital.

She should have just left everything at rehearsal and taken a cab. By the time Alex had parked and gotten inside, Tom was gone.

The nurse on duty gently told her he was brain dead when he came in. She wouldn't have been able to talk to him even if she had received the message when they called.

But at least she would have been able to hold his hand one last time.

She cried every time she thought of him lying in that

hospital bed alone. She tried to take comfort in the fact that he basically died at the scene and probably couldn't feel the pain, but it was still so hard.

She avoided concerts when Bruckner was on the program.

She grabbed her computer bag off the front seat of her little hatchback and went inside. Her dog greeted her with excitement. She let Sibby out into the postage-stamp sized backyard to do her business.

Alex was lucky she'd been able to keep the house. Most of her friends lived in small condos or apartments with no yard at all. A feeling of gratitude filled her as she got Sibby's dinner together.

For her own dinner, she pulled some leftover containers out of the fridge and plopped them unceremoniously in the microwave. When Tom was alive, she cooked for them, usually before heading to a rehearsal or a gig. She had loved taking care of him as her part of the marriage bargain. He made the money, and she kept the house.

It felt very nineteen fifties except that she would leave six nights a week. They didn't see each other much but always tried to have dinner together even if it meant Tom had to make an excuse at work at leave at 4:30. It worked for them. Really well.

She scooped the warm butter chicken and rice onto her dish and headed out to her usual spot in front of the television. She turned on the series she was watching while she ate, keeping one eye on her phone for messages from Michelle.

She was lonely.

January marked five years since Tom's death. She knew she should move on. Her friends made sure she didn't feel isolated during the pandemic, but with things moving back to normal for most people, she heard from them less than she had. It was understandable – they were getting back to their regular lives, just like she should.

The orchestra she used to play with was rehearsing right this moment, just a few blocks away. She should be there.

She didn't want to become one of those people who became obsessed with their dogs and work and just stayed home all the time. She was only thirty-six. She could find love again.

She just didn't know where.

Chapter 4

Alex didn't want to be with people anymore that day. She had pushed it out of her mind to focus on work, but the sadness kept pressing in on her, crawling through her veins.

The only way through was to embrace it.

Tom would have been forty today.

She had already exchanged texts with his mom to help her get through it. His mom had pretty much broken things off with Alex when Tom died. They liked each other well enough, but Patty told her she reminded her of Tom's death so they couldn't have a relationship.

She wasn't too broken up about it because they had never really been friends anyway.

It was a bit maudlin, but Alex had bought a cupcake and put a candle on it. "Happy birthday, Tommy." She blew it out.

Sensing her sadness, Sibby put her head on Alex's leg.

She laid her hand on the dog's warm head for comfort. Alex watched the single line of smoke snake toward the ceiling. Tears spilled down her face when she looked up.

Sibby snuggled closer. Alex clutched her dog and

indulged in a good cry. This wasn't the way it was supposed to be. They should be planning vacations together and arguing about whose family they would visit for the holidays.

Instead, she was alone crying with her dog.

Alex didn't believe in the afterlife. But just in case, she wanted Tom to know she still thought of him every day. "Every day, baby," she said out loud to the dark room.

If Tom could see her now, he wouldn't like what he saw. Sad and crying. That's not what he would have wanted for her. It was almost like he was talking to her. She heard the words as clearly as if he were in the room. "It's okay. Get back out there. You have so much love to give. Find someone to give it to."

She had felt like she heard him before. Those times, his words were "I'm sorry." This time, they were different. Encouraging. Forward-looking. *Brains are funny things*, she thought.

She knew he wasn't speaking to her from beyond the grave. Her mind was just telling her what she wanted to hear.

But maybe, just maybe, she should listen.

She wasn't doing herself any favors being alone. Was five years enough time to process his death and be ready for something new? She just didn't know. "How will you know if you don't try?" Tom had said to her when they had first talked about moving to Seattle. And when he had proposed. And when she had a big audition. It was one of his catch phrases. And just like those times, he was right.

Her phone rang. She checked the number and was happy to see that it was her grandmother. The woman who had raised her after her mother had died from a drug overdose shortly after Alex was born. She didn't know her father.

"Gram!" Alex exclaimed into the phone.

"I thought you might need a little cheering up today." She was starting to sound old. Not the vibrant woman Alex grew up with. She was eighty-three after all.

"Thanks for remembering, Gram."

"We all miss him, love. Remember how your grandfather would tease him?"

"Oh gosh, I remember when he came over to meet you both. When we got up to leave the table after dinner, Pops told him to leave the whipped cream on the table."

Gram's warm laugh flew over the line from Boston. "He was such a character." She paused and the silence stretched out. Alex thought about Pops. "I hope you're not sitting there being sad."

"I was until you called, Gram."

"We've both had some tough losses, but life has to go on."

"I miss Pops so much. And Tom, too."

"We both do, sweetheart, but you have to keep going. It'll get easier. There's always a way." That was Gram's mantra. *There was always a way.*

"It's been five years since Tom died. Three since we lost Pops." Alex trailed off.

"Yes, and we don't honor them by moping and being sad. The Potawatomi were the fire people. Not only did they tend the fire, but they honored it because it was pure. Be the fire and light, just like Pops wanted. You'll find your way, Little Eagle."

Pops was from the Potawatomi tribe of Native Americans. His Native name was William Flying Eagle. Pops left his small tribe in Michigan after high school and headed to Boston for college where he met Gram, and they settled in the outskirts of Boston to raise their daughter and two sons.

To honor his Native name, Pops called Alex Little Feather. She always loved it when he told stories about his elders and their traditions.

She got her musical inspiration and probably her skills from her grandfather. He liked to say that singing, dancing, and drumming were the ways that his tribe expressed themselves. She could hear his deep, sonorous voice in her head. "This is not a hobby for us. It is our heritage. As a Native person, your identity comes from how you express yourself in music and dance and what you create through it."

When she was little, she asked him why her skin was darker than most of the other kids, but not as dark as her friend Lily's. He told her it was because she was part Native American. "I am of the Potawatomi tribe, and you carry that blood. But you are also white. That makes you part Native, or Partawatomi." She remembered his deep chocolatey laugh.

Alex fingered the charm on the necklace her grandfather had given her when she left for college. It was about the size of a nickel and was made of silver. One side had the outline of flames. The other had the word *bodwadan* engraved on it. He told her it meant "the fire she lights."

She always wore it along with a gold necklace with a small gold charm Tom had given her. It was like a little blob. They used to joke about what it was. A meteorite, an ink blot, a crumb of cake?

Gram's voice pulled her back to the present. "It's late here, and you know I like my programs, so I'll let you go. Be happy, Little Feather. You know they both want that for us."

"Thanks for the call, Gram. We'll talk soon."

Gram was right. She needed to move on with her life. Stop grieving the past.

How would she know if she was ready if she didn't try? She was comfortable with the life she had made for herself. Comfortable, but not happy.

She dried her tears, determined to get out there. *But how?*

There was always a way.

Chapter 5

That Sunday, Alex drove her hatchback up the hill to Julia's welcoming house. Julia was back to hosting her monthly Steak and Bourbon brunches. Everyone agreed to take a Covid test before coming to brunch to ensure they weren't spreader events. So far, no cases had been traced back to brunch.

Alex had missed last month's brunch because she had Covid. Michelle insisted on an in-person meeting and half the team got sick. She was glad to be healthy and on her way to this month's brunch. She needed the infusion of positive female energy.

She didn't recognize the dog who greeted her at the door when she walked in.

"Okay, Zillah, that's enough." Julia rushed to calm the barking dog. "Welcome, Alex!" The yellow dog sat dutifully by her owner and lifted a paw at Alex.

"Aren't you pretty," Alex said shaking the offered paw. The dog looked like a German Shepherd but was blond all over. Alex noted that one ear was slightly shorter than the other like it had been cut off in an injury. It changed her look from fierce to cuddly.

"This is Zillah. We got her last month at the shelter and she's still learning her manners."

"Aren't we all." Alex tucked her long black hair behind her ear and followed Julia into the dining room. Zillah trotted along beside her. Several ladies were already sampling cheese from the appetizer plate.

"What're you drinking?" Melanie asked from the buffet table set up with a mimosa bar. "The bubbly with a splash of blood orange juice and grapefruit juice is my current favorite." She tapped her manicured fingernail against the champagne flute.

"That sounds lovely, Mel. Would you mind mixing one up for me?"

"Not at all, I'm here to serve." Melanie's short blond and brown hair poked out in all directions, reflecting her bouncy and optimistic approach to life.

Alex accepted the glass. She knew the rules. Get a drink and then mingle for a bit before glorious food made its way from the kitchen to the buffet table.

"Al! Get your scrawny ass over here for a hug." Gertie was a lawyer who had helped Kate, another brunch attendee who was now a best-selling author, get out of a tough situation at LampLight. Alex obeyed. Everyone was a little afraid of Gertie.

"Hey Gertie. So good to see you." Alex met Gertie's penetrating blue eyes, feeling a bit like she was being studied under a microscope.

A shout came from the kitchen. "Is that my girl Alex?" Angela bolted from the kitchen to embrace Alex, her long locs trailing behind her. "Give mama a hug. I haven't seen you in ages." It had only been two months. Angela was prone to exaggeration.

"Lady Ange, how are you?" Alex leaned in for an embrace. "You look fabulous." Alex took in Angela's dark skin and flashing eyes. "As always."

"Collagen. It's a miracle." Angela pointed a finger at her ebony cheek. "And of course, black don't crack."

Alex and Angela had a special bond. Angela was a singer who also had a day job. She understood the intricacies of balancing both. Her husband Jeremy was also a musician with a full-time job at LampLight.

"Okay, ladies, let's get this brunch going." Julia carried a hot frittata in each hand and set them on the warming trays already set up in the dining room. "Two frittatas on the buffet. Regular bacon and pepper bacon there too." She pointed with her now empty hands. "Waffles are in the third dish with two kinds of syrup in the little pitchers. Salad's on the table along with the currant scones, lemon curd, and clotted cream. There's a fruit salad that you can eat by itself or put on the waffles."

The ladies headed to the buffet to load up.

"Brie, the waffles are gluten free for you." Julia accommodated everyone's dietary restrictions. "They're made with rice flour."

"Thanks Jules. You always take good care of us." Brie's tie-dyed silk garment wafted in the breeze as she moved. Brie saw Alex eyeing her ensemble. "You like these?" She flipped her long blond hair behind her shoulder and struck a pose. "I call them my clown-eralls. They're like overalls but silky and fun colors. So good."

"Comfy-looking and stylish." Alex approved. "And the colors make your tats pop." Brie held her full sleeve of tattoos in front of her with a flourish.

By the time the first group went through the line, the rest of the attendees had arrived. Lesley, Kate, and

Margaret joined Julia, Alex, Brie, Melanie, Angela, and Gertie at the table.

"Where's Akiko?" Lesley looked fabulous as always in her flowy leopard print shirt. Her hair was back to its glorious wavy long length after growing it out after a particularly severe haircut a few years before.

"Down with the 'rona," Julia explained. "She hopes to be here next time."

They grabbed their food while Julia opened another bottle of champagne and brought out a coffee pot.

Brunch always reminded Alex of her grandmother's house. Gram didn't have much money, but she had inherited her mother's china and silver. They were prized possessions that came out every holiday and were then hand washed and carefully repacked in the small china cabinet in the dining room.

"AND THEN MR. MAN was all up in my business like he still thought we would get busy after that." Angela shook her head as she told the story of her husband Jeremy and his latest antics.

Alex wished Tom had still been here. He loved Angela and Jeremy. They were fun, lively, and musical. She missed their double dates.

"Thanks for the timing of this month's Steak and Bourbon brunch," Melanie said. "I've been missing my girls and your positive energy."

"To Steak and Bourbon." They all lifted their glasses.

"I told my husband I couldn't do something with him today because I would be here. I love him, but it comes down to this. Ladies, you're the ones who would come to the hospital if I was in a coma and tweeze my speaker wires when I couldn't do it myself."

Angela made tweezer motions with her fingers. "We got you, Mel."

"That's the definition of real friendship right there." Lesley nodded.

"Yeah, that's especially relevant since mine are starting to come in." Brie stroked her chin. "I guess that's what happens when you join the forty club."

"Welcome! At fifty, you can look forward to tweezing every day." Julia smiled amidst her sarcasm. "I have vivid memories of my mother sitting on the sofa with her mouth pulled to the side to stretch the skin on her chin while looking in the magnifying mirror perched on the end table and tweezing chin hair. I hate turning into my mother!"

Everyone laughed.

Except for Alex.

"Why so glum there, Al?" Aside from being hard core, Gertie was also observant.

"Sorry. It's nothing. I was just having a Tom moment. He would have turned forty this past week."

An awkward silence followed. Alex wished she hadn't been so transparent, but these were her closest friends, and she could just be herself.

"Is it time to get back into the dating scene?" Lesley asked gently, never shying away from pointed questions.

"Les! That's a bold move given she just said she's sad." Brie chided Lesley. She was the kindest in the group.

"No, it's okay." Alex smiled. "I know I should get back out there. It's just hard. Tom was my best friend. He still has part of my heart. It wouldn't be fair to someone else to try a relationship when I can't give it my all."

Gertie slapped the back of her hand into the palm of the other. "You can be sad and still get dicked. You don't have to choose just one." She pointed with each word.

"That's top-notch advice right there. Top. Notch." The ladies laughed.

"How long's it been now, four years?" Julia asked.

"January marked five years, but some days it feels like yesterday. Others, it seems like forever ago that we were laughing together."

"That sounds tough." Angela took her hand. Alex appreciated the outreach. Not being touched by anyone was surprisingly hard for her. "Honey, we got to get you a date."

You didn't argue with Angela once she made a statement. You just didn't.

"Yeah, you need to smack those cheeks." Alex wasn't even sure what Gertie meant, but it felt good to laugh about it with her friends.

"What do you want in a new man?" Margaret asked, her full head of chestnut hair bouncing in her excitement. "And none of that not being picky because we're old shit. Be picky. He's out there." Her freckles danced with her smile.

"Okay, um, stability is important." Alex thought about it. "I don't really care about looks. I like tall, at least taller than me. If he were musical, that would be a plus. I like to laugh. No kids, unless they are sixteen and up and I don't have to raise them. Has to like dogs, or at least my dog."

"That's a pretty good list. Why don't you stop there." Angela looked around the table. "Ladies, who do we know who's single, funny, musical, tall, and stable? Pick three of those traits and let's get some names. Julia, we're gonna need some paper, a pen, and a bowl."

Julia gathered the requested items as the conversation continued.

"My male friends are single for a reason." Brie joked,

but she sounded serious. "They're lovely to hang out with, but I wouldn't date any of them."

"How do we feel about recently divorced?" Margaret asked.

"How recently? Like, they've been separated for six months or they're thinking about breaking up?" Alex was good with some baggage but not loads of drama.

"Divorced two years ago after she cheated on him. Gabe doesn't talk about her much which might mean some issues."

"We all have issues," Lesley added. "Some are just more challenging than others. I say add him to the bowl!"

Kate made the next recommendation. "James has a really nice friend named Ross. He's tall, a little goofy – in a good way – and was single last time I checked. He's a data scientist and loves Excel. I don't know if he plays an instrument, but he sings."

"Contender! Write his name down and put it in." Angela pointed to the bowl Julia had placed on the table.

"Ross always brings a different person to your parties, Kate. What's up with that?" Gertie asked around a mouthful of waffles.

"Ross has terrible taste in women. He tends to pick beautiful, high maintenance women who boss him around. He likes powerful women, which is great, but he gravitates toward the ones who manipulate him rather than champion him. He needs someone like Alex to *respect* him while she tells him what to do." Kate laughed as she said it.

"Is Ross the one who always sings *Africa* at your parties, Kate?" Alex asked.

"The one and only."

"I've talked to him a few times. But yeah, he was always with a date, so I never turned on the dating material radar. That, and I wasn't really interested in dating again until now."

Alex's mind wandered thinking about Ross. After Kate left LampLight, she and James had more time on their hands and started throwing epic karaoke parties two or three times a year. Alex's rockabilly band had played one time to make it live band karaoke. The highlight for Alex was when Angela grabbed the microphone out of the lead singer's hand during *Ain't No Sunshine* and sang it like it was supposed to be sung. The lead singer had never gotten over it, but Alex understood. When someone is butchering a song you love, instinct takes over.

"Come on, we need some more names." Angela broke into Alex's reminiscences.

"What about that cute oboist Adam who plays like a dream?" Julia suggested. "His solo in Tchaikovsky's Fifth Symphony almost brought me to tears."

"Do we know if he's single?" Angela was all business. "He might be married."

"That's a hurdle, not a wall." Gertie's delivery was deadpan. She got a few odd looks from the group.

"Definitely a wall in my world." Alex nodded her head with finality.

"Just sayin'." Gertie shrugged.

"He might not even be straight. I'll do some digging." Julia picked up her phone to text him.

"There's this guy." Alex couldn't believe she had said that. Eight women leaned forward. "Cameron. He was a friend of Tom's at work. He's checked up on me a few times, and I always get the feeling he's looking for a little more."

"Boom chicka wow wow." Angela bobbed her head back and forth.

"Would that be awkward, or would you be okay dating

Tom's friend?" Julia wasn't afraid to ask the uncomfortable question either. One of the many reasons these Streak and Bourbon brunches were good for Alex's soul.

"You mentioned him, so there must be a little sumpin' sumpin' there." Angela pointed her fingers and made a little jabbing motion.

She made a good point. Alex must have been subconsciously considering him if his name popped into her head like that.

"Single!" Julia yelled out waving her phone. "And Adam is interested in meeting you, Alex. He's seen you at a few rehearsals and remembers you."

"Whoa, you're moving a little fast here."

"No she's not." Melanie shook her head and pointed at Alex with her fork. "We're on a mission."

Angela was focused. "My man Ty plays guitar in one of the bands I sing back-up in. Not so sure on the stability front, but he dances well and can groove like a motherfucker, so I bet he's good in the sack."

"I forgot that quality on the list."

"That's okay, because it would be weird if we could answer that about our friends." Margaret made a good point. "Although…" she trailed off, tapping her index finger to her lips thoughtfully. Everyone laughed again.

"You must have someone in your network." At Gertie's statement, all eyes went to Julia. "Cough 'em up."

"Some of you may remember my friend Carlos. We met at the dog park. Last I heard, he's still single."

"Oh yeah, back-up plan guy." Brie nodded.

"Don't call him that. He's actually really nice even though I chose Rob over him."

"In the bowl," Angela demanded.

Alex counted six names. "I can't date six men."

"Oh yes you can!" Margaret's eyebrows wiggled.

"I'm *not* dating six people at the same time. I can barely remember my own name sometimes, let alone six others."

"Okay, okay." Lesley waved her hands in a way that said everybody should calm down. "Alex, you're going to pick two names out of the bowl. That'll give you three choices since Adam is already on the hook."

Alex rummaged around in the bowl and pulled out a slip of paper.

"Gabe."

"I'll see if he's interested and will text an intro if he's in." Margaret picked up her phone. "No time like the present."

"One more." Melanie made drum roll sounds on the table with her fingers.

"Tyler."

"My sweet baby Ty." Angela nodded her head.

"The guitarist. Nice." Brie seemed happy that a musician made it.

Angela got out her phone. "I'll do the same thing as Margaret and text an intro. But before I do that, here are the rules." Angela leaned forward. "Before next month's brunch, I want you out on a coffee or happy hour date with each of them. You can report back to the group to see who has made the cut and pick another name if you rule anyone out."

Chapter 6

Alex settled into the chair in the conference room after plugging her laptop in. She had finally mastered the elaborate conferencing technology and had the presentation loaded for Michelle. All systems go!

LampLight had a very complex set of products and required multiple specialists to get involved in almost every deal. One person couldn't learn enough to answer all of the customers' questions. Alex knew that because she tried to teach it to herself. She had taught herself to play the accordion, for fuck's sake. She should have been able to understand the sales process from the one hundred and ten slide deck she read.

And re-read.

They had clearly put a lot of Type A control freaks onto the team to define the process and they all vied for control of the strategy. The result was a confusing mass of roles, responsibilities, and overlap. The project that Michelle was currently leading was designed to fix it. The word of the day was simplify.

Alex felt like they didn't know what that word actually meant.

This new plan was supposed to clearly delineate roles. Since everyone had their own taxonomy for sales, there were over thirty roles who could be involved in any given sale. Mass confusion.

This made her miss her music time. In an orchestra, jazz band, or even a combo, everyone knew their part. The second chair violinist didn't challenge the concertmaster for control over bowings. Each section had a leader, and the rest of the section followed their lead.

Simple.

Sure, there were challenges, but even when she was improvising in a jazz combo, there were rules. The singer was always right. Even if they sang at the wrong time, you skipped to where they were.

You played more quietly and without too much flash during other people's solos. You expected everyone to show up at rehearsal knowing their part and playing the shit out of it at the performance.

You listened to each other and responded in real time.

In orchestras, there were usually four movements. You played them in order. No one ever said, "Hey, let's play the third movement first." No! You played them as written.

Not so in the sales world. In-fighting, specialists wanting to sell their product first even when the customer had a different priority, and lack of understanding of each other's goals and the customers' needs was rampant.

And everyone spoke in sports analogies. The lead sales rep was the quarterback. Yeah, well, Tom made her watch enough football that even she knew a quarterback was only on the field with the offense. That made no sense when they were supposed to always lead.

This meeting was no exception. She started

daydreaming about how she would fix it. Maybe a music analogy would be better than a football one.

She could call the leader the conductor. Everyone followed the conductor, or the orchestra wouldn't play together.

She noodled on the concept while others droned on about how important their particular team was.

She continued musing. If the lead was the conductor, the sales methodology would be the orchestration. And the sales plan for what they would sell would be the arrangement. Each specialist team would be a section, like the flutes or the violins. And then each part would be an individual seller's role. That really worked because everyone had a different part. But classical music was not all that well known.

What if she tried jazz?

The lead seller would be the band leader. There would still be a chart, or song they were playing. The band leader would pick the order of the solos. Everyone had their own written part but some, especially the rhythm section of bass, drums, guitar, and keyboard, would improvise behind the soloist, supporting and helping them shine. Yeah, the sales team was a jazz band.

Alex's PowerPoint skills were not on par with the rest of the program managers, so she would describe it and then painstakingly create it in PowerPoint if people agreed. Or maybe she could just write it out in Word and let others make it pretty.

She tuned back into the meeting.

"Yeah, so the quarterback picks the plays and then the players do what they say." Eugene was working hard to make the analogy work.

"Then what do we call the special teams? The kicker doesn't do what the quarterback tells them." Michelle was getting into it. Alex was extra impressed that Michelle's brain could function with her hair pulled back into a severe ballerina-style bun all the time.

"We can call the salesperson the coach."

Everyone looked at Tanja. Alex read the annoyance on their faces.

"The coach is never actually on the field. That would suggest that the seller stays on the sidelines. No way." Eugene was dismissive.

"I'm from Germany. I don't understand American, football and neither will two-thirds of the audience." Tanja didn't budge.

"People, can't we just overlook the weaknesses of the metaphor and get on with the model?" Michelle was getting impatient, as usual.

"Uh, no. That's why we're stuck." Eugene's tone bordered on disrespectful to his boss.

"Yeah, Eugene. If we can't figure it out, how can we expect complicated sales teams with competing priorities to figure it out?" Alex tried to support Eugene.

"Yeah, it has to be dead simple." Eugene said the word of the day… again.

"Anyone else have an idea here?" Michelle sounded exasperated.

Alex was just a lowly program manager, faking her way in the techie corporate world, but she pretended she was on stage and went for it. She was playing the part of Alexandra, corporate wonk. "What if we use a musical analogy?" Alex walked through her approach.

At first, she was met with silence when she finished. Then Michelle chimed in.

"I love that, Alexandra. And then everything is orchestrated."

Michelle was misusing that word in a musical context.

Alex started to explain and then thought better of it. She let the conversation continue, only adding color commentary to further the discussion. It was still better than a sports analogy.

"Alexandra, could you write that up for us? I know you're a program manager and you should leave it to the strategists to do that, but I think you'll be able to handle it."

Alex chose to be complimented and ignored the jab.

"On it, boss." Alex had a full afternoon of checking in with people on action items. And she would be working late again to get this done, but it was important to move the conversation forward.

Also, she hated that most of her job as a program manager was making sure other people were doing their work.

She preferred to create something. Like a great performance.

ALEX SLOGGED through the first version of the model that night over some take-out Thai food after indulging in a walk with Sibby.

By about nine o'clock, she had taken the document as far as she could. Too tired to practice, she flipped the TV on and started thinking about her upcoming date.

Alex hadn't been on a date in over ten years. Not since she went on her first date with Tom in 2013. A lot had changed since then. She had changed since then. She was thirty-six. Not the perky little pixie she had been. Who was she kidding? She had never been a perky pixie.

Her first date was a Sunday coffee date with Tyler, the guitarist. Tuesday, she was meeting Adam on the one night he didn't have a rehearsal that week. She didn't know much about either of them, but with Angela and Julia giving them their stamps of approval, they were probably not serial killers. Or at least known serial killers.

What did you wear to a Sunday coffee date in February? Seattle weather was mercurial at that time of year, but it would likely be raining.

She felt like Tyler was doing her a favor going out with her, so she suggested a coffee place in his neighborhood.

How bad could it be?

Chapter 7

Alex walked into the cafe armed with a picture of Tyler and Angela on stage. The smell of coffee wafted to her along with the chatter from several groups of people. Most of the tables were taken, either by one of those groups or by stern-looking household escapees with earbuds and huge coffees trying to block out the world.

She didn't see Tyler. Should she get a coffee or wait for him? She didn't want the baristas to think she was a freeloader, just sitting there not ordering anything. She texted Tyler.

Alex: I'm here. What's your coffee order?

Tyler: Tall half caf w/2 Splendas, shot of vanilla. Be there soon.

That was a lot to process. He didn't want too much caffeine. He tried to balance out the sweet syrup with fake sweetener. Weird. She placed the order and waited for it to be ready.

A couple of minutes went by. In the interval, a few

tables opened up. She grabbed one and took the seat that faced the door.

Another ten minutes went by.

She hated cold coffee, so she started drinking her cup of black drip. As the taste hit her, dark and hot, she thought of her ordering issues when it came to coffee. In New England a regular coffee is milk and two sugars. In New York City, if you ordered a regular coffee, it was black. That had taught her to be specific in how she ordered whenever she moved.

She didn't know what a regular coffee was in Seattle. Maybe it was a tall half caf with sweetener and vanilla. *Doubtful.*

Another few minutes went by. Alex was glad she had texted Tyler for that coffee order. Otherwise, she wouldn't know he was on his way, and she would think she was being stood up. Not a great way to restart her dating life.

The door opened for about the seventh time, and Tyler was there. He was tall and wore glasses. He had a bit of a pooch she assumed came from beer. His light brown hair flopped over his forehead. He had a nice smile. They made eye contact. "Tyler?" she asked.

"No, I'm Damian."

"Oh." Alex was embarrassed. He looked like the guy in the picture. "Sorry."

"Blind date, huh?' he said.

"Yeah. At least I think so."

"Gotcha! I'm Tyler. Sorry I'm late. Is that my coffee?" He took the seat across from Alex. "Did Angela warn you about me?"

"Uh, no." Alex was really confused. *Why would he try to trick her and what should she have been warned about?* she wondered.

"You're a bass player, right?"

"Yes." Alex looked at him cautiously, wondering where he was going with his question.

"How many bass players does it take to change a lightbulb?"

"How many?" She restrained herself from rolling her eyes.

"None. The piano player does it with his left hand." Tyler laughed at his joke. A little too hard. Alex had heard that one a million times. A piano player's right hand usually played the melody while the left hand played the bass part. Hardy har har.

The joke triggered her mean side. "You play the guitar, right?" He nodded. "How do you get a guitarist to turn down?"

"We never turn down. We love it loud." Alex waited a beat. "How?" Tyler asked.

"Give 'em a chart." Alex raised one eyebrow and looked at Tyler.

"I don't get it," he said.

Alex flushed with embarrassment. She had over-estimated his musical knowledge. She didn't want to sound like a music snob. "You know, because most guitarists don't read music and play really loudly," she explained, absently fingering her necklaces. "If you give them music to read, they can't, so they turn down."

"Ha! I actually got it. I'm just messing with you."

Alex didn't like Tyler. She was down for a good joke, but not repeatedly at her expense.

"Dude, what's your deal?" she asked.

"My deal? I get nervous on dates. And then I try to be funny. It usually goes downhill from there." He grimaced. "I don't get a lot of second dates."

Alex reached for optimism. "Could we start again?" He

nodded and sipped what she assumed was now lukewarm coffee. "How long have you known Angela?"

"Ange? She started singing with us three years ago. Maybe four. We have a revolving door of lead singers. Angela sings back-up but will help out on lead at rehearsals."

"Why do your singers leave so often?" It was not a good sign for a band when singers left. It changed the whole sound of the group, and you had to get used to a whole new attitude from the next singer.

"Because they're singers. They're flaky. They warm up by singing do re me me me me me it's all about me." He imitated singing a major scale like "doe, a deer" in *The Sound of Music*.

Alex didn't like his blanket negativity toward an entire segment of performers. She sighed. "I don't think this is going to work."

"Yeah, I'm not surprised." His shoulders slumped. "You all say that."

Poor Tyler, she thought. "At least we can finish our coffee."

"Why? I guess I'll just use my left hand… or my right."

"Ewww." Alex looked at him like her brunch friend Melanie did when she said "rude."

Tyler grabbed his cup and left.

Alex just sat with her mouth open for a moment.

What the Hell was that? At least she had a story for the Steak and Bourbon crew.

SHE STILL HAD MOST of Sunday afternoon to relax and unwind. Maybe she would go catch a concert. Or maybe just chill with Sibby. They hadn't been over to the dog park on Mercer Island in a while. Maybe Julia was around, and

Zillah would like some socialization. Alex decided to go for it and texted her mentor and friend.

Alex: Up for some doggie play time on Mercer Island?

Julia: That would be great. Zillah is already tired from a romp this morning, so it's a great chance for socialization. Time?

Alex: Any

Julia: Aren't you supposed to be on a date?

Alex: Over

Julia: Cool. See you in 20?

Alex: Perfect

Alex got to the parking lot of the dog park. Sibby knew exactly where she was and was incredibly excited, wagging her fuzzy body from head to tail. Julia pulled in shortly afterwards. The two dogs hadn't met yet, so Alex waved from a distance.

Julia started walking over to them, Zillah's tail wagging excitedly. "Let's just both walk toward the off-leash area," she called to Alex. "They can get to know each other off leashes in there. Lower likelihood of drama."

Alex nodded and headed toward the fence. She went in and waited for Julia and Zillah. Seeing all of the dogs, Zillah held back a bit, but Sibby ran up to the fence that separated them. Zillah let out one bark and then resumed her happy body language.

"I think we're good to let her in," Julia waited for confirmation. Alex appreciated that Julia was sensitive to the dogs and their level of comfort. Like she was with people.

Zillah was a sweetie pie and let Sibby take the lead. After a few tail wags and some butt sniffing, they ran off together for a game of chase. Lovely.

"So how goes it?" Julia asked Alex. "We miss you at rehearsal."

"Yeah, I was working on a project for Michelle. Spencer knows I'm hit and miss these days," Alex said referring to the orchestra conductor.

"I know. I just like seeing you back in action with orchestras."

They were both quiet for a moment. Julia didn't sound even remotely judgmental, but Alex knew her friend was coaching her to reprioritize.

"What happened with your date?"

"Oh, I'll save that story for brunch. I'll just say there's a spot open for the next victim."

"His or yours?" Julia quirked an eyebrow.

"Good one. Both. He has been released to find his next blind date and I'm going to try my luck in Angela's Bowl of Men." Alex liked that turn of phrase to describe the group of names that Angela had collected at the last brunch. She collected band names from everyday conversation. "That would be an excellent band name."

"Yeah it would!" Julia agreed. "I look forward to that story. And work?"

"Work is work. It's so nice to have the money coming in. I need it to feel secure after what happened."

Julia looked pointedly at Alex. "It took me a long time to figure out that it's not just about money."

"I know, and I get it. Everyone is always saying there's more to life than money. But I feel like those people have never been broke or facing a mortgage payment they didn't know how they were going to cover. I've been there, and it's no fun. Add in that I have to go it alone, and it creates a real need to work."

"I know, and I feel bad because I got you into this situation."

"You? Feel bad? Are you kidding me? You solved a major crisis for me!"

"I guess."

"Don't 'I guess' me. Say what you need to say, Jules."

"I'm concerned you'll be mad at me, but you're right. It's the Steak and Bourbon Way to speak your truth. Here goes." Julia took a deep breath. "You haven't been as happy as you were when you were performing and teaching. You're like a shell of yourself. Barely making it through brunch without checking your phone. And the fire is gone from your eyes."

That hit Alex hard. She felt the tightening in her chest as the pain twisted through her. "You're right. That hurt."

"I'm sorry."

"No, don't be sorry, just give me a minute."

Julia and Alex walked in tense silence for a few moments. When Alex looked back up, Julia was staring at her with imploring eyes. "Are we okay?"

"Of course. Julia! Seriously. We can say anything to each other. If we can't be honest with our best friends, why have them?"

"Thanks, Alex. What do you think about what I said?"

Alex heaved a heavy sigh, her breath whooshing out of her chest. "I know you're right. But I don't see how I can continue to make money while also playing."

She listened to the sound of her feet crunching in the dog park sand.

"Maybe you could start small. Maybe take on a few students and join one orchestra? Like for real, where you tell Michelle to shove it up her ass, but only for one night a week?"

Alex thought about it. "Can I skip the part where I tell Michelle to shove it up her ass? I would probably have to try different angles and things until I did it just the way she wanted me to."

They both laughed.

"Thanks, Jules. You're a good friend."

"You've been there for me plenty of times. We need to hold each other accountable for following our dreams and making ourselves happy. Sometimes, you have to dig in and eat the shit, but sometimes, it's better to set boundaries and make good things happen for yourself."

"Gram likes to say there is always a way. I'm going to think about it. Maybe I can take on two or three students and teach on Saturday mornings. And I can join an orchestra that rehearses on Mondays. There's a lower chance of work drama early in the week that could stop me from attending rehearsal."

"That's the spirit."

"Look at Sibby and Zillah run!" They both stopped to watch their dogs chase each other with gleeful looks on their faces, stopping only to roll around in the sand and wrestle before running off again.

"Just like us at brunch, but with booze thrown in." Julia laughed and Alex joined in.

Chapter 8

"I was really impressed with the account orchestration model you laid out for the team, Alexandra." Michelle started their one on one with good news. Alex was a little shocked because they were usually a litany of small complaints and actions she wanted Alex to take that Alex found mundane.

"Thanks. I haven't heard much back from the strategy team since I documented it for them."

"They're running with it. And adding to it." Alex tried not to grimace at that. They were accidentally bastardizing it, but she had played with plenty of community orchestras who also butchered music. "It makes me wonder if you're in the wrong role."

That didn't sound good. Was her gravy train ending and she was being let go? A small thrill ran through her. This might be just the push she needed to get back into the music scene. Alex stayed quiet. She knew better than to interrupt Michelle when she was on a roll.

"I think you should take on more strategy work."

Strategy? Ha! Four years ago, Alex had never worked at

a software company let alone with a sales organization, and now they wanted her to do strategy work? Hilarious.

Alex chose her response carefully. "I'm not sure what that means."

Michelle marched on. "Your creativity and new approaches are refreshing. They breathed life into an organizational design project that had been stalled for weeks. You were the catalyst – the strategic bump they needed to move forward. I could use more of that on the team."

"So, I would stop doing the PM job and become a strategist?" Alex liked the idea of no longer tracking action items.

"No, you would do both roles. Over time, I could see if I could get you a promotion and a raise. We don't have budget for that right now, but if you're successful in the role, the money will follow. At LampLight, you only ever get promoted when you're already performing at the next level. This is your chance to prove you can do it."

"Wouldn't it be more fair to post the new role and let people apply for it, including me? I mean, the strategy folks are always saying they need more people and that others are dying to get on the team."

"No. This is faster. And it's better for you."

Alex assumed she was just confused by the corporate world. "That sounds great. Thanks for the opportunity. Can I think about it?"

"What's there to think about? I'm making this happen for you." Michelle sounded disappointed and slightly incredulous. Like she was upset Alex didn't jump on it.

Alex felt boxed in. Michelle said it was a great opportunity. Alex pushed the negative voices and questions aside and went for it.

"I accept the challenge," Alex stated with drama, head held high.

. . .

ALEX FELT icky leaving Michelle's office. The whole thing confused her. She would do extra work without extra pay, but she should be glad for the opportunity. And it didn't matter that other, more qualified people, would want a shot at the role?

This felt like the political favoritism she eschewed in the music world.

That felt dishonest. But maybe this was just how business worked. Maybe it was just how *people* worked. You could change the category from music to the corporate world, but people were still people. Power dynamics were the same. Once you got some power, it was easy to abuse it. Alex didn't want to become like that.

And she had sold another small piece of her soul to Michelle. Her idea to rejoin an orchestra was pushed away.

Her brunch friends hadn't abused their power. Or had they? She remembered that many of them had worked for or with Julia. And Julia continued to help them out, recommending them for new roles. And what about what Julia had done for her? How many favors had she called in to get Alex her job? She hadn't really thought about that.

Alex was part of the problem. Part of the machine of unfairness and subjectivity. But what would she have done without that?

Maybe she should just walk out of the whole thing. Yes, she'd be broke again, but she'd saved up enough money she could survive pretty nicely on a musician's earnings if no new expenses popped up. And then in a few years if things got tough again, she could get another corporate job.

She needed advice. She needed her girls. The next brunch wasn't for a while, so Alex did the next best thing.

She texted Angela.

Angela understood the joint pulls of money and music. She sold insurance which did not fulfill her, but she made the time to sing back-up vocals in several bands and frequent live music venues.

Alex: I need some work advice

Angela: You know I hate texting - calling

"Hey girl. What's all this about?" It was nice that Angela was willing to drop what she was doing and call her.

"I'm having a bit of a work crisis. You manage work and music so well. How do you do it?"

"Once I turn off that computer, it's like I turn off that part of my brain. I don't think about it."

"That sounds so simple. My boss constantly contacts me after hours and on weekends asking me for stuff. I feel like I have to respond."

"Mine, too. I just ignore him. I give them forty hours a week."

"Ignore him? That sounds so easy, yet I don't want to deal with the disappointed look my boss gives me the next day if I wasn't incredibly responsive."

"You've taught her you'll be responsive on nights and weekends, so she keeps doing it. What if you just stop?"

"I'll get a bad review."

"And then?"

"I won't get a raise."

"And then?"

Alex was stumped. "I guess I'd make less money than I could?"

"Yeah, but you still make a crap ton more than you

would as a full-time musician. You just plateau at a certain spot and ride it out."

That wasn't how Alex worked. She was always striving to be better at what she did. Not just in music, but at work. She'd taken the program management certification, after all. She wanted to improve herself. Angela was offering her a different approach – more like an existence rather than building towards something bigger at work. A way to make time for music. Interesting. "You've given me a lot to think about."

"Sweetie, I got to jump. Still within my forty hours this week."

"See you soon! Hugs to Jeremy."

Was it that simple? Just say no to more hours and only work eight hours a day? Go for the expanded job and set new boundaries with Michelle? Could she do that?

She'd be able to focus on music in the evenings and weekends. Maybe Alex could learn to not give into the pressure at LampLight of always being on call and working tons of extra hours. Maybe she could define new rules in this new job.

She would have to think about it later. It was date night. She had to get home and get ready.

▭

KATE HAD KINDLY AGREED to hang out with Sibby and feed her dinner so Adam and Alex could meet for a late happy hour directly after work. A full-on dinner was too much at this point. Kate only lived about a half mile away and loved dogs even though she didn't have one of her own.

She and Adam agreed to meet at a taco bar. Five-dollar margaritas and fifty cent tacos on Tuesdays. An easy bando-friendly decision. Even though Alex was making good money, she was still a bando at heart. That was what people in the band had been called in her high school. Non-bandos used it as a derogatory term, but lots of bandos had co-opted the term into something positive.

Bandos loved free food.

Cheap food was the next best thing.

She arrived at the restaurant and took in the wall mural of people dancing in brightly colored dresses. Sombreros were scattered in various places on the wall opposite the mural. A plastic banner of Dios de las Muertos skulls hung over the bar. She counted twelve different Tequilas before the door opened and Adam walked in. She felt a frisson of nerves. Especially after the semi-disaster of her coffee experience with Tyler.

But she knew Adam a bit. She often complimented his solos, of which there were many, after concerts.

"Hey Alex," he said, sliding into the red vinyl covered bench the server had just wiped down. "Thanks for meeting with me."

Meeting with him? Did he think this was an audition or a date? She guessed it was both. "Thanks for meeting with me." Clever. *Not.*

"I was happy to get Julia's text. I've been single for a few months now and was dreading hitting the dating apps again. Introductions from friends are always better."

Alex smiled. "I totally agree." She took in his brown eyes and dark skin. He had grown a mustache and trim beard since she last saw him. It suited him. His wire frame glasses perched on his nose. He was an adorable mix of nerd and musician with a hint of badass.

He was wearing a t-shirt under his fleece she had commented on at a previous rehearsal. It had a cartoon figure of an oboe wearing a swirling cloak that said "Oboe-

Wan Kenobi" underneath. It cracked her up. Had he remembered she liked it, or did he only have a couple of t-shirts?

"Have you been here before?"

"Oh yeah. Especially on Taco Tuesdays." She didn't have to be embarrassed about frequenting a cheap restaurant. Musicians often sought out the cheapest, best food in every neighborhood.

"Me too. And they just added birria to the menu."

"Traditional with goat or Americanized with beef?" Adam asked.

"I've never asked. I just know it's cheap and tasty."

Adam's eyebrows shot up. "I'm impressed. Most Americans I know won't eat goat. My Haitian grandmother often cooked with goat. It tastes so much better than beef – but the person cooking it has to know what they're doing."

"Have you ever been to Haiti?" Alex didn't know he was Haitian.

"I used to summer there with my grandparents. My parents didn't have much money, so it was cheaper to send me to Haiti than to pay for daycare or summer camps. I loved it." Adam got a faraway look in his eyes. "I would wake up in the morning and one of the housemaids would ask me which fruit juice I wanted with breakfast and would squeeze it fresh for me." He turned back to Alex. "Have you been?"

Alex appreciated that he asked and didn't assume she'd never been there. "No, but I've heard so many stories. My best friend from music school, Madou, is Haitian. I was assured that visiting her parent's house in Brooklyn was a lot like going to Haiti."

"Not exactly, but that's better than not having any connection to Haiti." He nodded.

"Have you found a good Haitian restaurant in Seattle? I haven't, and I miss the food. So much."

"Nope. The best Haitian food in Seattle is at my house." Alex almost asked for an invitation before she realized it would be a bit forward. "There used to be a place that wasn't too bad in the Central District, but they closed during the pandemic."

"Like so many other small restaurants. It wasn't just tough on us musicians."

"Amen to that, sister."

"What do you like to cook?" Alex asked.

"I'm famous for my *diri kolé*."

"Rice and red beans. *Bon bagay*. Good stuff," she added in case her Haitian Creole pronunciation was so bad he couldn't understand her. "I love that."

Alex had lovely memories of sitting in the avocado green kitchen while her friend's mother, Mama Rosie, sauteed the garlic and green onions before adding the beans and seasonings. Alex's job was to rinse the rice. Three times. Not one or two. Three times.

"Have you ever tried to make it?" Adam interrupted her reverie.

"Actually no. I loved every bite of food I had at my friend's house from soup joumou, to lambi to tassot cabrit. But somehow, it never seemed right to try to replicate it at home. First of all, I would get it wrong, but second of all, I felt like the respectful thing to do was to visit them to get my fix."

"Squash soup, conch with creole tomato sauce with onions and garlic, and fried goat? That's a major feast right there."

"It was always amazing."

"We do enjoy our food traditions in Haiti. I bet she loves cooking for you."

"For all of us. And her mother, who we all called Grandmère, cooked enough for thirty people every Sunday when she lived in Jacmel. The town knew they could come to the house and get food. Mama Rosie carried on that tradition in a Brooklyn way. Her house was full of visitors every Sunday, me included."

"When was the last time you had her food?"

Alex felt the twinge of sadness that she would never have Mama Rosie's food again. "Not since 2018 when I last visited Madou, before Mama Rosie moved back to Haiti. Clearly, I couldn't visit during the pandemic. She passed away from ovarian cancer last August."

"Oh, I'm sorry." He reached for her hand in an act of comfort. She enjoyed the warmth of his hand and the sentiment.

"Yeah, *mwen songé li an pil.*"

"Ou pale Kreyol. I think that was supposed to be 'I miss her a lot.' We can work on your pronunciation, but points for trying."

"Yeah, I don't speak it," Alex admitted. "I can say things like 'how are you' and 'I don't know' and 'nice shirt.' That's it."

"That's more than most white people."

She didn't feel totally white, but didn't want to correct him.

They placed their order.

"I HAVE to get to rehearsal. Not sure why you aren't on your way to one yourself, Alex. You're a great player. Can we do this again?"

"I'd love that." She smiled at him. His comment stung a bit, as she wished she was going to rehearsal, too. But

Michelle had given her a long list of to-dos, and she had to finish them that evening.

He left some bills on the table and leaned in to kiss her on the cheek. "Na wè pita."

"Yeah, see you later." She watched him walk out of the restaurant. He turned at the door and waved goodbye.

Alex enjoyed her date with Adam. Getting back together would be fun but also difficult to coordinate. Alex was only available on nights and weekends and that's when Adam had rehearsals and gigs. She'd figure it out.

She was one and one.

Tyler was out, but Adam was in.

Gabe was next.

Chapter 9

"I'm excited about this new opportunity." Alex tried to broadcast positive energy to Michelle.

"What?"

"The expanded role you offered me." Alex wondered if Michelle had forgotten.

"Oh, yeah, That. Please don't make a big deal about it. I'm just giving you the opportunity to demonstrate more value." Alex felt a bit let down. She thought this was a step up, but now Michelle was downplaying it. "I'm glad you're taking opportunities for advancement seriously. More responsibility comes with more hours and harder work, but I know you can do it."

Michelle probably thought she was being supportive, but Alex's response was increased skepticism.

She wasn't interested in working more hours. She wanted more time to focus on her music. Why did moving up have to mean more work rather than less? Shouldn't she be getting better at this and therefore it would require *less* work?

That's how it was with music. When you practiced

your scales and honed your technique, your sight-reading improved and your ability to play your part came more easily. Without practicing for long hours.

Why wasn't the corporate world like that?

Maybe dating would get easier with practice, too. She was going to find out.

GABE PICKED Alex up at her house. He pulled up right on time.

Alex gave Sibby a treat and locked the door behind her before hurrying down the stairs. Gabe was halfway up the stairs carrying flowers.

Wow. Flowers.

"You must be Alex."

"How'd you guess?" she joked.

"These are for you." He handed her the bouquet of daisies.

"Thanks. Let's go back inside so I can put them in water. Are you okay with dogs?"

"I am if they're well behaved."

Alex wondered what counted as well-behaved and hoped Sibby was still chewing on her bully stick when they came inside.

Not so much.

Sibby bounded to the door when Alex came back in and skidded to a halt as Gabe put his hands up in defense. "I'll wait outside." He slipped back out the door.

"Sibby, you be a good girl." Alex put the flowers in water and said goodbye to the dog again.

Gabe was waiting in the car, Alex's door open for her. She slipped onto the leather seat. She recognized the BMW logo but couldn't tell what model it was. It smelled expensive.

"Nice car," she said. "Thanks for driving."

"No problem. I take her out every chance I get."

"Where are we going?" Alex asked. Gabe had insisted on picking the restaurant and keeping it a surprise.

"Candles."

"Candles? Oh, that's way too extravagant for a first date." Alex slightly panicked. That was one of the very best, most expensive restaurants in all of Seattle.

"It's fine. I haven't had a date in a while, and I want to impress you."

"Consider me impressed." She wondered what he was trying to prove. She'd never been there before but had heard about perfectly grilled steaks and sumptuous desserts. Her stomach rumbled in anticipation of the great meal they'd have.

Alex couldn't help but contrast the display of wealth against her simple taco night with Adam. She was definitely more of a taco girl than a white cloth napkin girl.

The maître d' walked them across the slate floor toward the main dining room. The calming notes from a piano tinkled down into the space. She looked up to see a pianist tucked up in an alcove over the dining room entrance. The piano player gave her a nod when they made eye contact. She smiled back. Most people ignored musicians. Gabe did. She didn't.

The notes from the piano mingled with the sound of the salmon stream that ran through the middle of the restaurant. It reminded Alex of the opening of *The Moldau* by Bedřich Smetena. The piece described the Moldau river through music.

The host pulled out a velvet-covered chair for Alex. He handed her a menu once she was seated and unfolded her napkin for her. Quiet dinner conversation surrounded them.

The prices were hefty. And not how Alex wanted to spend her money. Gabe seemed to sense her discomfort.

"Don't worry about the prices. Order whatever you like. I want to treat you right."

"Was I that transparent? Being a musician creates a certain sense of fiscal conservatism." She thought that sounded better than "cheap."

"Are you saying I'm not careful with my money?"

She wondered why he sounded offended. "No, it's just that I could have three or four meals for the price of one here."

"Then just enjoy it. I have plenty of money."

Alex wondered what it would be like to feel that way. She was busy saving and squirreling it away so she could get back to her dream. Maybe being with someone like Gabe would take the pressure off. She wasn't looking for a man to pay for her lifestyle, but it didn't hurt.

They chatted for a few minutes. Gabe leaned forward and Alex mirrored his body language. She wondered what was up. It looked serious.

Gabe cleared his throat. "What're you looking for in a potential partner?"

Alex was taken aback at the pointed question. "Wow. You just kind of dove right in there. Um, I haven't really thought about it that much. I'm kind of new to the dating scene. Anything in particular you have to have or it's game over?"

"Yeah. Someone who doesn't cheat." Gabe's expression darkened like a cloud had passed over his face. He looked directly at Alex, unblinking. It made her feel like he was measuring her cheating potential. She didn't like it. "Have you ever cheated on your partner?"

"Of course not," Alex answered honestly." She looked back at the menu, hoping he would do the same. There was that one time in college, but she and her boyfriend hadn't said they were exclusive. She brushed that aside.

"Do you envision a scenario where you ever would, like if you were unhappy but didn't feel like talking about it or working to fix it?" Alex realized Gabe was no longer talking about her.

"She really did a number on you, huh?"

"You could say that. Twelve years together and then boom, she goes and cheats on me. I mean, I get that we were having problems, but that's no excuse for just banging the first guy who came along."

Alex was shocked at the rage pulsing off him. "That's a lot of anger to process. Have you spoken to anyone about it?"

"My friends. But they're kind of sick of me."

"I mean a professional. When my husband passed away, I went into a funk. I waited too long to seek professional help and wasted a lot of time on sadness."

"I'm not sad." He slanted his eyes at her. "I'm angry."

"They have the same root. There's hurt there."

"Oh, so now you're a therapist." His tone was sharp.

"No, I'm just sharing. It's hard."

"At least your husband had the courtesy to die. He didn't mean to hurt you. My wife broke my heart on purpose."

His words cut her like a knife. She recoiled and leaned back in her chair.

"I'm sorry. That was a really stupid thing to say."

"Not stupid, just callous. You're not the only walking wounded here." *Maybe they could heal together*, Alex thought.

"It's hard knowing she chose someone else. I guess I'm still processing it."

"Grief does weird shit to people. I hope you get the help you need."

"I just need to be in a relationship with someone else. Then I'd be fine."

"That sounds a little avoidant." Alex kept her tone gentle. Poor Gabe was still in the throes of despair and clearly wasn't ready for something new. He just wanted a distraction.

"Stop it with the counseling. I'm fine. I just don't want to be alone." There was that anger again. If he was this upset in the first twenty minutes of the date, she doubted it would get better as they talked.

"Okay, I think we're done here." Alex folded her napkin on the table. "I'm going to grab a ride home. You stay and finish. Good luck."

"Wait, please." Alex paused halfway out of her seat. "You're right. I'm being a total jerk. I just played this whole thing out in my head differently. Would you please stay?"

"I think you'd be wasting your money. This isn't going to go anywhere."

"I know, but I meant it when I said I was lonely. Please have dinner with me. Maybe I won't be such a jerk with the pressure off."

Alex knew she probably wouldn't be at this restaurant again in a long time, if ever. "Are you sure you wouldn't feel used if I stayed just for dinner?"

"No, absolutely not. And it would save me from eating alone."

Alex sat back down.

Chapter 10

"I had my three dates." Alex was at Julia's for Steak and Bourbon in February.

"Of course you did, because you're a rule follower and certified project manager." Margaret wiggled her dark eyebrows at Alex.

"Okay, who made the cut?" Angela jumped right into the meat of the discussion, clapping her hands together.

"I'm seeing Adam again. But Tyler and Gabe are out."

"My man Ty? What happened?" Angela leaned forward for the story.

"We just didn't click." Alex felt bad telling Angela he was kind of a dick to her. She didn't want to make it awkward.

"And Gabe?" Margaret asked.

"He's not ready for anything. He's still pretty wrapped up in the hurt with his ex-wife." She thought that was the most benign way to say it.

"I thought that might be the case. He can be kind of a jerk sometimes, but he's cute, rich, and single. Just how I like my men."

"Don't let Peter hear you talk like that." Julia referred to Margaret's devoted husband of almost twenty years.

"Two out of three isn't bad," she quipped. "But at least you tried with Gabe."

"Yep." Alex smiled at her.

"The rules say you need to have three guys in play, so pick the next names." Melanie jumped in. "Julia, did you keep that bowl?"

"Of course! I would never give up Angela's Bowl of Men." Julia dipped her head into the cabinet under the buffet and produced the bowl with the remaining names after winking at Alex.

Alex shuffled the slips of paper in the bowl and selected one. "Cameron."

"The aerospace engineer. Nice." Lesley approved. "You know I have a thing for engineers. Give him some glasses, and I'm on board."

"Alex might be soon, too." The ladies laughed at Gertie's comment.

She reached in again. "Ross."

"He's a cutie. I'm glad he's up next." Kate smiled.

"Only one name left in the bowl, and we know that's Carlos. Anyone else come up with new names?"

"Let me get through these before you add more!" Alex laughed and shook her head.

"Do I get to choose from Alex's leftovers if she finds true love?"

"You mean when, Les. When." Julia spoke with emphasis. "And yes."

"You make it sound so simple." Lesley sounded wistful, her large brown eyes seeming to focus somewhere far away.

"What is it with that word lately?" Melanie jumped in.

"It's like LampLight decided that fiscal year twenty-five is the Year of Simplification."

"Yeah," Julia agreed. "Having been at this company a long time, it seems like simplification is the highest priority… and it always will be."

"What do you mean?" Alex asked. She felt the prick of confusion in her brain.

"They talk about simplification, but every time someone new comes along, it all gets re-complexified again."

"Exactly! That's it! I keep trying to boil things down and summarize and the 'complexifiers' as I have learned to call the other strategists, just keep adding complexity back in!" It wasn't just her. Alex was thrilled to know others noticed it too.

"Simplification is an art, and you have the gift." Brie pointed a fork at Alex. "Like the story you told about using the musical analogy that actually works instead of the constant drumbeat, pun intended, of male-dominated sports analogies."

"I love that you always intend your puns, Brie." Kate nodded in her direction.

"Why is it like this?" Alex lamented.

"Because when you're in the thick of it and you think your value is measured in how complicated you can make something, someone coming along and simplifying it so that everyone understands is like magic." Lesley opened her hands palms up and pulled them down slowly, indicating the release of magic.

"Yeah, strategists love to design for edge cases so they can be perceived as smart." Akiko leaned forward. "It clouds the vision and removes the creativity of the teams implementing it if you make it overly prescriptive. And that's what headquarter teams love to do." She sighed heavily. "It's why I left LampLight. I couldn't figure out how to translate the complexity into easy-to-understand field training."

"Is that like me starting a story with 'this one time, at band camp' and then telling a ridiculous tale of teenage weirdness?" Alex made everyone laugh.

"Yep."

"How do these companies make any money?" Alex wanted to question the entire corporate structure.

"Because customers have become really patient over time and know the drill. And sadly, having worked at a lot of these big companies, they're all the same." Julia was on a roll. "Complicated sales models with sellers who struggle to get the right expertise to help. Customers have gotten savvy. They work with industry analysts, know what they want, and tell the sellers what to sell them. It's wild when you're actually out there in the accounts. Yet, the people at headquarters think it's things like sales orchestration models that make it all work." She rolled her blue eyes.

"That's just ridiculous!" Alex couldn't believe it. How could there be these huge teams who basically screamed into the wind? It was like playing music by yourself that you knew would never be performed for any other people.

She would hate to live in a world like that. Yet, she was paid to keep that world going.

It blew her mind.

Music was so pure in comparison. You practiced, you rehearsed, you performed. Rinse and repeat with an endless variation of pieces. Yet orchestras all over the world were struggling to increase audience size and most audiences had a lot of gray hair in them. Wild.

"This is why I go camping a lot. In the wilderness. Without any people around." Gertie took a swig of her drink. "People just muck things up."

"I like camping where there are a lot of people." Brie often had a different perspective from the other ladies. "I get my best stuff from groundscoring at concerts at the Gorge." Brie referred to a huge outdoor amphitheater in Washington state in the middle of nowhere.

"Groundscoring?" Alex was confused and had no idea what that meant.

"Yeah. There aren't any hotels nearby, so people camp. All the rich tech bros from Seattle buy expensive gear they never intend to use again. They just leave it behind." Brie's eyes lit up. "Then, the more frugal among us walk the grounds and scavenge for treasures."

"Totally," Gertie added. "I got a new three-person tent that way. Used once. Tags still on the bag. I pegged them as equipment deserters and called dibs on it before they left. They were glad to give it to me."

"You probably beat me to it." Brie joked.

"You're welcome to borrow from my garage any time." Brie and Gertie shared a laugh.

Angela approached Alex as they took their dessert plates into the kitchen. "Sounds like that new job is going to add hours, not subtract them. What happened to our forty hours a week plan?"

Alex felt a twinge of guilt. She had chosen success at work over getting back into music. "Change of plans." Alex wrinkled her nose.

"You know what's best for you. I'll support whatever decision you make, but I'm going to ask you to think hard about how to re-join an orchestra and take on a couple of students again." Angela gently poked her finger into Alex's chest. "You have music to share and new musicians to create. It sounds like that's super important to you, so please try."

Angela was right, as usual.

.   .   .

ALEX THOUGHT about it on the drive home.

She wondered where she would be if she hadn't befriended Julia. They had met in 2015 in a summer orchestra set up to play four rehearsals and a concert. Mahler's First Symphony. *The Titan*, as it was known. Julia sat next to Alex in the section, and they had hit it off. That could have been problematic because sitting principal meant Alex got the highly coveted bass solo in the third movement rather than Julia. There weren't many bass solos in classical music. Julia was a great sport about it.

Alex mentioned one day that she wanted to meet new people. Julia was a super connector – always matching people up who she thought could be friends or mentors. After the concert, Julia invited Alex to join her brunch group called Steak and Bourbon. "You serve steak and bourbon at brunch?" Alex had asked.

Julia explained that it started as a dinner group and morphed into brunch. They met monthly for bonding and conversation. Alex looked forward to each brunch as soon as the last one was over.

She wouldn't have gotten through Tom's death without the Steak and Bourbon crew. For a while, it was the only social activity she did. They rallied around her, taking turns visiting her, checking in, and trying to distract her. She owed them a lot.

They all came to her concerts when she got back into playing after what she thought of as her six-month mourning season. Julia even covered some gigs for Alex when she wasn't playing, gracefully bowing out when Alex could step back in.

Fabulous friends, every one of them. New people, like Kate, Akiko and Brie, had been added over the years.

Existing members would then decide if they could come back after their first time, kind of like an audition.

The group provided support, friendship, love, and psychological safety. No topic was off-limits. Alex learned a lot about most respectful interpretation in these brunches. Everyone freely expressed themselves without worry of offending others because love and friendship underpinned the entire experience. No one ever got mad. No one ever stormed out. You could agree or disagree with everyone's opinion, and no one held a grudge.

They were of different backgrounds, ages, races, sexual orientations, careers, and political views, yet they always had each other's backs.

Real female friendship.

It was another thing Alex missed when the pandemic hit. No gigs, no job, nothing. Luckily for all the brunch attendees, Julia didn't give up easily. During the pandemic, she and her partner Rob delivered brunch kits to everyone. The kits contained a box of scones, a bottle of orange juice, a bottle of champagne, and a chocolate bar. They all joined with their mimosas via Zoom.

The brunch ladies were amazing and supportive of each other, acting as each other's board of directors for decisions both large and small. The group seamlessly moved from advice about what color one of them should dye their hair to slavery restitution to vibrator recommendations to book reviews.

Alex had met amazing people through these brunches. Julia, Angela, and Gertie were all musicians or singers, and Brie was married to a bass player. They got her and understood how hard it was to survive during the complete stoppage of live music during the pandemic. The others helped her with work drama or just made her laugh when she needed it.

Alex could be completely honest with these fabulous ladies. She remembered with fondness how they had all helped her prepare for her interviews at LampLight. Even now, when she had been doing the role for four years, the group continued to mentor her.

The Steak and Bourbon crew helped her feel like she could do anything.

Like there was always a way, like Gram liked to say.

She would take Angela's advice. She would start back up with an orchestra and get a student or two back in her studio. She would combine music and corporate life.

She just had to figure out how.

Chapter 11

Michelle wasn't kidding about the extra hours. Meetings started at six-thirty or seven every day and ended well into the evening. Apparently at LampLight, strategy meant getting every single person's buy-in on every single decision. It was like no one could say "yes" but two hundred people could say "no."

Alex's plan to regularly re-join an orchestra was put on hold. Monday nights were when the Japan team wanted to meet. Tuesday night was India. Wednesday night was China. Thursday was Korea and Singapore. She was putting in sixty hours a week, well above her target number.

But she had worked out a way to start teaching again. She taught on Saturday mornings after taking Sibby to the dog park. It was the quietest time from a Michelle email perspective.

She now had two students, Dylan and Betsy.

Alex pulled her attention back to her second lesson of the morning.

"My mom is giving me crap again about not practicing

enough. I'm doing okay, right?" Betsy had barely made it through a Simandl bass etude in Alex's backyard teaching studio.

"Yeah, Betsy. You're doing okay." Alex thought honesty was best. "Do you want to just be doing okay?" She let the question hang in the air while Betsy considered.

"I don't have much fun when practicing but I really like being in the orchestra and playing with other people. I wish I could play songs I know, not this stuffy classical stuff."

Alex recognized talent in Betsy and didn't want her to give up. She had an idea to spark some energy in her young student. "Have you thought about playing the electric bass? Once you know how to play the upright bass, it's pretty easy to pick up electric. It's the same tuning and the same strings. You just play it on its side."

"How do you know that?" Betsy questioned.

Alex gestured to the three electric bass guitars hanging on the wall. "You think those are just for show?" She grabbed her favorite off the wall – a four-string blue Ibanez she'd had since college – plugged it in and played one of her favorite bass lines. She watched Betsy's face light up.

It got even brighter as she moved through the rest of the bass part.

"Can you teach me to do that?" Alex saw the flash of inspiration on Betsy's face. This was going to be fun.

"Let's work on a few things here in this lesson. Then, we can talk to your mom about making the switch since she's paying for the lessons. Meanwhile, I can send you home with an electric bass and a small amplifier so you can see what you think. Bring it back next week."

It was a great lesson and one of the reasons why Alex was a teacher. She bet she would work on orchestra parts with Betsy but then they'd switch to rock, blues, and jazz bass lines on the electric for most of their time.

She waved goodbye to Betsy after helping her load her upright bass and the borrowed electric bass and amp into her mother's car. Jeannie was enthusiastic about the electric and thanked Alex. "Maybe she'll be the next Carol Kaye."

"That would be amazing," Alex said.

"Who's Carol Kaye?" Betsy asked.

"Only one of the most recorded bass players in all of rock and pop music. She's on over ten thousand recordings and you've heard a ton of them. You just didn't know it was her."

"Wow. I'm going to look her up. Chick bass players unite!" Betsy raised her hand to give Alex a high five.

"Someone's excited," Jeannie said as she watched Betsy get into the passenger seat. "Thank you," she mouthed as she waved goodbye to Alex out the car window.

Lessons over, Alex turned her attention to getting her work done before her date with Cameron the next day.

Alex had known Cameron for over six years. He and Tom worked together, and they had gone out on several double dates. Cameron's marriage didn't make it through the pandemic.

Alex liked Lynda. They didn't have much in common, but she was certainly friendly and engaging when they hung out.

According to Cameron, spending all that time together during the pandemic exposed some tough spots in their marriage. They had jointly agreed they didn't want to work on them. After living together for an additional six months just to make sure, they sold their house and Lynda moved to Austin to take care of her aging parents.

Cameron kindly checked in on Alex every few months

after Tom's death. She appreciated it. She had never really thought about Cameron romantically, but he popped into her mind at the January brunch, and she liked to listen to her subconscious thoughts when she could.

After she pulled his name out of Angela's Bowl of Men, Alex had sent him a text message. She thought it was the most low-pressure approach. She wasn't sure if she should call it a date and state her intentions or just show up and see what happened. She didn't like the idea of potentially jeopardizing a friendship, especially one with a link to Tom. She decided on a Sunday afternoon, another indication that this was just two friends hanging out for coffee. That seemed safe. Then the conversation could go either way.

He had accepted immediately.

Alex had to get a bunch of work done today to ensure she could have her dog park time with Sibby and uninterrupted two hours or so with Cameron the next day. Michelle had already scheduled a 5:00 call with the Japan team on Sunday afternoon. That woman really must not have a life. Alex shook her head at the thought.

***

IT WAS CHILLY, even for late February in Seattle. People who lived in Seattle for more than three years knew not to put their sweaters away until July. They invariably needed to come out during the season locals called June-uary since it could feel like January in June.

Cameron lived on the east side of Seattle, so Alex picked a café close to his place.

Alex had developed the habit of being early when her grandmother used to drive her to rehearsals and always left late. It was tough to get a bass into a rehearsal without making noise. The embarrassment got Alex into the habit of fibbing to her grandmother about when rehearsals started so she would be on time. The habit stuck and now Alex was early everywhere. And you never really knew how long it would take to get across one of the bridges. Map apps changed their answers in real time.

Alex sat in the car for a few minutes checking her email. When it was only five minutes before their agreed upon time, she went inside. He was already there. And she hadn't seen him go in which meant that he was even earlier than she was.

"Hey Cam, great to see you." He stood and embraced Alex.

"It's been a minute. You good?"

"Yeah." Alex's discomfort melted away once she saw him. "Let's grab some coffee and chat."

As he placed his order at the counter, Alex tried to look at him through new eyes. Eyes that were looking at partner potential. He was good-looking in a boyish way, maybe a couple clicks toward bro with his short hair, but the nerd vibe counteracted it. His blond hair was starting to go gray at the temples. She hadn't noticed that before, or maybe it was new. His black metal-framed glasses hid his blue eyes a bit and gave him a studious look.

They sat at a low table in the middle of the café. "Alex, I'm really glad you called. I've been thinking about you."

"That's —"

He interrupted her. "I'm sorry to interrupt, but there's something I've wanted to say to you for a while and I've been sitting here building up the courage. If I don't spit it out, I'll lose my nerve."

Alex remained quiet. She felt her eyes bug out a bit and tried to neutralize her features.

He took a deep breath. "I really like you and think we

should try dating." He spoke quickly, like he wanted to get it all out into the universe.

"Actually Cameron –"

"That sounds like a no. I get it. I'm sorry. Forget I said anything."

"Cameron," she said again. "That's why I called you. I think there might be something here too and want to explore it." She smiled at him. She thought about reaching for his hand, but that seemed too forward.

They just looked at each other awkwardly for a moment.

"Wow," he said on a big sigh. "That's great news. I can't tell you how relieved I am you didn't laugh in my face."

"You were so kind to me after Tom's death. And the four of us used to have a good time together. It's strange to try to look at our friendship as something more, but I have this group of friends trying to hook me up with the whole world. You popped into my head, and I figured that it meant something."

"Remind me to thank your friends." Alex watched as a slow smile spread across his face. "Full transparency, I've had a crush on you for quite a while. Even before Lynda and I broke up. I, of course, would never have acted on it, I mean, you were with my friend. But now we're both single, so why not?"

"Why not indeed."

Two hours went by quickly.

No awkwardness, no barriers. Just two friends exploring what might be. There was an ease between them that came from a base of friendship.

Cameron took her hand on the table. She liked it.

"Have you been with anyone since Tom died?"

She stiffened a bit at the question, a mix of embarrassment and awkwardness. "No." She debated before asking him the same question. She decided to go for it. "Have you been with anyone since you and Lynda broke up?"

"No."

Tension hung in the air as they looked at each other.

"Would it be weird to, you know, mess around and see where it goes?" Hope sparked in Cameron's blue eyes.

"Yes." She saw part of the hope dim. "But that's a 'yes and.' It would be weird and welcomed." Alex gave him what she hoped was a flirtatious look. She wasn't sure she pulled it off. Weird and welcomed. *That would make a great band name*, she added to herself. Would it edge out "Angela's Bowl of Men" or "Dottie Brought Donuts" which were at the top of the current list? She pulled herself back to the moment and returned Cameron's gaze.

"We know each other, and it's safe since we haven't been with anyone else in a few years." Cameron made a great point.

"It's also safe emotionally since we're friends. I say we go for it." Alex was up for it and didn't want to think about it too much more. Alex felt her more carefree attitude from a few years ago ooze back into her psyche.

"Your place or mine?"

"Yours. It feels more neutral since we weren't there with Tom or Lynda."

"Okay, but let's not mention their names again tonight, okay?"

Chapter 12

This was the best of all worlds. She could release a little sexual frustration from five years of no sex in a safe place with a guy who'd had a crush on her for a few years. Win/win.

Alex followed him home.

He pointed to a visitor's parking spot at his condo complex, parked his car, and hopped out. She waited by her car door as he approached.

"You still want to do this?" he asked as he stood in front of her.

"Yes." Alex hadn't fooled around since Tom died. Five years. She heard his voice in her head like she had on his birthday telling her to go for it. She listened.

"Then strap yourself in." He moved in quickly, pressing her against her car door, his hands fisting in her hair. She kissed him right back, enjoying the feeling of his lips on hers. He parted her lips with his tongue and explored. Fireworks went off behind Alex's eyes.

When they broke apart, they were both panting.

"Wow. Who knew?" Alex wondered aloud.

"I suspected. I knew you'd taste amazing. I can't wait for more."

That lit a fire in Alex's core. "Then let's head inside. I like performing, but not for your neighbors."

He grabbed her hand and pulled her up the stairs to his condo entrance. She quickly looked at her watch. Ninety minutes before her meeting and she needed thirty of them for the drive home.

Cameron started kissing her again before he got the door open. But it was her turn to pin him against the door.

"Inside. Now." He told her. "I want to bury my face between your thighs." He reached behind them to open the unlocked door.

The "I'm newly single" vibe was all over his condo. The sparsely furnished living room. The huge television and an oversized reclining chair.

He grabbed her face with his hands and crushed her lips with his. He nudged her jacket off her shoulders and began exploring. She gasped as he kissed and licked his way down her neck, his hand caressing her breast. She felt the tension building between her thighs, a welcomed feeling after such a long time.

He gently pushed her down onto the leather chair. He took off his own jacket and knelt in front of her.

"Let's just get these off of you." She lifted her butt to allow him to slip her leggings off. He took her panties with them. She felt the cool leather on her backside. "Now scoot toward me."

She did as he asked. He placed his hands on her hips and kneaded as he nestled between her thighs. Once in position, he used his thumb to rub circles on her clit.

She threw her head back on the chair, her hips starting to buck in rhythm with his caresses. "Do you like that?" he asked. "Tell me you want more."

"Yes and yes," she panted. "More."

He inserted two fingers into her core. Alex opened her legs wide, hanging one over the arm of the chair. He replaced his thumb with the flat part of his tongue.

Why had she waited so long for this?

Sensations she hadn't felt for years bolted through her. She bucked against his mouth as he increased the pressure. She felt the warmth build in her center and the bunching of muscles. She knew what was next. "Don't stop."

He buzzed his lips on her clit, and she exploded in his mouth. She pumped against him until her hips stopped their natural rhythm. Then she just sat back basking in the afterglow for a few seconds. When she opened her eyes, she noted he used the time to take off his pants.

She liked what she saw.

"Your turn," she said, lifting off the chair.

"I won't argue with that."

They switched positions with her on her knees and him on the chair.

She cupped his balls in one hand and firmly grasped his cock in the other. She licked his head, noting that it was differently shaped than Tom's. She pushed that thought out of her head and focused on her task. She kissed his tip and then slid him into her mouth, slowly. She heard him groan and knew she hadn't forgotten how to do this.

His panting and moaning grew more fervent. She could have taken her time, but she knew the clock was ticking down to her meeting. She increased her pace to take him quickly to the edge. She felt the tremors before he exploded in her mouth with a triumphant yell. "Oh God."

He clutched her head with both hands to hold her in place. He threw his head back against the chair as he rocked in her mouth.

When he relaxed, she released him and stayed on the floor.

"That was even more amazing than my numerous fantasies about you. That was so hot."

"Right back at you. A lovely way to re-enter the scene."

"Care to stay for act two? The bedroom is around the corner."

She had the decorum to not check her watch again, but her internal clock said she better get going so she wasn't late to her meeting.

Who was this person, hurrying through a date to get back to work? Lame.

"You know, let's save that for next time." She didn't think he'd believe her excuse if she said she had to work. On a Sunday. "I have to go let my dog out."

"Next time bring her so you can stay overnight."

They shared a kiss at the door before she headed out into the dark February afternoon.

And back to her home office for her meeting.

Chapter 13

"Alexandra, could you take notes, please?"

Alex bristled at the request. She was a strategist now. She shouldn't be the designated note taker. That job should go to Aaron who was the more junior program manager. Why wasn't her boss helping her move into her new role?

She tamped all of that down, not wanting to look like she was putting on airs or wasn't a team player. She opened a notes file on the shared site and started typing.

She had been looking forward to getting out of the action item tracking and note-taking world. She would talk to Michelle about it in their next one on one. She couldn't perform her new duties and all of her old ones, too.

"We have to make it spell an acronym. It has to be catchy." Eugene was on a roll talking about their new sales methodology. "How about Sell, Advise, Listen, Execute. That spells SALE."

That made absolutely no sense to Alex. She tapped into her power as a strategist. "But you have to listen before you can advise and sell. That's out of order." She wanted this to make sense, not just be a gimmick. "Wouldn't it be better to call each step what it is rather than worrying about making it spell something?"

"No way. That's dumb." Eugene sounded dismissive. No one else seemed to notice, but Alex wondered why he was allowed to talk like that, unchecked. "If we don't make it memorable, no one will use it."

"If it doesn't make *sense*, no one will use it," Alex shot back.

"Alexandra, just leave it with the people who know the business to come up with the steps." Michelle tone was clipped.

Alex couldn't believe it. Why was she talking to her like that?

"Alexandra makes a good point, Eugene and Michelle." *Thank you, Tanja,* Alex thought.

Tanja managed the enablement team and had recently moved to the US from Germany. "Sellers aren't stupid, and they aren't children. HQ people love to make things cute but then they don't work. It can just be the steps we need to do in the right order."

That statement was especially powerful given Tanja's German accent.

"Then what do you suggest?" Eugene's tone was curt.

"Meet, listen, pitch, revise, contract, deliver, transform." Tanja counted each word off on her fingers.

"MLPRCDT? You can't pronounce that. It's not a word." Eugene wasn't giving up. "But I like that you added the element of transformation. That's important."

"Why are you so stuck on making it a word?" Alex asked.

"I just am." He looked at Alex with incredulity on his face. "That's strategy."

That was strategy? she thought. Wasn't strategy defining

a vision, gaining support for that vision, and creating a plan on how to accomplish it? That's what she learned in her Program Management class.

Alex was kind of over it at this point.

"Let's schedule a wallow to brainstorm this further." Michelle sounded like she was over it, too.

Alex didn't understand the term "wallow." Don't pigs wallow in mud? Why did people at LampLight use it to describe brainstorming? It was one of many entries on Alex's list of words that were made up or used incorrectly. *Did other companies do that or just LampLight?* she wondered.

The one that threw her in last week's design session was "non-goal." As she questioned the outcome of a project, she was told in no uncertain terms that her idea was a "non-goal." Why not just say "out of scope?" or "that's not what we're doing here." Why did everything have to get so complicated and uninclusive with these weird words?

"No, Michelle. We have to get this nailed down today or we'll jeopardize our training schedule." Tanja was firm.

Alex came up with a new option. "How about meet, update, design, pitch, iterate, transform."

"I like that." Michelle nodded. "It definitely describes the process."

"It also spells MUDPIT." Alex looked pointedly at Eugene. Perhaps now he would back off the word thing.

"Alexandra, I don't think you understand the spirit of this exercise." Michelle sounded angry, like she was mad she fell for Alex's joke. Alex was just having a little fun. If people were going to "wallow" wouldn't they be fine in a mud pit? She thought she was hilarious.

Alex could do this all day but decided that making fun of strategy was probably not the best approach. "Fine.

How about listen, envision, agree, document, execute, repeat. It spells LEADER."

"Now that's what I'm talking about." Eugene was undeterred by her mud joke. "And it brings in the element of repetition. Sellers should always be thinking about their next sale. I like it."

"But it doesn't fit with our musical theme." Michelle tut-tutted and shook her head. "And we lost the transformation element. Alexandra, you came up with the musical theme in the first place. Have you already forgotten? What else do you have?"

She wondered why Michelle was being so crappy to her. Alex thought out loud to fill the awkward silence. "The leader of the orchestra is the conductor, the maestro. Let's see." She looked at the ceiling for inspiration. "Meet, advise, envision, sell, transform, repeat, operationalize. MAESTRO."

"Love it." Tanja was on board.

"But we don't sell, Alexandra." There was that tone from Michelle again. "We advise and deliver end-to-end solutions."

"Okay then, change sell to solution." Alex controlled her eyeroll. Of course they were selling. Alex noted that no one seemed to notice that "solution" wasn't a verb. It was also on the list of words Alex didn't understand. When she would suggest ideas, people would say "we're strategizing, not solutioning" like that cleared something up for Alex's feeble brain.

She guessed that was the power of the English language. Any part of speech could be made into any other part of speech.

"That's it." Eugene smiled. "Done."

Tanja and Alex shared a questioning look. *Was this really strategy?*

Chapter 14

It was the following Saturday. Dylan was packing up his bass and Betsy was back for her next lesson. She had made amazing progress on the electric bass in a very short time. Alex started teaching her jazz scales and modes and had her writing her own bass lines for several tunes. She was a quick study, and it was obvious she had been practicing more between lessons.

"Did you know that Carol Kaye played bass with the Beach Boys?"

"Yeah, she played on a lot of their albums. She also recorded with Ray Charles, Simon & Garfunkel, The Supremes, the Four Tops, Frank Sinatra, and Stevie Wonder to name a few."

"Wow, that's cool… but what's an album?"

"It's a collection of songs that the artist meant to be listened to together." *But that's not important right now,* Alex added to herself in homage to one of her favorite movies – a joke she and Tom used to make all the time. "And she wasn't only a bass player. She played guitar, too."

"How come she's not more famous?"

"Well, that's kind of how it works when you're a studio musician. You play in the recording sessions and your name usually gets onto the back of an album, but you don't get the spotlight." Alex thought of all the studio sessions she'd done. Just another bass player in the morass of session musicians in New York. She had played way more than her share of jazz Christmas albums while living in the City. "And she lives right here in Washington State. She's from Everett."

"Maybe I can go visit her!"

"She's almost ninety, Betsy. I don't know if she accepts visitors. You can always admire her from afar or send her a fan letter."

"I'm going to do that! She's amazing."

"And she blazed the trail for a lot of female bass players."

"And me," Betsy added. "My mom said I can keep doing electric bass lessons. She's even going to get me one for my birthday. Would you help her pick one out?"

"I'd be delighted to. You'll need an amplifier, too. And there are some apps out there that let you plug your bass into your phone and use it like an amplifier through headphones."

"That's cool, but my mother says she loves hearing me practice and get better each week." That warmed Alex's heart. Parents who were supportive of their kids' musical endeavors helped so much. Like Gram.

"Happy to talk to her about some options."

Betsy's mother Jeannie was an executive at the local NPR station. It was always nice to get a behind-the-scenes peek at what they were up to whenever she spoke to Jeannie.

Alex helped them load up Betsy's equipment when Jeannie came to pick Betsy's up.

"The work you've done with Betsy is amazing," Jeannie said to Alex. "You have her listening to jazz and asking questions about who's coming through the studio." She was gushing.

"I'm so glad. I hear you want to buy her an electric bass."

"Yeah, I do. Honey, could you wait in the car while I talk to Miss Taylor?" Alex saw Betsy pull out her ear pods and hop into the front seat. "I want to encourage her as much as possible. I always wanted to play the drums, but my parents wouldn't allow it. I never want to block her."

"It's never too late to start." Alex smiled at Jeannie. "Betsy has a lot of natural talent. I think this is going to be a lifelong passion."

"It's too late for me, but I hope Betsy sticks with it. That said, I'm not ready to break the bank on her first bass."

"Oh no – I meant it the other way. She's going to have plenty of time to upgrade, so the most important thing about the one you buy now is how easy it is to play and how it feels in her hands. I'd be happy to take her over to the bass shop with your budget guidelines in hand and find her something. They have lots of used amplifiers, too. I'm also happy to just let her keep using the ones I lent her since she's comfortable with those. She can always upgrade later when a good one for her comes along."

"That's so kind, Alex. She's lucky to have you as a teacher. You really have a gift for sparking joy in your students."

"Thanks so much! I love creating new bass players and unleashing them on the world."

"And the way you talk. It's so lush and descriptive. Have you ever thought about going into radio?"

"You know, people have told me I have a great voice

since I was twelve, but I've never really thought about it much. I did a few shows for my college radio station. I don't know, my voice always sounds a little nasally in my head."

"I'm going to think about this a bit. I feel like there might be something here." Jeannie narrowed her eyes at Alex like she was already brainstorming. "Mind if I come back with a few ideas?"

Alex didn't really know what she meant. "Happy to help however I can."

Alex watched them drive away. She went back to their conversation about Carol Kaye. She was one of the most famously unknown bass players of the last hundred years. People knew names in rock like Geddy Lee from Rush, John Paul Jones from Led Zeppelin, and Flea from the Red Hot Chili Peppers. Few people outside the music world knew of Carol.

The story went that Carol had her first kid when she was sixteen and her music teacher was the father. Maybe it was true love, but Alex remembered all too well how it felt at sixteen to have authority figures make advances. One of her teachers had tried it with her. She knew at the time he would give her the advantage in getting into college because he made sure she knew he would give her a good college recommendation. She didn't succumb to his advances but always wondered what would have happened if she did.

She literally shuddered at the thought, as she had at age sixteen. It was a common tale. It had happened to her. It happened to Madou. It really could happen to anyone and was way more common than people thought. She would talk about it with Betsy, so she was prepared and didn't feel alone if it happened to her.

She wanted to protect Betsy. And all the other female bass players. And female musicians.

More importantly for now, Betsy was making amazing progress. Alex knew in her bones that she had made a good decision to re-prioritize teaching. She loved watching Betsy respond to learning electric bass. She was soaking it all up and becoming a better musician.

If she could help Betsy learn how to navigate the inevitable sexual predators she would encounter and help her stick with music, Betsy might become the next Carol Kaye. There was always a way.

⸺

"HEY GRAM." Alex called her grandmother most Saturdays. It was a tradition that started when Alex left for college, and it had stuck. During college, she was usually out gigging in the evenings. Daytime on Saturdays tended to be a quiet time for Alex in between rehearsals and gigs… and now work.

"How's my favorite granddaughter?"

"I'm your only granddaughter." It was a conversation they had many times.

"Even if I had twelve, you'd still be my favorite."

"Safe bet since it's highly unlikely you'll have more at this point."

Her grandmother was quiet for a moment. Alex's older uncle had been killed in Desert Storm and her mother's younger brother never wanted to have kids with his partner. Alex didn't know what had happened between Steven and Pops, but it was bad enough that he wasn't part of the family.

Alex's heart twisted for her grandmother. Two dead children and one estranged. Alex had encouraged her grandmother to reach out to Steven now that Pops was gone, but she wouldn't do it. Alex had never met him, so she thought it would be weird to try now.

Gram's experience with her children influenced Alex's decision to never have them. Watching the pain they caused her was so awful that she had no desire to repeat it. It's not like her real mother had been a model for her. She was lucky to have Gram.

"You're so like your mother. I imagine she would have looked just like you if she had lived to be your age."

Alex hadn't been watching the calendar. With everything going on, she had missed marking her mother's birthday.

Alex had no memory of her. She had lived with her mother until she was three years old when her mother, who liked to be called Amethyst even though her name was Geraldine, dropped her off at Gram's place. Amethyst had a recurring drug problem for which Gram had begged her to seek help. She was in and out of rehab for years, but it hadn't worked. Amethyst was briefly married to someone named John Taylor which is how Alex wound up with the last name. They never heard from him after Alex arrived, and Alex never went looking.

Gram and Pops had stepped in and had been all the parents Alex ever needed. Because of Amethyst's drug problem, Gram had volunteered at and monetarily supported a recovery center in their town. Gram didn't have much money, but she had a lot of time since she retired from nursing. She gave most of it to the center.

She told Alex it helped fill the void left by Amethyst's death and the decisions she made on her journey. Gram thought that if she could help even one kid keep their mother, it was worth her energy and investment. Alex admired that about her.

Alex's job was to pull Gram out of her funk when this mood struck. "Gram, my favorite student just left. Her name is Betsy. You'd like her. I'm just starting to get her hooked on playing the electric bass."

"If I had recognized your mother's musical talents earlier, perhaps I would have helped her get hooked on music instead of drugs and alcohol."

It had been a poor choice of words on Alex's part. "Gram. It wasn't your fault. You tried and tried to help her. The grief counselor said we should focus on living for today instead of grieving the past."

"You're right. And I just said goodbye to a lovely young woman who made it through the program and is moving into a group home. She's on track to get her two kids back. I have a good feeling she's going to make it."

"Two more kids you're helping. You're so amazing."

"I get it from my granddaughter. Tell me more about Betsy." Alex distracted her grandmother with stories for the next half hour.

Then, she put in several hours of work so she would have time for her next date.

Chapter 15

Alex's heart wasn't engaged in her date with Ross. The data scientist with bad taste in women. She already had two potential partners in the wings with Adam and Cameron. She didn't need to add more complexity. She thought about cancelling, but then what would she tell Kate?

She decided to just push on through. It was only coffee.

Alex didn't know any data scientists. All she had to go on were stereotypes, and she didn't want to rely on those and create biases before she even met the guy. All she knew was that he was a motorcycling friend of Kate's husband James. Kate had known him for several years. Her only criticism of Ross was his poor taste in women. Alex wondered where that came from.

She and Ross planned to walk around Green Lake. She had learned through their text exchanges that he had started the same habit during the pandemic. They would walk and talk which would give them something to do.

They didn't match at all on paper. He was into data, and she was creative. Kate called him goofy. She wondered what that meant. Alex could be goofy, but it was rare. She was pretty strait-laced. She could see why Kate and James liked him with her penchant for Weird Al and his love of puns.

Alex felt a lot of pressure dating friends of her friends. If she didn't like the guys, they might see each other at parties or make Kate, Margaret, Julia, and Angela feel uncomfortable.

She had to stop focusing on the negative and just enjoy being back on the dating scene. Her friends wouldn't judge. They would want her to be happy.

Since it was March, chances were good it would rain on their walk. They had a back-up plan to meet at a bistro if it was pouring. Seattleites were used to drizzle – only pounding rain had them heading inside.

Sunday morning was cloudy but not rainy, so Alex decided to take Sibelius along with her for the walk. It would help her assess the dog-friendly part of her criteria.

Alex pulled her windbreaker over her head, grabbed Sibby's leash and headed out the door. It was only a half mile walk to their meeting spot, so she would leave her hatchback in the garage.

The perennially cloudy, steely gray sky greeted her. But she always smiled when she walked Sibby. She was very people-friendly and was getting there with other dogs. Sibby had an uncanny ability to sense when someone was interested in meeting her and when they preferred that she just walk by. Alex wished she had that kind of intuition.

The two of them walked down the sidewalk, dodging overgrown bushes and brown foliage. The sidewalk gardens and front yards were just starting to come back to life after the wet winter. In another two months, she'd be marveling at the vibrancy and color.

She loved this neighborhood. It was safe and diverse.

Lots of teachers and blue-collar workers in addition to the techies.

Sibby spotted another dog. "Does your dog like other dogs?" Alex called out. She knew better than to approach a strange dog.

"Oh yeah. Please come and say hi."

Alex kept walking toward them. Sibby's tail wagged vigorously at the little black and white dog. The dogs sniffed each other and tried to play with their leashes still on. Alex coaxed a reluctant Sibby away from her new friend, happy with the socialization progress. "Have a great walk!"

They continued to the bottom of the hill and the path that led along the lake to the restaurant she and Ross agreed to use as their back up plan. Looks like they didn't need it after all. As she approached, she could see Ross in an orange raincoat out front.

"Hey Alex. I see you brought protection." Ross bent down to greet the dog. "Who do we have here?" Sibby was already happily getting scratches behind her ears by the time Alex started the introduction. He was clearly comfortable with dogs.

"Hiya. This is Sibelius. Not much of a guard dog."

"Sibbay-what?"

"Sibelius. A Finnish composer." He looked uncomfortable. "He's pretty famous for a composer but not exactly a household name."

"Got it, like naming her Euclid for a math person. I get it. Speaking of getting things, can I get you a coffee for our walk?"

"That would be great. Just an Americano or drip coffee – whichever is easier."

"Your wish is my command." He gave her a lopsided

smile like he was trying to contain a laugh. "Be right back."

She watched him walk away. He was tall. She liked that. His sandy hair was too long and hung over his face, probably a carryover from not getting haircuts during the pandemic. His orange rain jacket hid his body, but unless he had let himself go during the pandemic, she knew he was on the husky side, but not in a bad way. A way that suggested he liked to eat.

He came back quickly.

"Want to walk and talk?"

"Sure, and thanks for the coffee."

"Is it okay if I give Subbalaylis a cookie? They had a jar at the counter."

"Sure, thanks for that, too." He asked Sibby to sit before giving her the cookie. Another point in the positive column. "It's actually Sibelius. You can just call her Sibby."

"That's easier to remember, thanks." He smiled at her. He didn't seem to mind the correction. He had expressive green eyes. She hadn't noticed that before.

"So, um, what do you do for fun when you aren't at Kate's karaoke parties?" Alex thought that was a good starter question.

"I work a lot." Ross ran his hand through his hair. "I'm a data analyst. You know, spreadsheets and predictive models and artificial intelligence, oh my." He said it like Dorothy in *The Wizard of Oz*.

"Sounds like you need a brain and some courage for that."

"And a heart. Especially with AI. You can do a lot of damage based on the data that gets input into these models if you aren't also looking out for humanity."

"Lots to explore there. What do you mean?"

"Like if you create a predictive model that automatically approves loans and you feed it historical data, then it could decide that only white people in a certain economic echelon get approved because that's who was historically approved. If you don't check the biases in the data, you could inadvertently train a model to be a racist."

"Wow. I hadn't thought of that. It doesn't come up much in the music world."

"Oh, but it does. There's a ton of chatter out there about AI being able to replace composers. I mean, you could ask it to write a symphony in the style of Sibby-what's-his-face and you might not be able to tell the difference between the one he wrote and the one AI wrote."

"Whoa. That's scary."

"Yes and no. It's still evolving and will for quite a while. I focus more on the ways it can automate mundane activities so people have more time for their more creative pursuits."

"I get that. I wonder all the time why my job hasn't been automated."

"I thought you were a bass player." Ross sounded confused.

"I am, well, I was. I'm not playing much these days. I have a day job to pay the bills. I basically manage other peoples' action items, with a soupçon of strategy thrown in."

"That sounds kind of boring compared to being on stage."

"Yeah, it is, but the music scene is just starting to recover after the pandemic. I feel like I need to leave the paying gigs for musicians who didn't have friends like Julia and Kate to help them with alternate careers during the pandemic. I'll get back into it in time." *Would she?* she wondered.

"That's altruistic of you." Ross sounded impressed. "Do you just keep practicing in the evenings to stay sharp?"

"Yeah. There's a free service for orchestra parts, so when I feel like playing a certain symphony, I can download the part and play along with a recording."

"That's so cool. I'd love to hear you play sometime. What kind of music do you play?"

"I like to say I play ABC." Alex had created that acronym in college.

"ABC?"

"It stands for Anything But Country."

"Ouch. There's a lot of great country music out there."

"Yeah, okay. But the two-note bass parts and whiny lyrics annoy me. I tried to expand my horizons by playing in a Rockabilly band before the pandemic. At least that was country-adjacent. I'm growing." Alex laughed. So did Ross.

"How mature and self-aware of you. I remember that – you played at one of Kate's parties. That was so cool." They shared a smile. "But I have to ask, out of all the instruments out there, why did you pick the bass?"

"I actually tried the violin first. During rehearsals, I would sit in my section and look longingly at the basses lined up on the opposite wall of the music room. There were three basses and no bass players. The instruments were abused by the kids. When the conductor wasn't there, they would de-tune or bang on them. I wanted to save them. One day, the conductor asked if anyone would be interested in trying to play one. I jumped at the chance."

"He just offered it to you?"

"Most people don't want to play the bass, especially in sixth grade. They're hard to transport. And it's not flashy to be a bass player. You don't get solos or features. It's not sexy. Anyway, I took it home for the summer and my grandparents got me lessons. I loved it."

"What do you love about it?"

"Everything. The bass lays the foundation for the entire orchestra. Like you're the floor the entire orchestra is built on. We help the orchestra be better. It's why I didn't pursue a solo career. I love what a group can do together – something that's bigger than you as an individual."

"Shit, you're going to make me cry. That was beautiful. And says a lot about you as a person." He smiled at her. "How did you get from orchestra to playing rockabilly at Kate's party?"

"Because every group needs a bass. Orchestras, jazz bands, even wind symphonies. I started playing in every group I could in high school. Community orchestras, the pep band at basketball games, chamber music ensembles. You name it."

"Marching band. Can't play in a marching band."

Alex laughed. "You wouldn't think so, but I dated a kid in high school who played electric bass in his high school marching band. He set up an amplifier on the sideline and connected through a wireless interface. Mikey." She sighed at the memory. "He introduced me to the band Rush and blow jobs."

"I love Mikey. I've never met the guy, but I love him."

"Anyway, since you can play in just about any group, there's never a shortage of work for a decent bass player. Except when the entire world shuts down for a pandemic."

"Good point. That must have been hard. I just switched to working from home and carried on."

"It sucked. Julia saved my bacon and got me a corporate gig. And the rest is history."

They fell into a comfortable rhythm sipping and walking. Whenever there was a lull in the conversation, Sibby would invariably fill it by wanting to greet another dog or getting attention from a friendly passer-by.

"I've never had a dog. Now I see the appeal. You can meet a ton of people by walking around with a cute dog. If this doesn't work out, maybe I could borrow Sibby for a few walks."

Alex decided to joke back. "Why do you think this wouldn't work out?"

"Just being prepared. I mean, we're not very compatible on paper. You're a musician from the East Coast and I'm a data scientist from the Midwest. I'm usually attracted to the wrong women, and I have a history of getting dumped or worse, staying in relationships too long even though I'm not happy. So now I'm thirty-nine and single."

"Thirty-six and single." Alex waved her hand at Ross. "What's wrong with us? There must be something."

"I'm going with not meeting the right people." Alex looked down at her shoes at Ross' comment. "What? Did I say the wrong thing?" Ross looked concerned.

"No, sorry. I'll just get this out there. I did meet the right person."

"But he left you to join a cult?"

"No." Alex have him a wry smile. "He died. Five years ago."

"Oh shit, I'm sorry. That wasn't in the brief I got from Kate. Big detail to not share. Sorry for being flippant and making a joke."

"Forget about it. Let's focus on the positive. It is possible to meet the right person. I just have to do it twice."

"Okay, then let me introduce myself again. Hi. I'm Ross." He extended his hand for a handshake.

"Not meet the same *person* twice." Alex playfully batted his arm and chuckled. She started to understand why he and Kate's husband James got along. They were both goofballs.

Ross won a second date.

Chapter 16

Alex was on her way to Michelle's office for their one on one. They were usually one-way conversations where Michelle dictated action items and Alex executed them.

But Alex was doing strategy now and she wanted to address why Michelle wasn't supporting her more in meetings. She wasn't quite sure how to approach it. She would figure it out, hopefully in the next ten steps down the hallway.

"Come on in," Michelle said when she saw Alex at the door. "We have a lot to talk about."

Alex opened her laptop, ready to take notes. "There's something I would like to discuss first." Alex looked pointedly at Michelle.

"Let's go over that after I get through my list. I'm sure we'll have plenty of time." Alex recoiled a bit. *If we have plenty of time, why not start with my list*, she wondered in vain.

"Okay." Alex was annoyed with herself for capitulating. "What've you got for me?"

"First, we need to talk about the March update email for Craig." Craig was Michelle's boss' boss' boss. Michelle always freaked out when she had to send him email updates. She was a fan of the laundry list and Alex had already learned from Julia that Craig preferred three bullet points of results and the top two areas where help was needed along with a very specific estimate for the business results the help would unlock. Period. That's it.

But instead, there would be eight rounds of back and forth before Alex took Michelle's gobbledygook and added an executive summary on top, which would of course, be the only part that Craig read. *Here we go again,* Alex thought.

"And I need you to lead the strategy session this afternoon. I've been called into another meeting. I know you can handle it."

"Thanks for the vote of confidence." Alex wondered why Michelle supported her strategy work in private but not in public. Something to ask about when they got to Alex's list. "What do you want to get out of the meeting?"

"You're in charge of the strategy now. I'm tired of the in-fighting. Make it stop. Get everyone to agree on the final version and land it."

That was a lot. They'd been trying to do just that for a few weeks now, and Michelle wanted her to do it in one meeting?

"Okay, I'll do my best." Strategy was apparently a lot easier to do than Alex thought. She believed she needed to deeply understand a topic, have studied it, have become knowledgeable about it, come up with ideas, test them, and then implement them. Kind of like practicing a piece of music until you mastered it and then performed it in a recital.

No. At LampLight, it seemed like whoever yelled the loudest and held out the longest led the strategy. She decided to test that theory as the account orchestration model continued to evolve. "Okay great. I know who isn't onboard. I'll meet with them to hear their concerns and come back with a final strategy."

Alex knew it wouldn't be the final strategy. Nothing ever seemed to be final here. She kept seeing documents from other projects called things like Project X – final. Then two days later, it would be called Project X updated final. It was like a Tchaikovsky Symphony. Just when you thought it was over, there was an entire additional page of music.

"Great. That's all the time I have for us today." Michelle dismissed her with a smile.

They never got to Alex's questions.

▭

ALEX STARTED the meeting to finalize the strategy. She leveraged her program management expertise and had created a list of open items that needed closure to land the strategy. They would take them one by one and get through the list.

"Okay people, we need to get this done by the end of the week so there's time to develop and deliver the training before the strategy goes live in July."

"Alexandra, what do you mean by done?" Murphy from the sales team asked.

"Done, like complete. All open items closed. Everything documented. We've been swirling on the same open items for a few weeks now. We have to close them out."

"That'll never happen in this meeting." He shook his head dismissively.

"It has to. The fiscal year deadline isn't going to move. Legal needs a month for their review, and the enablement team doing the training says they need a month after that to fully develop the documentation. Then, they need a month to deliver the training around the world." Tanja held her ground, as usual.

"They can do the training in two days if pushed." Alex wondered why Murphy was being like this.

Alex saw Tanja's scrunched up face.

"Okay, but why would we push them?" Alex asked. She touched her flame charm for emotional support. "We want people to be able to take the training when they need it in between closing business. We don't want to cram it into the last few days of the fiscal year. We all know it won't get done because closing deals will be more important. We'll miss revenue in the first quarter from the delay."

"So we just go live later. No big deal." Alex found his tone very annoying.

Alex didn't understand this lackadaisical attitude toward deadlines. In music, there were scheduled performances with audiences. They didn't move. If the orchestra or the soloist wasn't ready, the show must go on. Why wasn't it the same here? Where was the sense of urgency?

"Everyone, let me just try a musical analogy." Alex went to her safe place.

"Great, another one." Murphy rolled his eyes. There was a collective groan from the team, led by Eugene. Alex chose to ignore it.

"Let her speak. This is important." Alex appreciated Tanja's support.

"You have to practice your part before a performance. Let's say this is the world premiere of a new piece of music. Groups don't just sightread concerts."

"Sightread? Your musical jargon makes no sense." Eugene sighed.

She knew exactly how he felt navigating the bizarre world of LampLight's misused vocabulary. "That's what it's called when you first see a piece of music. Even ringers called in as substitutes at the last minute have to come to at least one rehearsal and the dress rehearsal before they're allowed to perform. Soloists arrive in town the week before to have at least two practice sessions with the orchestra. You don't just go in cold."

"Why not? What's the big deal?" Murphy was clearly not a musician.

"The musicians don't play together, the piece sounds terrible, the composer is unhappy if they're still alive, and most importantly, the audience never comes back. We're the composer of the piece, the sellers are the musicians, and the customers are the audience. If we don't prepare the musicians to sound good and play together, the audience isn't coming back."

"Actually, that makes a lot of sense." Eugene sounded surprised. Alex chose to ignore the tone and take the win. "I keep thinking about it like we're the musicians. But we're not. We're the composer."

"And the orchestrator and the arranger. It has to all be written into the parts or the musicians will be confused. They get to ask questions in the rehearsal. Everything has to be done before the rehearsals can start."

"This is making a lot more sense. If we follow that logic, we really do need to get all of the open items completed this week, or the arrangers won't have time to translate it into all of the parts. Right, Alexandra?"

"Now you're getting it, Eugene!" This time, the group nodded. "So let's hit item number one." Alex clapped her hands together, feeling the zing of triumph. "Who gets to decide which solution to sell first?"

"Easy." Murphy leaned back in his chair. "The seller with the solution that's most behind on revenue in that subsidiary for that quarter gets to take the lead."

Alex's victory was short-lived. She saw it very differently. "Murphy, if you bought a ticket to hear Madonna and once you were in your seat, you found out that it was actually a Rush cover band, would you stay and listen to the concert?"

"No, that's just dumb." He pursed his lips at her.

"But that's what you're saying. A customer tells us they want to improve productivity, and we say, that's great, but what you *really* need is a new security platform. No. We sell what the customer asks for first and surround it with the prerequisites they need. Then, we add-on solutions afterwards."

"Fit that into your little music analogy, Alexandra." Eugene challenged her.

Alex thought for a moment. "Okay, you're at the Madonna concert and you know there's an opening act. Even if you don't like the music, you stay and you listen because you really want to hear Madonna. And maybe you'll even decide you like the opening act because it was chosen to go with Madonna, so you're more open to hearing and liking it."

"You got game, girl." Eugene changed his tune. "This really is just like a musical performance!"

She wondered if this was her new career. Going from team to team and explaining things through analogies and metaphors with a musical twist. Why did people with MBAs in business strategy and marketing and everything else need this to be explained in such simple terms?

TANJA PULLED her aside after the meeting. "You know, Alexandra, things have really taken off since you started helping with strategy. Have you thought about switching teams? You have such a great way of simplifying and explaining. My team is hiring a training strategy position. I think your skills are wasted on action item tracking."

Tanja's comments matched Alex's internal talk track. "Thanks, I'm flattered."

"Think about it. The job will be posted next week, and I'd love for you to interview. It's a level higher than you are, but I think you have a great case for an on-hire promotion given your work here."

"Awesome. Right now, I have to get to work documenting our final decisions and writing up an update for Craig. I'll talk to Michelle and see what she thinks."

"You shouldn't do that." Tanja's tone was serious. "You don't have to tell your manager when you interview. Wait and see if you get the job before you piss her off. She can get prickly, and I would hate to mess up your relationship with her."

That sounded odd to Alex. Wouldn't it be better to involve Michelle in the process? But, she figured Tanja had a lot more experience than she did, so she agreed.

"Great. I'll leave you to it." She watched Tanja walk away.

Alex was beaming. This strategy thing was working out. Michelle was right. It was a great skill to have added to her repertoire. *And someday, more money.*

Chapter 17

It had been a couple of weeks since their first date. Adam had decided to follow-through on the Haitian food angle and offered to cook for Alex.

Her stomach grumbled as she thought of the good food she was about to eat. She reminisced about her semi-adopted Haitian family as she drove south to Adam's place. She thought about the first time she met Mama Rosie and Papi. Her friend Madou, a nickname for Madeleine, was an amazing pianist at music school. It was hard to get in as a bass player, but at least ten times harder as a pianist since piano was such a popular instrument.

They both showed up for jazz band auditions and were glad to see other women there. Even though it was 2004, there weren't as many women in jazz as either of them would have liked. They were put into a rhythm section together for the audition and clicked. They could read each other incredibly well even in their first jam session. Madou would play a comp chord, and Alex would answer with a lick. They traded fours, each building on the others' themes.

They had been inseparable for those four years.

Madou grew up in the Midwood neighborhood of Brooklyn. It was a little over an hour on the subway to get there from the upper West Side where they both studied. Alex and Madou made that trip at least once a month. From the first moment Alex entered Madou's house, she had been accepted as part of the family. Before she could even introduce herself, Mama Rosie grabbed her in a bear hug.

Papi was one scary-looking dude. He was a plant floor foreman who would answer the phone with a gruff "Why are you calling my house." Once Alex said it was her, his tone would change to warm and loving. His tough guy demeanor was just an act to keep people in line. He was a massive, cuddly teddy bear with an amazing laugh and huge heart. And he was a jazz fan. Alex and Papi talked for hours about their favorite players and recordings.

Alex had learned a lot in their house. A lot about the Haitian culture and a lot about being a minority. Growing up in a relatively affluent suburb of Boston and passing as white, Alex was usually surrounded by white people. She knew people of color in the youth orchestra she played in during high school. But they weren't close friends. In Mama Rosie's house, Alex learned about acceptance. No one ever questioned why she was there or who she was, this skinny little white girl. She was just accepted as part of the family.

Alex had taken French in high school, but she wasn't fluent. She spoke to Madou's older relatives in broken French since she clearly didn't speak Haitian Creole. It didn't matter. They used hand gestures and smiles and somehow understood each other. They taught her some key phrases.

And the food. Mama Rosie was famous for her cooking. And her house was the center of the family. There were always pots bubbling and excitement in the kitchen which was the center of the house even though it was located in the back. If you weren't helping her chop ingredients or watch the plantains frying on the stove, you had to get out of her kitchen.

Alex spent so many hours in that house and as part of Madou and Mama Rosie's family. Mama Rosie and Papi moved back to Haiti when Madou's youngest sibling graduated high school. She hadn't had good Haitian food since.

Alex pulled up to the curb near Adam's house in Columbia City. It was a single-story bungalow on a narrow street. Most of the houses in view were well kept with tidy lawns and relatively fresh paint. Every fifth house or so looked like they could be making meth inside. It was a great neighborhood.

She grabbed the bottle of Barbancourt Haitian rum and the red wine she brought and walked up the path to the front door.

Adam greeted her with a warm smile and accepted the bottles. "Ooh, the good stuff," he said as he looked at the rum. "They did teach you right."

"It smells great in here." Alex smiled as the smell triggered memories of Mama Rosie's kitchen.

"Griot and pikliz with rice and beans."

"Yum. Do you fry or bake your meat for the griot?"

"I marinate and bake the pork shoulder and then broil it to get it crispy on the outside. It's a little healthier that way. A little."

They shared a chuckle. "Can I get you something to drink?"

"How about some of that wine?"

"The griot will take another few minutes. I'll join you

in that wine while we wait." He pointed to the couch. "Why don't you have a seat, and I'll bring you the wine."

"Sounds good." Alex settled onto the soft green sofa. There was a throw over the back knit in soft colors that looked homemade.

"The orchestra is in full swing again. Why aren't you back with us?" Adam asked as he handed her a glass of wine.

"Timing. I have to go into the office on Mondays and Wednesdays for my day job. I work until seven and then have to get home for my dog. I can't get to a seven o'clock rehearsal on Wednesdays. I miss it." Alex subconsciously clenched and unclenched her left hand, her fingers itching for the neck of her bass.

"Day job? But that's all it is. Not who you are."

She had used the term day job because that's what musicians called jobs that paid the bills while they gigged on nights and weekends. Hers was actually more like a day, evening, and weekends job. "Yeah, my hours keep getting worse, and now I'm kind of stuck."

"Why can't you just arrange your schedule to leave at five on Wednesdays?"

"Because that's one of the days we do reviews with the teams in Asia. We meet with them from three to six and then I have to compile all of the notes."

"You should be focusing on a different kind of note."

"Good one. I make so much more money in my corporate gig. And I was struggling to make ends meet as a musician."

"If you were serious about being a musician, you wouldn't let money worries stop you. You would get back in there." His tone sounded pretty judgy to Alex. But he had a point.

Alex didn't understand how he could be so certain. "I like the money. I'm alone now and have to do it all myself."

"I get it, but you know how to maximize earnings as a musician. You teach during the day and rehearse or gig at night. It's tiring, but when you love what you're doing, you get energy from it. Don't you miss it?"

"Like a limb." Was that the problem? She had gotten comfortable playing in tier two and three orchestras and keeping the house for Tom. At a hundred and fifty bucks a service, she made enough to contribute, but Tom's salary paid the mortgage. If she had to teach for eight hours a day and then head to rehearsals or concerts six or seven nights a week and barely scrape by, would it turn from something she loved into a grind? "Yeah, I miss it. I still teach on Saturdays."

"That's not the same as playing. You have to decide whether you're going to suckle at the teat of capitalism or get back to your craft."

"I know." Alex was uncomfortable under Adam's steady questioning. She wanted to change the subject. "The griot smells like it might be done." She went for the redirect.

"Oh, right." Adam jumped up and ran into the kitchen to check the meat. "Nice save. It's just right. I'll meet you at the island with a plate. Marinade on or next to the griot?"

"On the side please. The scotch bonnet pepper can be a little strong for me."

"I get it." He set a steaming plate of crispy pork, rice and beans, and a cup of spicy pickled cabbage in front of her.

She leaned in and sniffed deeply. "It smells wonderful." She stayed where she was, letting memories of Mama Rosie's kitchen fill her with warmth.

"Kind of hard to mess it up."

"Don't sell yourself short. I'm having a moment here." She kept her eyes closed.

"Kiss and make it better?" He looked at her with hope in his brown eyes, the judginess gone.

Alex leaned in for a kiss. His lips felt nice and warm on hers, but the earth didn't shudder under her feet. Maybe she was just distracted by the smell of the food.

"Now let's dig in," he said, pulling away about an inch.

Alex was left wondering what would happen after dinner.

Chapter 18

"Did I pass the test?" Adam raised his eyebrows with the question.

"What test?"

"Did my griot get a passing grade?"

"Oh yeah," Alex said, wiping a bit of stray sauce from the corner of her mouth. When she looked back up, Adam was staring at her mouth. "What? Do I have something in my teeth?" She ran her tongue across her teeth to check.

"No, just admiring the view." Adam's smooth voice and sexy smile sent a zing to her core. "Shall we take this to the couch?"

Alex froze for a moment. She had an inkling where this would lead. She liked him. She liked him a lot. He pushed her to examine her life instead of just accepting her explanations about her corporate self. But she was kind of involved with Cameron. And then there was Ross, too. She set that aside. "I'd like that."

He took her hand and led her toward the sofa. He stopped to put on some music.

Sade. *Sex music*, Alex thought. No one put on Sade just

to listen to it. "Paul Spencer Denman. Sade's underrated bass player. I mean, listen to that line." Alex started to sing along and mimicked the slide in the bass line with her left hand.

"Bass players. Always singing the bass line and thinking people know what song they're singing." Adam reached out and grabbed the hand she was using to play air bass.

"Oboists," she shot back. "Always singing the melody and thinking that's the important part." She chuckled and pulled him down on the couch. *Just go with it,* she told herself.

Adam turned toward her and reached out to tuck her hair behind her ear. "Now I can see you better," he said as he leaned in. Their lips met in a warm kiss. Alex pressed against him and poured herself into it. He wrapped his arms around her and pulled her closer.

Alex traced his lips with her tongue. It surprised her that she could feel the callous on the midline of his upper lip where he rested his oboe reed. She couldn't stop the giggle.

"What, you don't like this?" Adam asked as he pulled away.

"I haven't kissed a woodwind player in a long time. I forgot about the lip callous. You've been practicing."

"I'd like to continue another kind of practicing if you don't mind." He laid her back on the couch and spread his hand over her breast.

Alex let the warmth envelop her as she kissed him back. He wasn't exactly lighting a fire in her, but it was lovely to be with him like this in the comfortable living room where the smell of their Haitian dinner lingered in the room and on his tongue. She sank into the sofa and let the coziness fill her. They kept kissing for a few minutes. She enjoyed the slow pace.

"Want to watch a movie or something?"

Alex was surprised by the sudden change as Adam sat up. Was she that bad of a kisser? She was suddenly filled with awkwardness. "Um, what time is it?" She fumbled to look at her watch. "It's almost nine and I have an early meeting. Guess I'll head out."

He walked her to the door. The mood had shifted. "Everything okay?" she asked. They could be honest with each other.

"Tout bon." It didn't seem to Alex like everything was fine.

"You sure? Something seems off." She tried to probe a little deeper.

"Nah, just tired." He looked at her with a pleasant smile on his face.

"Thanks for dinner. You make a killer griot."

They shared a smile before Adam opened the door for her.

ALEX PONDERED the end of the evening on the drive home. She'd been enjoying herself. Maybe she'd been out of the scene too long and had forgotten how to kiss. She used to be good at it. Good enough that several men came back for more. Tom had never complained. They'd had an excellent sex life. She couldn't have forgotten everything. Then again, she and Cameron hadn't spent too much time on that part either.

She had to admit there were no fireworks. Just sweet, comforting kissing.

Maybe Adam wasn't into sweet, comforting kissing.

For her, it was another nice and easy re-introduction to being physical with someone.

She felt safe and comfortable. That was a good thing.

But maybe she was supposed to be a lioness and pounce on him.

She would get input from her friends at brunch that weekend.

"YOU KNOW, I don't mind that I've gained a little weight." Julia sounded pretty upbeat about it at their monthly brunch. "I mean, that's what happens when you hit fifty, right?"

"Or forty," Gertie added.

"Or thirty," Alex chimed in.

Julia continued. "There is one time in particular it bothers me."

"When you have to squeeze into Spanx for dresses that used to fit you?" Margaret asked.

"Nope. I just buy a new dress."

"When you see yourself naked in the mirror? Girl, I've stopped looking." Angela chuckled as she said it.

"You're gorgeous, so stop that. But not that either. It's when Rob and I are going at it and body parts hit and make noises they didn't used to. You know, like…" Julia demonstrated by pulling her cheek back and forth rapidly to make a splatting sound. The ladies started laughing. "It was okay when it was like slap slap slap." Julia repeatedly slapped the back of her right hand against the palm of her left hand. "That sound is okay. It's the sound of sex. But when it's my belly slapping his when I'm on top, it kind of ruins my mood."

Margaret spit some of her mimosa across the table, tears falling from her eyes as she laughed.

"I don't even remember what sex sounds like." Alex said with a sigh.

"We're working on that. Who's in the lead this month?"

"March results are in." Alex played it up for the brunch ladies. "Two dates with Adam, one with Ross, and one with Cameron."

She received nods of approval.

"You've been busy," Lesley gave her a thumbs up.

"And?" Angela's eyebrows couldn't go any higher.

"All three are in. It's crazy."

"Poor Carlos, languishing all alone in that sad bowl."

"Is he single?" Lesley asked. "I want in on this, too."

Julia looked a little guilty. "I haven't asked. Since he didn't get picked, I didn't follow up. I can ask for you the next time I see him at the dog park."

"No, let's wait and see how this plays out for Alex."

"Alex, pros and cons. Who's in the lead?" Akiko was all business.

"I don't know. Whichever guy I go out with moves to the top of the pack. Adam gets me. He's a musician and we discovered a mutual connection to Haiti, or at least the culture and food. We're both really close to our grandparents. Ross is hilarious and immediately put me at ease. And then Cameron was easy to hang out with also. The downside with Cameron is he's so much like Tom. I don't want to date him just because he's like Tom."

Gertie cleared her throat. "Dating Cameron because he's a lot like Tom is dumb." She paused. "Not dating Cameron because he's a lot like Tom? Also dumb." Gertie had a way of simplifying the complex. Maybe *she* should work at LampLight.

"I just can't separate them in my head. I mean, we used to hang out together. I'll never know if I like Cameron for who he is or if it's just the comfort of having him remind me of Tom. I don't want to second guess myself all the time."

"Then don't." Brie made it sound easy. "Just take it as it comes. Life is precious and you just waste time second-guessing when that energy could be focused on creating new memories together." That sort of sentiment was more potent when coming from a doctor who treated cancer.

"How do they compare in bed?" Margaret asked, wiggling her eyebrows and leaning in.

"Margaret! I just started seeing them!"

"And?"

"I did make out with Adam earlier this week." Nine women moved in to hear the story.

"It was really nice."

"Wah waaaah." Gertie made the game show loser sound and put both thumbs down.

"Oh come on, comfortable is good." Alex wanted to defend Adam.

"Yeah, when we're talking about bras, not men." Margaret's wisdom elicited nods from the table.

"Margaret makes a good point," Brie nodded. "There has to be a spark."

"Was there maybe just a long fuse that needs to burn for a while before it explodes?" Julia was being positive.

"It didn't feel like that. We just sort of kissed for a few minutes and then it was over."

"Girl, you've been in a sex desert for five years." Angela shook her head. "If he didn't make you want to rip your clothes off and jump him, something is definitely wrong."

"Wrong is a strong word for it. It was really nice to be held." She thought about their lovely moments on the couch with the soft throw. Angela looked down at her drink. Alex wasn't fooled. "Ange, I can feel your eye roll from here."

"Busted. Part of this experiment was to, Gertie, how did you put it?"

"Smack some cheeks."

"That was it. If he doesn't make you want to go there, I would take him off the list."

"That's harsh. He made me dinner and we had a lovely time."

"You can do that with me," Angela added.

"Smack some cheeks?" Gertie sounded intrigued.

Alex gave Gertie a stern look amidst the giggles from others. "Sex isn't everything. He's kind and sweet and funny. He gets me. We have a cool connection to Haiti. Cut him some slack."

"You're the one dating him, so you should make your own call." Kate's no-nonsense attitude was on display.

"Or go jump Ross and Cameron and see if they make your blood hum." Margaret pursed her lips and nodded sagely.

"Cameron kind of jumped ahead on that plan."

"Now you tell us?" Margaret pretended to be affronted.

"How'd he do?" Lesley asked.

"Very well, I'd say. We traded head. He wanted to, and I figured he was a safe bet for getting back on the horse, so to speak."

"Save a horse, ride a cowboy," Gertie belted out. "I'm adding that to my karaoke party list, Kate."

"And?" It was Melanie's turn to ask for details.

"Rocked my world. And I clearly hadn't forgotten how to do my part."

"Talk about burying the lede!"

"No, we haven't done that yet." Alex tried for a sex

joke. She usually left that to Gertie and Margaret. They were so much better at it than she was.

It took a while for the laughter to die down.

Kate was the first to recover. "That reminds me. You're all in for our party next weekend, right? We wouldn't want to miss Gertie's new song."

"Cheers to that!" Lesley led the toast.

Chapter 19

Alex decided to go for the role on Tanja's team. It had taken a while for it all to get scheduled, but the interviews were finally on the calendar. Breaking up with Michelle would be hard, but once Alex saw the level and salary of the new job, she had to go for it. Clearly, Tanja thought she had the chops.

She dusted off the advice she had gotten from the Steak and Bourbon crew before her first interview at LampLight to prepare.

- Practice some answers about where you did well. Check.
- Get a story or two together about when you failed and what you learned. Check.
- Ask what success looks like for the interviewer. Check.
- Ask the interviewer how the role supports *them*. Check.
- Go for the close – ask for the recommendation. Check.

She was good to go.

Alex dressed to impress for the interviews. She didn't spend a lot of money on clothes. Julia helped her buy a few pieces that went with anything once the pressure was on to go back into the office. Alex had plenty of black pants from her orchestra days. She added no-iron dress shirts in various colors and prints and basically wore them every time she had to go into the office. She was more comfortable in all black orchestra dress or the studio wardrobe of jeans and t-shirts.

She marveled at the women who looked like they stepped out of a fashion magazine every day. She had neither the money nor the inclination to be like that.

After returning from her early morning walk with Sibby, Alex chose a light pink dress shirt and her typical black pants. She topped it with a gray jacket. Professional but a little fun. She added a dash of mascara and was out the door heading across the water for her day of interviews.

The armpits of Alex's shirt felt sticky with her nervous perspiration. She was jittery.

She didn't really understand why. She was perfectly happy in her current role. She hadn't even wanted the new job. But once she saw the salary increase, she was hooked. If she got the job, she could try to start it with a fresh mindset.

Like Angela.

She took a bracing breath and knocked on the door of her first interviewer.

THE FIRST THREE interviews went smoothly. She knew all the interviewers because they were from Tanja's team and were key stakeholders. They felt more like conversations than interviews.

Maybe that's how the corporate world worked.

They all asked her the same questions. Almost like they hadn't coordinated before the interviews. This was way too easy.

Alex knocked on the final interviewer's door. She hadn't worked with Blair before. He managed field landing for changes to partner strategy on Tanja's team. His sandy brown hair was cropped close to his head and his blue eyes seemed very round in his face, like he always wore a look of surprise. He broadcasted overgrown frat boy – the college bros Alex had learned to avoid in New York City.

"You must be Alexandra. Come on in. I've heard good things about you. It would be great to have you under me."

Her eyes squinted involuntarily as she tried to figure out his comment. "Nice to meet you, Blair. I thought this role reported to Tanja. Has something changed?"

"Not so far." He winked at her. She was skeeved out by his look, a shiver running down her spine.

"Make yourself comfortable." Blair certainly did as he opened his legs, clasped his hands behind his head, and leaned back in his chair, giving Alex a full view of his manspread. "Need anything?"

She kept her eyes on his. "No, I'm good. Thanks."

"We'll see about that," he said. "Tell me about your strategy experience."

Alex didn't really know what to say. She almost blurted out that she hadn't done a strategy role before, but remembered Julia's advice to let the interviewers do most of the talking. She likened it to going through customs. Say as little as you needed to and don't offer information that wasn't requested. "I'm the lead strategist on the new sales model on Michelle's team." She was proud of her answer — totally true yet with no dates.

"What would you want your title to be in this role?" He slanted his eyes at her.

"Title? I'm not worried about that. The Business Strategy Manager title in the job description is just fine."

"Is it though? And what if there was a re-org and you wound up working for me?"

Alex swallowed her first answer. "I care more about the work I do than the hierarchy." She decided not to tell him about her desire for better work/life balance and wanting to leave work behind every day.

"Maybe it's a cultural thing. Culture has a big impact on views of hierarchy," he mansplained. "My background tells me that working for a peer would be like going backwards. What's your background? Hispanic? Asian? It's tough to tell."

She wondered what this had to do with the strategy role. "My family has been in the US for at least four generations." She'd learned that revealing she was a quarter Native American led to a whole lot of questions that had nothing to do with business. "What can I tell you about my experience to prove that I can rock this role?" Alex went for the redirect.

"What do you do for fun?"

He clearly wasn't going to take the hint.

"I'm a musician. A bass player. I mostly play jazz and classical."

"Cool. Tell me how jazz is like leadership."

That was actually a very cool question. Perhaps he wasn't a total loss. "Bass players set the feel in a jazz combo. My job is to lock in with the drummer and support the soloists. Most people can't even pick out the bass part — it's just there, supporting everyone. If anything goes wrong,

I lean in and get people back together. When the horn players need a break, I take a solo." She took a breath, assuming he would interrupt her, but he didn't. Another point in the "not a total dick" column. "Playing bass in a jazz band is all about leadership. Setting the feel is like creating a vision. Locking in with the drummer is like building the foundation. Supporting the soloists is like people management. And knowing when to fade into the background and when to lean in is how you scale. And lastly, playing by yourself is fun, but nothing beats the teamwork you feel when the combo is grooving."

"Whoa." Blair leaned back even further. "I feel like I need a cigarette after that answer. It's certainly better to play with others than just with yourself. You have my vote." Blane nodded his head slowly at Alex.

That's not what she meant. She'd had plenty of time with creepy musicians to know just what he was doing. As much as she wanted to respond, she knew it would just make it worse.

She was again reminded of Julia's advice from her first interviews. She told Alex not to sell past the close. Once someone said they would hire you, get out of there as soon as possible because any additional discussion could undo the yes. "Great. Thanks for your time." Alex high-tailed it out of his office.

After checking her email in the hallway, Alex headed for the parking garage. She needed to get out of there. And felt like she should have a shower after that interview. Blair was just plain gross.

Alex was suddenly back at a summer orchestra rehearsal when she was sixteen. She had come to the rehearsal right from work and was dressed for her job as a front receptionist at a law firm. The principal bass player was an older guy who gave her the creeps. She wasn't sure why until that day. Usually, she sat on a stool at rehearsals and concerts because it was more comfortable for a three-hour rehearsal and gave your hands more freedom because you didn't have to support the instrument. He kept telling her to sit down, but she couldn't sit on a stool in a professional pencil skirt without hiking it up and she was not going to do that.

He decided to do it for her.

He reached over and pulled the hem of her skirt up. He laughed and said, "there you go – now you can use your stool" as he looked her up and down.

She yelled at him to never touch her again and continued with the rehearsal. She remembered the shame burning her cheeks. Why hadn't she thought about appropriate attire for rehearsal? Why had she sat close enough to him that he could reach her? What could she have done to avoid the situation?

Back then, it never occurred to her that it was entirely his fault for being an old letch. In her mind, she had brought this on herself. The shame.

She didn't say a word about it when she got home. She just tried to put it out of her mind. She didn't think much of it when the phone rang that night.

It was one of the cellists in the orchestra. He had seen what happened and asked Gram if Alex needed help or wanted to press charges. He said he would testify on Alex's behalf.

Since she hadn't said anything to her grandmother, Gram had no idea what the nice man was talking about.

When Alex told her, Gram explained that men got away with that, and she had to make sure she didn't do anything to encourage them. Alex had put her shields up, started dressing like a frump, and making sure she was always ready to fight off whoever tried anything.

She didn't like having that feeling again in a work setting.

Luckily, very few people were even in the office and her afternoon meetings were all with people outside of Bellevue. It didn't make sense to sit in an office alone for the calls when she could be at home with Sibby.

And it was Taco Night with Adam.

She headed home.

⸻

"I'VE BEEN INVITED to audition for T3BO." Adam bubbled with excitement when they sat down with their tacos and margaritas. "This year's concerts are in Washington D.C. and Paris."

Alex's bad interview experience was pushed from her mind in an instant. She knew all about The Black, Brown, and Beige Orchestra, referred to in the musical world as T3BO. The group was the best of the best of people of color that got together every two years to play a concert in the US and a concert in an international location. The caliber of the musicians was very high, and it was a fabulous networking opportunity even though it wasn't a paying gig. "That's an amazing opportunity. Congratulations!" Alex was thrilled for Adam. She put down her birria taco to toast him with her five-dollar margarita.

"Don't congratulate me yet. I don't have a spot, just an audition."

"It's still super prestigious to get an invitation."

"Like usual, it doesn't pay, but participants get free transportation to the cities and free room and board. And this year, each musician can bring a guest along, as long as they pay their own way there. Guests get free room and board too." He gave her a meaningful look. She wasn't sure he was inviting her and also not sure she was ready for an international trip with him.

"That's amazing. Who's conducting this year?" Alex tried for the gentle redirect.

"Nkechi Touati."

"No way. She came to my music school my sophomore year. We did Mahler Two. She was so commanding on the podium but also playful. Easy to follow."

"It's great they got a female and black conductor. In past years, it's been a black orchestra with a white conductor." Adam pursed his lips and shook his head. "I didn't like that message."

"Can't do much better than a first-generation American with a Tunisian father and a Nigerian mother who used every opportunity to train with the best and reach the top of the game. If you haven't read her memoir, you should."

"Preach." Adam made it a two-syllable word and added a finger wag.

"What's she conducting?" Alex knew it would be a popular piece.

"The anchor work is *La Symphonie Fantastique*."

Alex gasped and clapped her hands. "That's one of my absolute favorite pieces. Love, a ball, shepherds in a meadow, an opium-induced hallucination, dancing with witches, and a guillotine. All wrapped up in a fun bass part. Who could ask for more?"

"There are two other pieces."

"Hit me."

"It's a bit on the nose, but we're also doing Duke Ellington's *Black, Brown, and Beige*."

"Oh my gosh, so few people know about his orchestral works. I played the Martin Luther King, Jr part of *Three Black Kings* in high school."

"T3BO had it re-orchestrated for full orchestra." Adam ran a chip through the salsa.

"Amazing. What's the third piece?"

"*Candide Overture*."

"Brilliant." Alex bubbled. "A French book by Voltaire made into an operetta with music composed by Leonard Bernstein." Alex clutched her hands to her chest and looked up and the ceiling. "The perfect combination of American and French."

"You're so excited." Adam smiled at her exuberance. "Too bad you're too white to audition."

"Yeah, sadly, my Native American blood doesn't show enough on my face."

"It explains the nose."

"Very funny, Adam. When's the audition?"

"By next week. They're doing it all virtually. I just send in a video of me playing a few excerpts from the Mozart oboe concerto and three orchestral excerpts of my choosing for a total of twenty minutes of playing."

"How pandemic of them," she said with a smile. "What are you going to use?"

"I have some ideas. What do you think?"

Alex thought about it for a moment. There were hundreds of great oboe parts to choose from, but which ones would best showcase Adam's musicality and talent? "I loved the way you captured the lyricism of the oboe solo in the Brahms Violin Concerto when we played that, what, before the pandemic? Wow. Time flies."

"That's a good one. How about the poco piu mosso in the third movement of Shostakovich Five?"

"Totally haunting." Another of Alex's favorite symphonies. "Definitely a different feel than the Brahms. Is it too obvious to play the third movement of the Berlioz? I mean, that solo is in the concert."

"Yeah, but I think everyone will do that. I need something fast. And not totally conventional. Something that sets me apart."

"How about the second section of the Shostakovich Festive Overture? It's so blisteringly fast, the woodwind part always mesmerizes me when I perform it – when I'm not managing nasty page turns, that is."

"Interesting." Adam looked pensive. "It's so nice to talk to you about this. I'm not sure why you know so many great oboe parts."

"Because I listen during rehearsals and performances. As a bass player, it's my job to keep everyone together."

"That's a very jazz mentality." He shook his head and pointed his index finger at her. "The conductor keeps everyone together."

"In great orchestras, yes, but in the tier two and three groups I perform with, there's a lot of playing to your ear instead of watching the conductor's baton, so I have to help push or hold back when people aren't watching."

"Oboe parts are so difficult, we tend to pay the most attention to the people around us - the flutes, clarinets, and bassoons – so we can play in unison. And block out the horns behind us."

"I'm glad my ears are above their bells. It must be so loud to sit right in front of the trombones."

"Yeah, it's one of the reasons I don't play English horn very much – you sit at the end of the section, usually right in front of the trombones. Trumpets are bad enough."

Alex laughed, warmed by talking with someone who understood her secret music world like no one at work, Cameron, or Ross did. "Back to the audition, do you have to work those excerpts up, or do you already have them under your fingers?"

"I have some work to do, but mostly it's making sure

everything I want to showcase fits into twenty minutes and then doing a few takes."

"Let me know if I can help. I can push stop and start on the video if you need it." They smiled at each other over the empty basket of tortilla chips.

Alex thought about Adam's comments about her being too white to audition. She had never felt all-the-way white. Her coal black hair and almond-shaped eyes gave her an exotic look. Exotic enough that Blair had asked about her background.

She pushed that out of her mind to focus on Adam's great news.

____

Chapter 20

____

Alex and Ross approached Kate and James' condo for their annual Cinco de Mayo party. They had each been there separately, but they had never arrived together. It felt a little odd but also nice to have a date.

The Cinco de Mayo theme was on display with tiny taco-shaped lights around the doorway. It reminded her of taco dates with Adam. A tinge of guilt that she was out with another man pushed into her brain.

"Is that a storm trooper helmet decorated like a Dia de los Muertos mask on the door?" Alex studied the brightly colored storm trooper mask.

"Yeah, I don't get it." Alex and Ross looked at each other for a moment in confusion.

The door opened and James was on the other side wearing a sombrero and a brown robe. "Hello. I'm Obi Juan Kenobi. Juan like J-U-A-N. May the Fourth Be With You."

"Ohhhh," they both said together.

"It's a combo theme," James added with a smile.

"Cinco de Mayo and May the Fourth be With You. On May Fourth. Get it? Come on in!"

The party was already in full swing. Alex saw Kate in the kitchen with Julia. Lesley, Gertie, and Melanie were there. Angela was on the microphone crooning *Killing Me Softly* while Angela's husband Jeremy stared at her with an adorable expression of love. She sounded amazing. It made Alex wonder why she only sang lead at karaoke parties but was a back-up singer in her bands. It didn't add up.

Alex saw some stormtroopers and another play on the joint holiday theme – Juan Solo who was a guy dressed in a sombrero sporting a pencil-thin black mustache while wearing brown pants and a vest.

Julia approached them wearing a wig with two buns and a pasted on unibrow.

"Let me guess, Princess Frida?"

"Exactly. I thought about Lando Kahlo-Rissian but I already had the wig." They laughed together.

"What can I get you to drink?" James asked.

"You're always so attentive, thank you James. I'll have some bubbly if there's some open. If not, a margarita would be great."

"Ross?"

"I'll have some sort of beer that's not a porter."

"Coming right up." James dashed off to get their drinks.

"I'm going to go say hi to Kate. Meet you back here in a minute." At Ross' nod, Alex was off on a mission to find the host. Alex found her in the kitchen cutting up a large hunk of meat.

"Roasted tauntaun?" At Alex's surprised look, Kate continued. "Just kidding. It's beef brisket. It smells better on the outside."

"What's a tauntaun?"

"It's an animal that lives on Hoth. Han Solo stuffed Luke Skywalker into one to keep him warm?" She looked questioningly at Alex who stared at her blankly. "That's okay. You know lots of music stuff I don't understand."

"I'll need you to explain your t-shirt, too."

Ross came up behind her at that moment. "Hilarious, Kate! Mos Eisley Space Cantina! The bar on Tatooine where Obi Wan takes Luke to meet Han Solo. You brought the Mexican cantina theme and the Star Wars theme together. Brilliant!"

"Thanks Rossypoo." Kate hugged him without touching him with her meat-covered hands. "Welcome to the party."

"Rossypoo?" Alex raised her eyebrows at Ross.

"It's just something she calls me. Let's forget about that."

"I think we missed the memo about the costumes." Alex was a little uncomfortable. If she'd known, she would have supported Kate's theme.

"I wouldn't say we missed it, Bob."

"I don't remember a character named Bob in Star Wars." Alex felt so out of the loop.

"Mixing movies – that's from a different movie."

Alex was missing all the jokes tonight. She would have to watch more movies.

Ross rebounded quickly. "What do you want to sing?"

"Me? I only sing back-up – no solo stuff for me. Bass player. Remember?"

"Not even a Juan Solo?" He looked at her like he was waiting for her to laugh. She was reminded why he and James were good friends. It was clearly a mutual love of puns. "You've been to parties here before. There's no pressure to be good."

"I just heard Angela sing Roberta Flack better than Roberta Flack. The bar is high."

"Don't worry. When too many good singers in a row go, Kate jumps in and does some Weird Al to lighten the mood and make room for other singers. I'll definitely do some Toto tonight, but I've been working on a Roy Orbison tune I might want to debut. It depends how much I drink."

"Then I'll stay sober and drive your drunk ass home so I can hear some Roy Orbison. *Blue Bayou? You Got it? I Drove All Night, It's Over?*"

"Alex, how can you rattle four Roy Orbison tunes off the top of your head and not know what a tauntaun is?"

"You heard that? How embarrassing." Alex blushed, the embarrassment lodging in her cheeks.

"Not embarrassing, just different experiences. And I would do *Crying*."

"A classic. And high." Alex was impressed. "You can sing that high?"

"We'll see, won't we." Ross giggled and strode away.

Ross took the microphone while Alex grabbed a seat on the couch between Akiko and Brie. Ross pressed some buttons, and the strains of the song came over the speakers. The opening was nice and low, and Ross started strong.

People crowded around the sofa to listen.

He took a big breath as he got to the chorus. "And I'll always be…" And then, unlike Roy Orbison, Ross didn't even have to switch to a falsetto to hit the refrain. "Cry-eye-eye-eye-ing over you," soared out across the living room. The crowd went wild.

Ross took a big theatrical bow when he was done and handed the microphone to Gertie who had teed up a Bjork song next.

"That was amazing," Alex gushed as he came toward her.

"Thanks." And with that, he leaned in and kissed her. Right there, in front of everyone. She decided to go for it and kissed him back, his voice was that good.

"Ahem, I'm trying to sing here." Gertie shouted at them, but her tone was good-natured. "Get a room!"

Chapter 21

Alex had been through several review cycles before. They were very straightforward. She wrote up her part of the review, listing the top accomplishments from the quarter and an area for improvement. Michelle would then add some innocuous comments that Alex was on track and send it back to Alex.

The "review" part of their review meeting lasted only as long as completely necessary for Alex to say she understood Michelle's comments, and they would return to discussing the action items at hand.

It wasn't so much a review as a check-the-box exercise.

Alex didn't mind. She got her mentoring from the Steak and Bourbon crew.

Michelle apparently hadn't had time to write up her part because it was still blank in the tool when Alex checked before the meeting. She guessed they would do it in real time.

"Have a seat, Alexandra. We have lots to discuss. I just sent your completed review back to you."

"Oh, I just checked, and it wasn't there."

"I said I *just* sent it."

What was with that tone, Alex wondered. Clipped and negative. Even more than usual.

Alex refreshed her screen. Michelle's comments popped into the document and the review status said *Approved*. That was odd. Usually they did that together.

Alex read the first paragraph and froze.

"Alexandra is not completing her program management assignments in a timely manner. She has a lot to learn about how to create and lead a team through strategy projects if she wants to be successful."

She looked up at Michelle, feeling her brow furrow in confusion. Confusion was followed by frustration. "Michelle, what's this?"

"This? It's an accurate reflection of your capabilities." Michelle placed her hands in front of her, like her little ballerina feet would in third position.

"Hang on, I don't understand." Frustration was replaced by anger, seeping into her veins. She tried to keep her tone light. "You've piled on the work and told me to focus on strategy, yet in my written review, you say it's bad that I did just that. In our meetings, you give me feedback that my strategy is good. But then you write that I'm bad at it. What's going on?"

"What's going on is that I am trying to coach you. Help you be the best strategist you can be." Michelle's smile looked like a smirk to Alex.

How does cutting me down in writing accomplish that? she wondered. Instead of asking that, she tried a softer version. "Wouldn't it be better to have a verbal conversation about that rather than putting it in writing in my review? I'm doing the best I can to step up in the strategy role." Alex's frustration leaked into her tone and tried to express itself through tears. She felt the burn in her eyes.

"And your best isn't good enough." Michelle looked like a nursery schoolteacher telling her student to color inside the lines. "You have a lot to learn."

"Like what? And who's going to teach me?"

"Really, Alexandra. You're a senior person and need to be a self-starter." Alex just cocked her head and looked at Michelle. *Was this a parallel universe?* "I still don't understand." Alex tried to control her tone.

"Alexandra, if you ever want to get another role in strategy, you have to improve. I would hate to pass on a problem to another team."

There it was. Busted. The interview for Tanja's team.

"Anyway, Alexandra, the review is already completed, approved, and posted. Let's get back to our real work."

Alex froze. This wasn't the way it was supposed to go. She was supposed to be in the driver's seat and tell Michelle to stop treating her like crap. But now she felt like she was lucky to have this job.

Alex closed the review document and opened her notes file. "Okay, I'm ready."

▭

ALEX SAT at her desk after the review. The betrayal was sharp. Her blood boiled. How could Michelle have turned on her like that? What could she do about it? Complain to HR?

But what would she say? That her manager had given her a stretch project and then punished her for not doing a good job? She would just look like an idiot for biting the hand that fed her.

Alex was glad she would be heading to Steak and Bourbon in a couple of days. They could help her decipher what happened.

In the meantime, she could focus on date two with Cameron to get her mind off her shitty review. Given how they launched themselves at each other, Alex figured that some hot sex was in the cards.

AT HOME that evening preparing for her date, Alex studied the dresser at the foot of her bed. Seattle Craftsman bungalow houses were small. But what they lacked in size, they made up for through charm.

That charm was blocking her lingerie collection.

She had to turn sideways to get around the queen-sized bed. But she and Tom wanted to get the biggest bed they could into this small room. She couldn't open the bottom drawer of the dresser at the foot of the bed unless she stood to one side. That's where she had moved her infrequently used items. Her lingerie fit into that category.

She performed the gymnastics to reach the bottom drawer and pulled out her favorite lacy bra and matching panties. She had last worn it for Tom.

Holding them in her hand created a wave of hurt. She had to take a break and sit on the edge of the bed, overcome by emotion. She laid a hand on his side of the bed.

For a year or so after Tom died, she had continued to sleep on her side of the bed.

But now she used the whole bed and slept right in the middle. She even found herself lying diagonally across it some mornings. She wasn't exactly sure how she got into that position, but it worked for her. Maybe it was time to move back over and make some room for someone else.

She patted his side of the bed and continued to get dressed for her date.

She slipped the orange lace bra and panties on and added jeans and a sweater. She grabbed a lint roller and tried to de-Sibelius the red cashmere. The sweater was ancient. It was a gift from her grandmother, but it still looked great. She pulled her eagle pendant and Tom's charm out over the collar, added some lipstick, and was good to go.

Kate had agreed to watch Sibby. Alex wasn't sure if she'd be coming home or not.

Anticipation filled her.

She grabbed a Lyft to the restaurant to make it easier to go home with Cameron.

He let her choose the restaurant and she went for an afghani-inspired tapas place. Alex missed the food scene in New York City and sought out interesting places for great food in Seattle… when she could afford it.

She was waiting at the bar with a smoked orange margarita when Cameron arrived. He went right in for a nice kiss. "Want to have a drink before we head to the table?" Alex motioned to the bartender.

"Nope. I'm in a hurry for what's after dinner." He gave her a sexy smile. They were on the same page.

Rather than ordering another drink, she closed out her tab and the host showed them to their table. It was so easy to talk to Cameron. He caught Alex up on all the news from Tom's old team at work and Cameron's recent promotion.

Dinner went by quickly.

"Want to look at the dessert menu?" Alex handed him the small white cardboard list.

"I'd rather get out of here and pick up where we left off a few weeks ago." His eyes smoldered. "I've been having trouble thinking about anything else. Can we go?"

"I thought you'd never ask." Alex tried for a coquettish smile. She probably didn't need to try to be any sexier – he already seemed ready to go. She felt the power of her sex appeal flowing through her veins for the first time in five years.

"Where did you park?" Cameron asked, putting on his jacket and helping Alex into hers.

"I didn't because I was hoping to go home with you."

She saw his shoulders drop as he released his breath, like it was the perfect thing to say.

AS SOON AS the car was parked at his condo, Cameron launched himself at her. She met his heat, opening her mouth to welcome his tongue.

"Ow!" she said as she rapped her head on the arm rest on the door. "Maybe we could take this party inside?"

"Good idea." It took her a while to disentangle herself. Cameron hopped out and opened her door. She all but fell out, still trying to sit up in the twisted seat belt.

Finally free from the vehicle, she chased him up the stairs.

Just inside the door, he pressed her up against a closet door and placed his hands on her face. He kissed her greedily, licking into her mouth with his tongue.

Just like last time, he lit her up.

She could feel her reaction throughout her body – the tingling and throbbing of physical excitement. It matched the intellectual connection she had with him at dinner.

She was surprised they weren't awkward together given their history. She pushed that out of her head, so she didn't make it awkward.

"Let's try to make it all the way to the bedroom this time." He pulled his hands about a half inch from her face, like that was all the distance he could stand.

"Lead the way."

She looked affectionately at the chair where he had

gone down on her as they passed it. Maybe there was more of that waiting for her inside the bedroom.

They started tearing each other's clothes off. First his shirt and then her sweater. She wished she had thought that through better when she picked one of her favorite sweaters to wear. She hoped the cashmere survived. But even that one thought was soon pushed out of her head by his roving hands.

Cameron reached for the button of her jeans and slipped her pants down her legs. Still kissing, she undid his pants to release him. She wanted to see and feel all of him.

He toyed with the waistband of her lace panties as she reached her hand into his boxer briefs. She found him hard and ready.

Alex was loving this. She had always enjoyed sex and celebrated every sensation. She wanted to take it slowly and savor the experience, but it seemed like Cameron had different ideas.

"I want you. Now." He spoke through clenched teeth. "On the bed."

He backed her up to the bed where they fell next to each other on the soft mattress. She pushed him onto his back and stripped off his underwear. She knelt over him for a moment. "Still too many clothes," he said.

She peeled off her underwear and unclasped her bra as he watched. She did love a good performance. She ran her hands from her full breasts down to her center. "Anything you'd like to sample?"

His response was a guttural groan as he grabbed her and yanked her down to him. He flipped her onto her back and teased her nipples into hard peaks. He replaced one of his hands with his mouth as he reached for her core.

He drove two fingers into her. She opened her legs

wide to encourage him to move to her clit. He did so without any direction.

She writhed against his hand as his fingers curled into her just the right way. She pumped against it, riding the energy coursing through her, ready for what came next.

She felt the sensations building, the telltale tightening in her core. And then she was coming. And coming. It lasted a good, long time.

When she could breathe again, she reached down to stroke him. He throbbed in her hand, ready for action.

"Condom?" She wasn't able to put whole sentences together yet.

He produced a condom from the nightstand drawer. She wondered for a moment if this was a common occurrence for him but was glad he was prepared. The one she stashed in her pocket was too far away right now anyway.

Straddling him, she rolled it down his length. Her long hair hung down around her face, touching his chest. "Ready?"

"Oh yeah," he said. She positioned herself over him and glided down in one fluid motion. "Yes!" she cried as he filled her.

She set a slow pace, taking him in and out slowly.

"Ride me. Just like that." His hands were on her hips, guiding her.

She increased her pace and felt her muscles gather for another good orgasm as she stopped at the bottom of her slide, taking all of him in.

Then, she pumped harder and faster, ready for another big release.

His groans became more intense, and she realized they would go together.

"Yes! Yes!" he cried. "I love you, Lynda."

Chapter 22

Lynda? She wasn't sure what to do. He kept going. Did he not notice he called her by the wrong name?

Fighting to get her mojo back, she restarted the ride. She didn't have enough time to get back in the zone before he exploded inside her. She continued pumping until he was quiet beneath her, panting.

"Did you go again?"

"Um, no," she said.

"Okay, finger time."

He didn't realize what he'd said.

She lay back and let him finish her off. No reason to waste a good build-up.

When their breathing was back to normal and the silence grew uncomfortable for Alex, she asked the question that was bouncing around in her head. "You want to talk about what happened?"

"You mean mind-blowing sex? That was amazing." His hand fell limply on her chest.

"I mean what you said right before you came."

"Oh, I have no idea what I said."

"You said, 'I love you Lynda,' and then you, you know…" She gestured with her hand to indicate ejaculation.

"No," he cried, sitting up. "Oh God, I was thinking about her. I mean, I haven't been with anyone since we were together. I'm so sorry."

"It's okay, but I think you might want to give her a call. Sounds like you have some unresolved feelings for your ex-wife."

"She's not my ex yet," he added a little too quickly for Alex's taste. "We never actually got divorced."

"Oh."

"I mean, she's living in Austin, and we're separated, but we haven't officially filed, and I guess I need to confront the fact that I don't want her to."

"Awkward time to figure it out." Alex tried not to laugh.

"Want to stay over anyway?" he asked with a sheepish grin.

"Nah. That was really fun, but it'll only get more awkward if we continue. What if you get back together and she wants to hang out?" Alex grimaced inwardly at the thought. "Let me know how it works out when you talk to her."

"I'm such an idiot." He shook his head. "I guess I should thank you. For the great sex, and for the realization. I think I need a strategy where Lynda's concerned."

I guess I am a strategist, Alex thought to herself with a laugh.

HER LITTLE HOUSE was quiet when she got back because

Sibby was at Kate's. It was only nine o'clock, so she called her friend.

"Nothing to worry about," Kate sang into the phone. "Sibby and I are cuddling. Focus on your date."

"About that," Alex couldn't contain her giggle. "I'm already home."

"What? No sex?"

"Oh, there was sex. But he called me his ex-wife's name."

"Ouch. I'm coming over."

"You don't have to do that. I'll swing by and get Sibby."

"James and I will take your mind off it."

Alex headed out on the short walk to Kate's. The evening had turned colder, but it wasn't raining, which was a small miracle for May.

It served her right for dating three guys at the same time. The universe was punishing her for not making a choice.

She was tired of making choices.

Her whole life seemed to be a series of trade-offs and choices with none of the options being what she wanted.

When she backed off at work, she felt guilty for wasting the chance Michelle had given her. She had to choose money over music.

When she tried to dig in and go for a new role, the very person she was trying to support blocked her progress. She had to choose loyalty over money.

When she found someone who understood her culturally and musically, the chemistry wasn't great. When she wanted to laugh with Ross, she felt guilty for cheating on Adam. She had to choose between great sex and great companionship.

When she tried to get back into music, she only had

time for the low-tier orchestras who didn't mind her erratic work schedule. She had to choose bad music over no music at all.

At least one choice was now off her plate. She didn't have to keep Cameron in the mix. He made that choice for them. In the most hysterical way possible.

Alex looked up in the dark to see a short person with a dog shaped a lot like Sibby walking toward her.

Kate placed a hand over the headlamp she was wearing so she wouldn't blind Alex. "Al, is that you?" she called out.

"Yep. Nice of you to meet me halfway."

"It was time for Sibby's bedtime pee trip anyway. And I thought you might not want to be around guys for a while."

"That's sweet. I'm actually fine about Cameron. I got the sex I wanted, it just ended kind of awkwardly."

"I'll say." Kate handed Sibby's leash to Alex. "Mind if I walk with you for a bit?"

"That'd be great. We'll walk back towards your place since I have my vicious attack dog with me to protect me on the way home."

They both laughed as Sibby wagged her tail at someone coming up behind them on the sidewalk.

"Evening."

"Evening." The man patted Sibby on the head and kept walking.

"Want to talk about it?" Kate asked.

"Nah. I have a more important question for you. How did you know it was time to choose to follow your dreams?" Alex's voice sounded small in her ears, not like her usual velvety tones.

"I didn't. I struggled with it for months. You remember those brunch conversations. Everyone else could see exactly what I should do, but the voices in my head, like my mother, my upbringing, my boss, told me something else."

"I get that."

"I had to stop the noise and really listen to my heart. Getting paid to leave my job based on the toxic work environment I was in certainly made it easier because I had a cushion. And I had James."

"Yeah, your support system and financial position were stable. You could take more risks. I'm alone, so I can't."

"It certainly didn't feel stable while I was going through it. Things always look easier from the outside."

Alex took a moment to absorb the power of that statement.

"That said," Kate continued, "it's easy for me to stand here and tell you to follow your heart. You have to get there on your own. Spend the time thinking about what you really want and then make it happen."

Alex stopped to clean up after her dog. "I feel like my job is a lot like what I'm doing right now – cleaning up poop." They shared a laugh. "I want to play music more, but every time I try to leave work early or do something for myself, Michelle lays on a huge guilt trip."

"The same Michelle who blocked you from getting your new job? She is not your friend. Don't let her make you feel guilty."

"But she gave me the job that saved me."

"And you've paid her back in hard work well above your job requirements for four years. Maybe that's enough."

"Easy for you to say because you've already made your dreams come true."

"That's how I know you can do it, too. I believe in you

and so does everyone in Steak and Bourbon. And your grandmother. You're not alone."

"Thanks, Kate."

Kate stopped and put her hand on Alex's shoulder, a look of great solemnity shown in her blue eyes under the streetlamp. "And I'll never call you Lynda."

Chapter 23

"But Michelle has been my sponsor since my first day at LampLight." Alex heard the whine in her voice. "Why would a sponsor do that?" She tried to rinse her anger away with the effervescence of the mimosa at May's Steak and Bourbon brunch.

"Uh, because she's not a sponsor." Gertie looked at Alex with her patented no nonsense expression.

"This is so confusing! Isn't your boss supposed to help you move up the ladder?" Alex shook her head.

"Lecture time!" Julia sang out. "There are four kinds of stakeholders you need to have in your network. Mentors, coaches, advocates, and sponsors."

"That sounds like a lot of people. I don't like people, present company excluded," Gertie added.

"The same person can play multiple roles, but you have to be clear on the functions. Let me go over it. Mentors give advice. They tell you how they would do things to help you avoid issues or learn. Very clear. Mentors give advice."

"Like you do for this group."

"I like to think of myself as a coach, but yes, I mentor,

too. Coaches facilitate your own learning to help create transformation. A coach doesn't tell you what to do. They ask powerful questions and make you discover the answer for yourself."

"Oh, you *are* a coach."

"Thank you. I do try to control my advice-giving and not tell people what to do."

"And sometimes it works." Brie joked. The brunch group laughed good naturedly.

"Advocates recommend you for a job. They do more than just give advice. They help."

"This is confusing. You're an advocate, too." Alex felt her brow wrinkle.

"Stop using Julia as an example." Margaret jumped in. "It'll only confuse you."

"I have a unique role in this group." Julia smiled as she looked around the table.

"Yeah, Julia has done each of those roles for all of us." Melanie nodded.

"Thanks, but the last role is the tricky one. Sponsors. Sponsors give you or get you a job."

"You did that for me, too."

"This isn't about me!" Julia sounded slightly exasperated. She did not like having attention on herself and everyone at the table knew it. "You can ask people to be the first three roles, but sponsorship is earned. And it takes time and effort to develop sponsors."

"Yeah, it's bad when you think you have a sponsor and it turns out they're just an advocate, or worse, a mentor." Brie scrunched up her lips with a look of disappointment. "I didn't figure it out until the person I thought was my sponsor suggested someone else for a role I thought they were helping me get."

"Ouch."

"Yeah, ouch indeed. It set me back, like, six months on my promotion path. But I'm clearly over it now," Brie added in a tone that suggested otherwise.

"Sounds it." Gertie said, pulling air through her teeth like she was in pain.

"What I'm hearing is that you think Michelle is a mentor, advocate, and sponsor, but she's actually a predator."

"A predator? But that wasn't on your list." Alex was confused.

"Right, because you don't need those. And worse, she's a predator in sponsor clothing. She acts like she's helping you, but she's really just holding you back for her own benefit."

"That's not fair. She gave me this great opportunity." Alex felt like she should defend Michelle.

"With no increase in pay and no promotion." Akiko shook her head and gave Alex a disgusted look.

"But isn't that how the corporate world works? She told me to keep it quiet, so others didn't get jealous."

Alex was met with rueful stares from the group.

Lesley jumped in. "No. She told you to keep it quiet, so HR didn't figure out she was messing with the system. She should have posted the role, interviewed people for it, and given the successful candidate the proper title, level, and compensation."

"She lured me in with promises." Alex flumped back in her chair.

"Yep. And did she deliver on anything other than the extra work?" Gertie's mouth turned down in a questioning frown. Like she already knew the answer.

Alex thought about it. "No."

"And that crack about if you want to get another job? Someone told her you were interviewing, so she gave you a shitty review in writing to block you." Akiko cut right to the chase.

"I haven't heard yet whether or not I got the job. There's still a chance. That's too much negativity. Michelle wouldn't do that!"

"Wouldn't she?" Julia didn't sound surprised. "Ladies, are we surprised by Michelle's behavior?"

A chorus of nos rang out around the table.

"What's going on here?" Alex was befuddled. "Why aren't we sticking together?"

"An age-old question." Melanie said sadly.

"I bet if we went around the table, each of us could pinpoint a woman early in our career who fucked with us and held us back. Picked on us, belittled us. All to make themselves feel better."

Angela spoke first. "Yeah, mine told me I had to pay my dues just like she had after she lied to the higher-ups about something she did and blamed on me. Leanne. I still get angry when I think about that bitch." Angela sounded like the pain and anger were still fresh.

"Mine repeatedly cut me down in public and praised my male colleagues. When I confronted her, she told me there was only room for one powerful woman on the team and she was there first. I quit the next week." Akiko shook her head, clearly thinking about her experience.

"Seriously? All of you?"

Hands went up all around the table.

"Women should do better by each other." Melanie nodded sagely.

"I used to think they didn't do it on purpose, that it was some weird case of societal pressure or something. But it happened too many times to ignore." The group nodded at Lesley's comment.

"Is it subconscious?" Alex didn't want to believe that

women would turn on each other. Female bass players were pretty rare, especially when she was a kid, and tended to stick together.

A horrible thought struck her. "Oh my gosh, I've done that." Alex was astonished at her behavior when she looked at it through this new lens.

"How so, girl?" Angela asked. "I don't believe you."

"I hate playing in all-female jazz bands. I was always good enough to play with the boys, so I did. I almost always said no when asked to be in all-female jazz bands because I thought they were just as sexist as all male bands."

"That's different. You weren't saying you *wouldn't* play with them because they were women."

"No, but looking back, maybe I should have played in the group so that I could hear them in action and be a better advocate and sponsor for future gigs, to use Julia's nomenclature."

"I'll give you that one," Angela said pointing at Alex with her glass. "So what are you going to do about that?"

"Shit." Alex placed her hands on her cheeks and looked down at the floor. "I just never thought of it from their perspective. I could have been leading the charge instead of leaving them behind."

"Enough beating yourself up, Al. You were good enough to play with the boys. So you did. And now you have a chance to work on that. I would give that your attention rather than beating yourself up about the past." Brie made it sound so easy. She loved Brie.

"Class A mentorship right there," Gertie said with a nod to Brie.

"Yes. And maybe I'm better off without that job I interviewed for anyway so I have time to work on something with women in jazz. One of the interviewers was super creepy and kept making sexual comments. I wouldn't enjoy working with him."

"What'd he say?" Akiko asked.

"He asked how I'd feel about 'working under him' and asked what I did for fun. It was double entendre stuff – you know, comments meant to make you wonder what he meant without being obvious? And he spent the interview manspreading. It was gross."

"Oh, girl that's nothing." Angela swung her long locs behind her shoulders. "Try being a powerful black woman in an office full of old white men. Just walking to the bathroom emasculates them."

"I thought that stuff just happened in the music world." Alex was saddened to hear that it happened everywhere.

"Like what?" Akiko asked.

"In college, I auditioned for a cover band. I learned three tunes in two days. And this was before iTunes and instant access to music. I had to just use my ear. I lugged an amplifier and an electric bass to a tiny apartment on the Lower East Side."

"Just that sounds difficult."

"You get used to it. I rocked my parts, and the rest of the band was grooving along, as noted by the head bobbing and nods in my direction from the drummer. But at the end of the session, I was unceremoniously told by the lead singer that I had the wrong equipment."

"No dick?" Gertie asked.

"Exactly. I asked him if he meant my small amplifier or the fact that I didn't have a penis."

"Did he come clean?"

"Oh Hell no. I thought I would shame him into

confronting his bias. Instead, he looked at me and just said 'both, really. You play great but you just don't match the image I have in mind for our bass player.' No hint of irony, no shame. Just a blatant disregard for my talent over a stereotypical mold."

"That's rough. What a douchebag." Melanie's disgust was obvious on her usually smiling face.

"Yeah well, my friend was the guitarist in that band, and they never went anywhere anyway."

"Maybe they would have if you had been in the band."

Brie said what Alex had thought for years. "I like to think they wondered that too."

"What did you do?"

"I lugged my equipment back to the Upper West Side on the subway. What else could I do?"

"Knee him in the balls on the way out." Gertie always made them laugh.

"That would have been a better exit." Alex nodded at Gertie.

"How about on my second week of work in my first job after college when my client commented on how well my ensemble matched and asked me if my underwear matched, too? When I gave him a 'fuck you' look, my boss' boss said, 'be a sport, Julia, and tell him what color your underwear is' and then told me I needed to learn to play along."

"Did you at least knee him in the balls?"

"Gertie, do you regularly knee co-workers in the balls?"

"No, I win cases against them. Same same."

Akiko picked up the thread when the laughing subsided. "Or this guy at LampLight who didn't like that no one had nametags in a meeting we were in together. I was the only women in the room. And the only person of color. So clearly, I must have been the admin. He looked around at everyone and when his eyes landed on me, he asked *me* to get the nametags."

"I'm glad I wasn't in that room. Did he survive?" Margaret asked.

"I calmly and politely told him that I couldn't do that because I was the next presenter and that it was Christopher's meeting as I pointed to the meeting host."

"Douchebag!" Lesley yelled.

"Nice job, Akiko."

"I've got one. I was on a client site and the guy who paid for the contract called me perky." Melanie spoke up this time. "I told him a lot of people called me that. His answer was to look me up and down and say, 'if it were up to me, I'd call you breakfast.' I'm pretty sure his balls shriveled at the look I gave him."

"Melanie, that's awful."

"Oh my gosh, was he fired?" Alex was incredulous.

"Honey, no. I told him not to speak to me like that and asked my boss to be removed from the project."

"Douchebag!" Lesley yelled again.

"Sadly, the next client was worse."

Alex sighed. "Sexual harassment and discrimination are rampant in music. Interesting to know it's the same in the business world."

"Yeah, power is power. It's not a man thing. It's a power thing. I have a friend who's a ballet dancer." Brie stopped to sip her drink. "His industry is mostly women, and he was harassed by those women just as badly as men do it in other industries."

"I had no idea."

Angela gave her a sad look. "We could go on all day, child."

The mood turned sad.
"Okay ladies, this is getting heavy. New subject."
Melanie was always great at topic intervention.
"I've got one," Lesley volunteered.
Alex appreciated the redirect.
Until she heard what it was.

Chapter 24

"I am on a quest to find out what guys want in a relationship." Lesley looked at Alex. "You know, to help us find loooooove. What do you think they want, ladies?"

"Why do you ask? Things not going well?" Margaret sounded sympathetic

"Let's just say I'm thinking of becoming a lesbian."

"At least you can share clothes with your partners." All eyes turned to Gertie. "What? You just have to choose your partner based on size."

"Ooh, ooh. I know the answer." Kate sounded like Horshack from *Welcome Back Cotter*.

"Lesbians?"

"That was college." She continued, leaving Alex wondering if she was being serious. "I was out with James and a few of his friends, including Ross, after they went motorcycling, and I asked them to design their AI Girlfriend."

"Is that a thing?"

"Sure. AI can do anything, right? Anyhoo, I thought

I'd get some insight into Ross' deepest secrets that I could, of course, share with Alex."

"Did you, now? Spill." Angela sounded even more interested than Alex.

"Trevor, whom you don't know, said there would have to be two girlfriends. One for companionship and one for sex."

"Douchebag!" Melanie said, continuing Lesley's theme and making her classic "rude" face. "That's just wrong."

"I know, right?" Kate agreed.

"Let me guess, one has boobs so big you can't see her chin." Gertie rolled her eyes. "And the other has two butt holes."

Margaret could barely speak through her laughter. "Wow, Gertie. Your faith in men is an inspiration to us all."

The giggles erupted again.

"Okay, okay, okay. Calm down ladies because I did get one gem from Ross. He said he wants someone who needs his help."

"Douchebag!" Margaret yelled. That joke didn't get old.

"Help with what?" Akiko asked, her voice full of suspicion.

"I pressed for details. Emotional support, chopping down trees, pushed around in a wheelchair. What kind of help?"

"What was his answer?" Nine women leaned in.

"Any." Kate said with finality.

"I don't know if that's good or bad." Alex was confused.

"Yes," several of them said together.

"You're no damsel in distress, Al." Alex loved that Akiko used the nickname this group had given her. It made her feel like she belonged.

"He didn't say helpless for fuck's sake." Angela pursed her lips and nodded her head sagely. "He just wants to feel useful. Jeremy's like that too."

"There are worse things than wanting to help." Julia added. "That's not a red flag for me."

"Especially if the help he wants to provide is always raising the bar on the quality or quantity of your orgasms." Gertie slammed her fist on the table.

"Gertie, I'm sensing a trend here. Is there something you'd like to share with the group about your sex life?"

"Which one?" Gertie deadpanned.

They all laughed again.

As the ladies took their dishes to the kitchen and another successful meeting of the Steak and Bourbon group wrapped up, Julia took Alex aside.

"Would it be okay if I spoke to Michelle? I mean, I got you into this mess in the first place. I could just touch base with her and see where her head is at. She doesn't know about our personal connection."

"I don't think I want to know, Julia. She has her reasons. I'll just put my head down and keep working."

"I hear you, but she shouldn't treat you like that, and I want to coach her for your sake as well as others. Can I?"

"Julia, you know I trust you. Do what you think is best." She gave her friend a hug and headed out the door.

TWO BUTT HOLES. Alex couldn't help but laugh every time she thought of their conversation at brunch. She needed that time with her girls so much. It carried her through other not-so-great times.

This was one of those times.

It was the end of another grueling week. Alex was working at home and looking forward to a glass of wine and a cuddle with Sibby that evening. She would probably fall asleep on the couch if she tried to add watching TV to that plan.

She had one more meeting. Tanja scheduled a thirty-minute chat with the subject "update" at 4:30. Alex didn't think that was a good sign. She dialed into the meeting and waited for Tanja.

"Hello Alexandra. Thanks for your push to get the strategy done. The training schedule is on track because of you."

Alex knew this was not the reason for Tanja's request for time, but she played along. "No problem, Tanja. Just doing my job."

"And it's a great job. You're doing a great job." She emphasized the words.

Alex remained silent, hoping Tanja would get to the point. It worked.

"Speaking of jobs, you were everyone's top choice for the role on my team."

"That's nice to hear." Alex perked up. Maybe her worries were for nothing. Maybe she was about to get this new job, and she could start on her plan to build her network of stakeholders and actual sponsors just like Julia said. Michelle wasn't the evil witch her friends made her out to be.

"I wrote up your job offer." Something Alex couldn't read flickered across Tanja's kind face on the screen.

"I'm listening," Alex prompted, not sure where this was going.

"And then my boss asked to see your review history before he approved the offer." She paused, looking uncomfortable. "They were so good up until the most recent one. He knows Michelle and asked her about you. I don't know what she said, but I know he came back with a no hire. I'm so sorry."

The Steak and Bourbon crew was right. As usual.

"That's really disappointing."

"Tell me about it." Tanja shook her head. "I would have loved to have you on my team." Tanja looked like she kept the next comment to herself. "At least we still get to work together."

"Thank you so much, Tanja. I appreciate that you stuck your neck out for me."

"I will again if the opportunity comes up. Take that bad review seriously and see what you can do to turn it around. Most hiring managers don't look back more than one or two. You can go for another role in a year or so."

Tanja was trying to be supportive.

Alex felt boxed in.

The review was a lie. But there was nothing she could do about it but hunker down and keep working. Tanja knew her and even she wasn't able to get her boss to look past the bad feedback. Michelle had fucked her. Hard.

"Thanks Tanja. Have a great weekend."

The call ended.

Alex sat and stared at her computer screen. *What was she going to do?* What could she do?

Were there any consequences for Michelle's poor leadership?

Probably not. She just got to keep on going, ruining other people's job prospects to keep them on her team.

Pouting probably wouldn't solve anything.

But four people had picked her as their top choice for a strategy role. With a higher salary. She should be making more money and getting that promotion.

But the fiscal year-end was approaching rapidly, and

with that bad review, Michelle clearly wasn't going to promote her like she had promised.

Alex checked herself. Technically, Michelle hadn't promised her a promotion. She just told her she would see once Alex had been in the role.

Alex wished she had asked her friends for guidance before agreeing to take on the role with expanded scope and no benefits. And before keeping her job search a secret from Michelle.

This corporate stuff was just as bad as music. She had truly believed that the business world was objective. Was a meritocracy. Tough way to find out that people are people.

She remembered what Angela said about leaving work at work and focusing on her life instead.

It was time for action.

It was time to dust off her bass and get back out there.

She would try to coast through fiscal year 2025 by phoning it in at work and closing her laptop every day at five to focus on her music.

Fuck Michelle.

▭

THAT SENTIMENT LASTED ABOUT AS LONG as her "commute" from her home office to her kitchen. Michelle had given her a chance. It wasn't Michelle's fault Alex turned out to have some real talent. It must be hard to live with that kind of jealousy.

What was she saying? It was like an abusive relationship. Alex was making excuses for Michelle's bad behavior and taking the blame. She didn't recognize herself. But she had told herself the story for so long. Poor Michelle, a perfectionist ballerina pulled in so many directions. She needed Alex to help her. And Alex felt privileged to get the opportunity.

But she had already paid that back. She excelled in her job and worked on self-improvement. This was bullshit and it was time to end it.

Today was a good day to start.

"C'mon, Sibs. Let's go to the park. Mommy needs a walk." Her dog was more than happy to oblige.

By the time Alex returned from the park with a happily exhausted dog, she knew which orchestras she would approach, how she would add more students, how she would get back into the studio scene, and which musicians she would contact to put a jazz combo together.

It felt good to be creating a strategy for herself instead of some stupid sales methodology.

Chapter 25

Saturday morning, Alex was out in her studio waiting for Betsy to arrive. She was planning which new electric bass parts to work on with Betsy after they went through her orchestral parts for her high school orchestra. That was the agreement with her mom.

Betsy wasn't old enough to drive herself to lessons yet. Alex looked up to see Betsy and her mom Jeannie in the doorway, Betsy with her upright and Jeannie with Betsy's electric.

"Welcome Betsy. Jeannie, nice to see you."

"You too, Alex. Are you going right into another lesson when you're done here, or do you have a few minutes?"

"I can make time, Jeannie. What's up?"

"Just something I want to discuss with you."

"Great. See you in an hour." She turned to Betsy. "How's it going on the Beethoven?" Alex loved that bass part. It didn't look like Betsy shared her enthusiasm.

"Okay, but I love the bass part you showed me for *Red Clay* and have been playing along with the Freddie Hubbard recording you pointed me to."

"She's really all about the electric now, Alex, and that's fine with me."

Alex loved seeing supportive parents and beamed at Jeannie.

"Well then, I think I know what to do in today's lesson, Betsy. Do you know what popping and slapping sound like?" Alex strapped on her electric bass, flipped open her music app, and played the bass line from *Play that Funky Music* along with the tune. It was simple enough for a beginning slapper to play but sounded really cool.

Betsy's eyes were like saucers. "Can you teach me to do that?"

"Yep, and it'll only take you ten minutes to master it. Let's do it."

Alex caught Jeannie's smile as she closed the door behind her.

THE HOUR WENT BY QUICKLY.

"My thumb hurts, but it's the pain of progress!" Betsy looked at the side of her red thumb with pride.

"You build up a callous. You'll see. Just keep at it. And listen to those recordings I texted you."

"I'll start listening now while you talk to my mom." Betsy put her ear buds in and sat on the small chair in the studio. Jeannie came into the room.

"Alex, remember that chat we had about opportunities at the radio station?"

Alex nodded. "Of course. I was intrigued."

"I found some of the radio programs you did back in college. You certainly downplayed that little tidbit about your radio background."

Alex blushed. "It didn't seem like a big deal. I did some

guest DJ spots late night. I think of myself more as a performer than a radio host. It wasn't anything magical."

"You're wrong there. You connected with the audience and sounded great. And you know your way around the equipment. Things have changed in the booth but not so much that you couldn't pick it up in an hour or so. It gave me this idea that you could sit in as a guest host for our Thursday night jazz program."

"Thursday Jazz Jams? I love that show."

"What are you doing this Thursday?"

"Sitting in for Keith?" A ripple of adrenaline ran through Alex's chest.

"Not quite. Sitting in *with* Keith. He wants to reduce his hours, maybe do the show every other week instead, and I thought you'd be great as his substitute. You would do it with him once, so you could learn the ropes while trying out your voice again on the air. Get back into the groove."

Back in the booth? She hadn't really thought about it much, but it could be really fun. "Has Keith already picked a theme?"

"Keith rarely picks the theme more than a day in advance since his knowledge is so vast. And you would be along for the ride – you wouldn't have to pick the tunes unless you wanted to. Just have some witty repartee and tell some stories about playing, and you'll be good."

"That sounds amazing. Thank you."

"Be at the downtown studio at five on Thursday, and you'll go on the air with Keith at seven."

"Does he want to talk first?"

"Nah. He's not a planner and he knows you're coming."

THE REST of the weekend was fabulous. Gram was thrilled to hear about the radio opportunity, and she had a fun-filled afternoon with Ross on Sunday.

But Monday morning at work, it was like her epiphany from Friday night and her great intentions disappeared in a poof.

Alex struggled through another PowerPoint presentation. Her skills were improving, but it still took her longer than others to make things pretty.

She tried not to care and to grab onto her new attitude.

Music first, corporate gig second. Alex over Alexandra.

She reminded herself that with that bad review, she wasn't going to get promoted at year-end anyway, so why keep trying so hard?

Right! Forget about advancement. Forget about these fake "opportunities" she was being handed. This was bullshit.

She needed to focus on her music.

It would be a tough adjustment, but she had to try.

She had already heard back from her network and had leads on orchestras and studio gigs. A theater offered her a five-week-long gig if she could commit to seven shows per week.

Game on!

Her phone buzzed with a text from Adam.

Adam: Can you talk?

She called him to find out what was going on.

"What are you doing the first week of June?" Adam sounded excited.

"Working."

"Want to go to Paris?"

"You got the gig with T3BO? Woo hoo!" Alex jumped up from her desk and pumped her fists.

"Yeah, but calm down, girl. It's just a gig."

"No it's not and you know it."

"Okay, you got me," Adam admitted. "I'm so damned excited."

"You should be. But I won't woo hoo again. Out of respect for my elders."

"Ha ha. Two years does not an elder make."

"It seems like more when you tell me to keep it down. Next you'll be telling me to get off your lawn."

"Doubtful." Adam paused before continuing. "Anyway, do you want to come to Paris with me?"

"Holy shit. I haven't been to Paris in years. That would be amazing. Are you sure you want to take me? I mean, this is kind of new. And that's in less than three weeks!"

"Did I stutter?" Adam chuckled to show he was teasing. "I was going to take my mom, but her knee surgery got pushed out, so now she'll join me in D.C. in October instead. You're my first choice as an alternate. You'll understand that I'll be in rehearsal most of the time and won't expect me to entertain you, but we'll still have time to hang out and have some fun. And the concert is at L'Opéra."

"I would love to hear you play there. Since they mostly do ballet, I've never heard a concert in that venue – only at La Bastille."

"Come with me. It's basically a week. Monday is a travel day, I have rehearsals on Tuesday, a day off on Wednesday, rehearsals Thursday, Friday, and Saturday with a concert Saturday night. We would fly back on Sunday. You'll have to pay for your plane ticket, but the hotel is covered, and we get a daily meal stipend."

"I'll talk to my boss later today. Can I give you an

answer after my meeting? I'll know in just a couple of hours."

"Sure."

"I'll text you when I know."

"I'M glad you asked about vacation, Alexandra." Michelle was back to being her previous nice self. If Julia and the Steak and Bourbon ladies were right, it was because Alex didn't get the job and was staying put, so Michelle had gotten what she wanted. "I meant to bring this up last month and it slipped my mind. I was reviewing the team's vacation usage, and you were at the top of the unused vacation list. You can roll over one hundred hours of vacation, but you have over three hundred. You'll lose it if you don't use it by the end of the fiscal year."

"Use two hundred hours of vacation in six weeks?"

"Yeah, vacation is there to be used. Now, it would be pretty hard on the team if you took it all, but you should plan on a week off before July first."

Alex did the math. Forty hours was a lot less than two hundred. She had been working too hard to notice that she hadn't had a break.

"Okay, I'll be taking the first week of June off. And I need to leave early on Thursday."

"That's fine about Thursday, but a full week off in June? That's really soon. It'll be tough on the team if you're out so close to the end of the fiscal year."

Which is it? Alex wondered. Take your vacation or not? Michelle had disagreed with herself in the course of two sentences.

"It's a great opportunity that just popped up and I want to go."

"Opportunity? Like a new job?" Michelle sounded defensive.

"No, a musical opportunity."

"I didn't think you were doing that anymore. You need to be dedicated to your job."

"It's not for me, it's for my… boyfriend." Alex stumbled on the word.

"Oh, okay then. Go for it."

That made no sense to Alex, but she had what she wanted – permission for a week off.

She raced down the hall to an open conference room to call Adam. She was so excited she had to tell him right away. "I'm in."

"Awesome. I'll buy the tickets, and you can pay me back."

"We're going to Paris!" Alex shook her hands back and forth in excitement. It was tough to sit through her last meeting of the day.

Chapter 26

"That's right, Michelle. I'm done at two today. I told you in our one on one that I had a commitment this afternoon." Alex stood her ground with Michelle, trying to turn over a new leaf.

"But I need this updated by tomorrow." Michelle sounded positively affronted that Alex didn't jump on her request.

"I hear you, Michelle, and I'm sorry, but I can't be in two places at once, and I'm needed elsewhere."

"You're needed here! How long is this 'commitment' going to take?" She put air quotes around "commitment" seeming to Alex like she was degrading it.

"Again, Michelle, I have to go. I will get that done first thing tomorrow."

"But I promised it to the team in Europe first thing."

Alex held back from telling her to do it herself. "I understand what you're saying. I have to go and will do my best to get it done first thing tomorrow morning. The European team could probably have it by close of business their time. That's the best I can do."

"We've talked about your best not being good enough."

Yes, Alex thought. Those exact words were in the review that cost her a promotion and new job. Alex looked at Michelle with calm clarity, the way she looked at a student or parent having a tantrum. She was good at waiting it out.

As the silence stretched out, Michelle's face contorted through several expressions from anger to acceptance.

"Fine."

Alex pushed her guilt away and walked out of the office.

SHE ARRIVED at the radio station, hardly able to believe she would be on the air in only a few hours. She had settled herself with quality time with Sibby before her big radio show. Sitting on the floor with her dog after a romp at the park had centered her. She visualized a successful evening and remembered that a lot of people were rooting for her.

The Steak and Bourbon crew would be listening. What great friends. They were always there for her. Always.

And Gram, of course.

As her hand grasped the metal door handle on the front door of the station, a feeling of great importance settled in Alex's chest. This was an amazing opportunity. One she hadn't gone looking for but was thrilled to try out.

Jeannie was waiting in the lobby.

Alex greeted her with a hug. "I didn't expect to see you here tonight!"

"I had to come and support my experiment. And to make sure everyone treats you right." Jeannie gave her a mischievous smile. Alex wasn't used to people throwing their weight around for her. "Let me introduce you to Keith."

Jeannie led Alex down a long, narrow hall plastered with broadcasting awards on each side. They stopped in front of a solid wooden door that said Studio A. The "on air" light was off.

"A for Alex. Let's do this." Jeannie opened the door. Alex's nerves jangled from head to toe. She touched her necklaces for support.

"Welcome, Alex. I hear you're my next victim." Keith looked like an aging rocker. His blue eyes crinkled at the corners as he laughed. He had long silver hair, parted in the middle and pulled back in a ponytail. His mustache and soul patch had just a hint of the red his hair used to be.

"Behave yourself, Keith," Jeannie chided him.

"Nice to meet you, Keith. This my mic here?" Alex showed she wasn't intimidated and took her seat at his nod. "Are we talking for a while or should I gear up?"

"Let's do a quick sound check."

Alex put on her headphones and turned the bass up on her voice. She knew that would accentuate her natural tone.

"Testing, one, two." Alex said. The dark-haired woman in the booth, likely the producer, gave Alex an OK sign. Alex waved back and smiled.

"She's a natural," Jeannie said to Keith, beaming at Alex from the doorway.

"You sound pretty good, Alex. What do you want to talk about tonight?"

"You're in charge. I'll follow your lead, Keith."

"I like you already."

. . .

"LIVE IN THREE, TWO..." The producer counted down on her fingers, leaving the one silent as she hit the live button. The On Air sign lit up and the theme music started playing.

Alex thought her heart might beat right out of her chest. She had the metallic taste of adrenaline in her mouth. *Keep it cool,* she thought. She knew to take a few deep breaths and hold them to keep her voice steady. She blew out with her mic turned off and turned it on as the opening music ended.

"Welcome to Thursday Jazz Jams. I'm your host Keith Keys. I've got a local bass player with me tonight on microphone two, Alex Taylor. Welcome Alex."

"Thanks, Keith. It's great to be here." She waited for him to continue.

He slanted his eyes at her. Remembering Jeannie's comment, Alex wondered if he was going to fuck with her.

"Taylor," he said slowly. "Are you related to any of the famous Taylors? James Taylor? Martin Taylor? Cecil Taylor? Taylor Swift?" He laughed, almost like he was trying to throw Alex off.

She was made of tougher stuff than that. "No, not that I know of, but Doctor Billy Taylor, the legendary jazz piano player and composer, came to my high school. He was in town for a local jazz festival and swung by a few schools to encourage students."

"Is that right?"

"Sure is. We were working on *Sweet Georgia Brown*. It was a suburban high school, so we played it pretty square." Alex sang a few bars to demonstrate. "After he listened for a few measures, he cut us off. He looked at us and said, 'no no no. You got to play it like you say it. SuWEET JOE-ja brown.' My conductor looked at him and then back at the all-white high school band and said, 'uh, they don't say it like that.'"

Keith's laugh echoed over the transmission lines.

THE TWO HOURS went by quickly. Alex had comments on a lot of the bass players in the recordings Keith chose and they kept up their banter and stories.

"That'll do it for Thursday Jazz Jams. I'm your host, Keith Keys along with my guest today, Alex "Sweet Georgia Brown" Taylor. Join us next week when guitarist Frank Vignola will join me in the studio. Until then, keep your temper cool and the jazz hot."

"And we're clear," the producer said from the booth.

Alex removed her headset and looked at Keith. "Did I do okay?"

"More than okay." Keith let out another belly laugh. "Alex, that was great. And you can play, too?"

"Yep."

"Next time, bring your bass. We'll jam."

Next time? She celebrated internally for a moment. "I'd love that."

He looked her up and down. "If I wasn't old and married, I'd be jealous of your talent, but ask you out anyway."

"Thanks Keith. If I wasn't young and smart, I might accept that date."

He laughed again, wiping tears from his eyes. "Come back anytime."

She smiled back, waved at the producer, and walked out of Studio A.

Jeannie was waiting outside, giving Alex a slow clap. "I knew you'd be good, but I had no idea you'd be *that* good."

"Thanks Jeannie. Keith made it easy."

"No he didn't, Alex. He kept trying to trip you up, but you danced circles around him."

"I've met musicians like him before. It wasn't too hard to break through his crusty exterior."

"That's a great way to put it." Jeannie nodded. "I'm putting you forward as his regular substitute. We need to shake things up."

"I'm good at that." Alex beamed at her.

Angela, Kate, and Brie were waiting for her with a big bouquet of balloons in the lobby. "Al! You were amazing!"

They engulfed her in a group hug.

"Let's go celebrate your Seattle radio debut!" Angela called out.

"We'll be the first members of your official fan club." Brie handed her the balloons.

"See Alex?" Kate leaned in for a hug. "Not alone."

Chapter 27

"You drove him back into his wife's arms? Classic." Margaret tipped back her glass.

"It wasn't quite like that, but man, it was weird. And funny."

"That happened to me once." Gertie paused to think. "Twice really. The first one didn't count because I had already forgotten his name by the time we hit the sheets and he said the wrong name. Fair's fair." She held up her hands like she was balancing a scale. "The second one was a lesbian. And I was the one who broke up their marriage."

"That's a little different." Akiko looked at her quizzically.

"Is it?" Gertie cocked her head to the side. "After a few months, she went back to her wife, so it sounds the same to me."

"All's well that ends well." Lesley nodded at Gertie.

"It was tough to explain the Birkenstocks, the Subaru Forrester, and my collection of Dixie Chicks CDs, but my proclivity for blow jobs helped my next partner understand that I was into dicks, too."

"Thank god for blow jobs," Angela added.

"Said no woman ever." Lesley shocked the crowd with her comment. "They're entirely about power, not enjoyment."

"And?" Kate quipped, causing the group to titter. "Sounds like you have a story there, Lesley."

"I'll have to examine why I feel that way." Lesley looked thoughtful. "I guess it's because I realized I was good at it and boyfriends in high school never broke up with me. I figured that was why. The power of the high school blow job."

"Another great band name," Julia said to Alex.

"So that's your sexual baggage. Nice." Gertie got some odd looks from around the table. "Oh come on, we all have weird shit that happened to us when we started experimenting. Some of it turns into our kink and some of it fucks us up. It all makes for good brunch stories."

"I'll bite," Brie said. "I have three older brothers. They all used to invite their friends over. Our house was like a combination of nerd camp and a locker room. There was this one guy. Jerrod. He was three years older than me, and I thought the sun rose and set on this guy. Looking back on pictures later, all I saw was a pimply kid, but back then, my friends and I thought he was positively dreamy. But of course, I was his friend's baby sister. Completely off limits. Except one time."

"Oooooh," Margaret rubbed her hands together.

Brie continued. "Jerrod came over while my brother was at the orthodontist, and I was home alone. One thing led to another, and I practically threw myself at him. I was thirteen and wanted my first kiss. We didn't know what we were doing, but we jumped in. He wore too much cologne, but his lips tasted like Chapstick and heaven. Then my mom came home with my brother and the moment was over, never to be spoken of again. As nasty as I know that stuff is, the smell of Polo by Ralph Lauren still gets me going."

"That's what I'm talking about." Gertie slapped the table. "Kinky for cheap men's cologne popular in the eighties. Love it. Who's next?"

"In high school, a guy went down on me for the first time in the dark back corner of his parent's backyard. Gave me a thing for having sex outside." Akiko looked lost in the memory as she nodded her head.

"Outdoor sex is the best! Only a pool makes it better." Margaret raised her glass at Akiko.

"Or the ocean."

"Good one."

"How do you do that and know that people aren't watching?" Alex asked.

"You don't."

"That's my kink, or one of them." Gertie smirked. "I like when people secretly watch."

"Girl, I never know if you're being serious or not."

"It's one of those." Gertie took a swig of her drink.

Alex headed to the mimosa bar for a refill. She brought the bottle of champagne with her and offered to top up people's glasses.

When she returned to her seat, Lesley was in the middle of a story. "Give him a set of crotchless overalls and he'd be all set for the party." Alex wondered what she had missed. Never a dull moment.

"Crotchless overalls? Wouldn't that be a skirt?" Gertie had a good point.

"No," Brie chided. "There would still be legs. Now, overall chaps would be more like a skirt."

"It's important to align on taxonomy," Margaret added.

"Speaking of taxonomy, how goes it with your new gig, Melanie?"

"Pretty well. It has been funny to try to create a companywide standard for what we call what we sell. We aren't supposed to call them products because we also sell services. We aren't supposed to call them services because we're primarily a products company. The team aligned on solutions. But no one really has any idea what a solution is. Is it a product? A service?"

"It's a combination of both to solve a business problem." Julia spoke with confidence, as always.

"Yes, exactly. So what do you call the pieces that make up a solution? Pieces doesn't work, because then you can't sell one by itself without it sounding incomplete."

"Component?"

"Same issue."

"And round and round we go." Melanie's exasperation was clear.

"The easiest thing is to call it what the customer wants to call it."

"Well said, Alex, except we have to call it something in our marketing collateral and then the seller can change the word once they find out what the customer wants to call it. We literally spend hours debating this stuff. It's maddening."

"And the second you get one group to agree, another team undoes it." Margaret added her experience.

"Exactly. It's so dumb and we waste so much time on it."

"We're doing the same thing on my team," Alex added. "Whatever you land on, could you make sure it starts with the letter S?"

Everyone looked at her, puzzled.

"I had to make our sales methodology spell a word. The stuff we sell has to start with an S to help the acronym make sense."

"Stuff? Nice and generic." Lesley laughed.

"Shit?" Gertie retorted. "Nice and generic."

"It would be great if it could be that easy."

"Hey, that's the name of my sex tape." Gertie loved that joke and used it often.

"Nice and generic?"

"No, 'that easy.'"

As usual, the group laughed with gusto.

Chapter 28

Alex and Adam made their way through customs to get to where the drivers were assembled. Alex had decided to splurge on a car and pre-paid for a ride to their hotel. The three times she had been to Paris previously had all been on a musician's budget. She had some cash now and with a free hotel, she was ready to show Adam some of the finer things.

She spotted the driver holding an iPad with her name on it and walked to him.

"Bonjour. Je m'appelle Taylor."

"Bonjour, la voiture nous attend," the driver said.

"The car is this way," Alex explained to Adam as she started to follow the chauffeur.

"You said you didn't speak much French," Adam said as they followed the driver.

"Oh, I can nail my name, ask where the library is, how you are, and order breakfast. It's enough to get around, but I'm certainly not fluent."

"You sound pretty good to me. I have some high school

French, and enough to get along during summers in Haiti, so I'll try to keep up."

Soon, they were racing in a Mercedes down the highway. Since Adam hadn't been to Paris before, Alex pointed out a few sights as they went by.

"If you look right between those two buildings, you can just make out Sacre Coeur up on the hill. And the Eiffel Tower should pop out in about five minutes just over there." She pointed farther south.

They drove around La Périphérique on their way to the west side of Paris.

They exited the freeway, went under an underpass, and were suddenly surrounded by white limestone edifices with wrought iron balconies. Gargoyles graced every corner with bakeries and coffee shops clustered around their bases. "It's better than in the movies," Adam said as he took it all in.

Julia watched as Parisians and tourists mingled on the street, the Parisians looking chic in their scarves and boots while the tourists gawked and stared at maps.

"Nous sommes proche."

"Merci, Monsieur," Alex said to the driver. She turned to Adam to explain. "He says we're getting close." The driver pulled to the curb.

"C'est juste là." He pointed down a tiny alley.

"It's right down there." Alex translated for Adam.

They popped out of the car to retrieve their luggage and Adam's oboe. "Merci encore une fois et bonne journée à vous!" The driver waved and sped away.

"What did you say? I want to learn some phrases."

"Just thank you again and have a good day."

"I only ever said 'merci' in Haiti."

"What I said is just a little more formal. Merci would have been just fine, too."

They walked down the alley where the driver had pointed. The cobblestones were slightly uneven, so they had to watch their step. Classic French limestone surrounded them on both sides. The driver definitely couldn't have made it down this tiny street.

After about twenty feet, they went through a stone arch that opened into a courtyard. Three-story buildings surrounded them. They found number fourteen Rue Saint Charles and a big red door with a keypad. Adam entered the code he had been given by the team at T3BO. A human-sized cut out in the bigger door opened with a buzz and they stepped through into a small foyer with a tall staircase.

"3A. Third floor. Looks like it's a walk-up."

"Good thing you didn't have to bring your bass."

"Right?"

They hoofed up two flights of stairs and put the code in. The door didn't open. Adam tried again. "It's not working."

"Wait a sec, isn't there a weird floor numbering thing in parts of Europe?"

"Oh right. The third floor is the fourth floor because they call the ground floor the rez de chaussée." Adam looked at her with surprise. "What? There are a lot of things hanging out in my head that you just have to say the right words to unlock. That was on the essay portion of my AP French test."

They tried the code on the next floor up and the door buzzed. "Success!" Adam said with glee. "You're a genius. I would have called the orchestra support line."

"Et voila." Alex gestured grandly with her hand to usher Adam into the apartment. She saw a small sitting room with a kitchen tucked in the back. Eight-foot windows with a view out to the quiet Parisian street greeted them. There was a small balcony with just enough room for two people to stand, if they were brave enough to try it. "Are you kidding me?" Adam asked as he gawked. "We get to stay here?"

"It's so cute!" Alex exclaimed as she was drawn to the windows. "There's a park across the street."

"Let's see what's behind this door." Adam opened the door to reveal a small room with a queen-sized bed tucked against two walls. "There's another door in here."

"Probably the bathroom." Alex turned the knob expecting a small bathroom to match the rest of the apartment, but it revealed a short staircase. "It's some stairs. Let's check it out."

Alex walked up the eight stairs in the narrow staircase with Adam right behind. She opened the door at the end and found herself looking at rooftops. "It's a deck!" They went outside, the fresh air helping to revitalize a sleepy and jet-lagged Alex. An iron bistro table and chairs were set on the right side of the tiny deck and there was a wooden shed on the left. A sign on the door read "W.C."

"Oh my gosh." Alex didn't realize she had spoken out loud.

"What's wrong?"

"That's the bathroom." Alex pointed at the door.

"No way. Up here?"

Adam peered inside. "Turkish toilet. But there's a sink and a small bathtub with a hand sprayer."

They looked at each other with horror. Alex had never used a Turkish toilet. Adam spoke first. "I bet this was the servant's quarters back in the day."

"That would make sense. Top floor, bathroom outside. At least we have this view. It's amazing."

"I'm going to try it out." Adam closed the door behind him. Alex was glad she'd used the restroom at the airport.

She'd have to use it eventually, but she could put it off for now.

She turned her gaze to the cityscape stretched out in front of her. She could see the Seine River from here. And the Bois de Boulogne. The view was southwest according to the sun, so it was away from the famous monuments, but it was still amazing.

She was in Paris.

Chapter 29

"Have fun in there." Alex dropped Adam off at the rehearsal hall at the Cité de la Musique on the opposite side of Paris. It was attached to the musical instrument museum where Alex would spend the next couple of hours. She especially wanted to visit the octobass. She had heard one played before but had never seen one and they had one at the museum.

The park where the rehearsal space and the museum were located was built in the nineties, so it didn't have the typical Parisian architecture. Instead, it was all glass and angles. But she was interested in what was inside.

She splurged on the audio tour. She could put in the number for each instrument and hear it being played. It was wonderful to hear the old instruments. She loved the way they had curated the museum.

After seeing dozens of violins, guitars, harps, and keyboards, Alex found the octobass. It was mounted to the wall and stood over eleven feet high. The player would stand on a platform to work the bow and use a system of stoppers at shoulder height to manipulate levers that acted like mechanical fingers on the strings to make the notes. It could be tuned a full octave lower than a modern double bass.

She was in awe. Hector Berlioz was one of the only composers who was a fan of the octobass - the same composer Adam would be performing with T3BO.

She wished she was playing the Berlioz. She had first learned it in high school. There was something about playing a piece in your formative years as a musician that locked it in. The youth orchestra she played in during high school had performed it. They spent four hours every Saturday for four months working on it. When you hear a piece of music for that long, you get to know everyone else's part in addition to your own. The *Berlioz Symphonie Fantastique* was one of those pieces for her. She practiced the bass part for hours. Many parts were exposed and important – not your typical background part. She loved it.

God, she missed playing in great orchestras.

She needed to make more time for music. Period. She only had two students these days and they had lessons on Saturdays. She had to stop working so much and figure out a way to make commitments to orchestras. Community orchestras would always have a place in her heart, but when players only had one volume setting, and it was loud, the music lost its emotional connection. She had settled for too long. It was time to get serious again.

She wandered through the harp section and found a small recital space. An accordion player was sitting on a small stage with his instrument.

"C'est privée?" she asked, wondering whether this was a private room.

"Non. Allez-y." He beckoned to her to come in.

"Je suis deso, mais je ne parle pas francais." She knew how to say, sorry, I don't speak your language in about seven languages. It had come in handy when she was traveling with various groups.

"Canadienne?"

She laughed when he guessed she was Canadian.

"Non, Americaine."

"Oh, hey. What do you want me to play?" he asked in perfectly unaccented English.

"Oh wow, are you American?"

"Canadian," he said with a smile. "I'm from Toronto."

"Are you doing a concert?"

"Well, I'm supposed to be, but there's no audience so that makes it kind of tough. What would you like to hear?" Alex thought for a moment. "And please don't say 'la vie en rose.' I have to play that all the frickin' time."

"How about a tango, maybe *Por Una Cabeza*?"

"Great choice. How do you know that one?"

"I used to play bass in a tango orchestra, and it's pretty famous from the Arnold Schwarzenegger movie."

"Rock on, sister." He started moving his fingers deftly over the keys while squeezing the accordion closed and then pulling it open to fill it with air. A dramatic tune to begin with, he cheesed it up which made her happy.

He was really good. She knew thousands of musicians, but it always impressed her to hear one who had mastered their instrument and could play with unbridled joy.

He went from *Por Una Cabeza* to *Tico Tico*. He played it way faster than the original, his fingers flying over the keys. Alex couldn't keep her shoulders from dancing along.

"What else do you play other than tango?" he asked after he finished his second tango. Since it was still just the two of them in the room, Alex thought it was unconventional but okay to talk to him between songs.

"I call it ABC. Anything But Country." She paused

while his musical laugh filled the small space. "Unless I'm being paid, and then I play what's in front of me."

"How altruistic of you. I don't mind country, but with this thing, I get a lot of polka, gypsy music, and Brazilian." He smiled at her. "I don't think Johnny Cash used much accordion."

"How did you get into it?"

"My last name's Yankovic. It kind of goes with the territory."

"Are you related to Frankie or Weird Al? You know they aren't actually related to each other."

"You just get more and more interesting. I suppose if you go back far enough across the boundaries of eastern Europe, we're all related, but no, he's not my grandfather or anything. I watched *Polka Varieties* as a kid and was hooked."

"Oh my gosh, I remember that show. It's how I learned the words to *She's Too Fat for Me* among other polkas."

"So cool – not the lyrics to that totally obnoxious song – but cool that you know tangos and polkas." He smiled at her. She felt this one all the way to her toes. "I always wondered about the name, though. Isn't 'polka varieties' an oxymoron since they all sound the same?" Before her laughter died down, a woman and a small child entered the room. "Back to work. I get off at four if you're still around. My contact info is on my sign." He pointed to a QR code on a sign at the edge of the small stage and started the next tune.

She smiled at him, and he smiled back as his hands caressed the accordion. She felt warm in places she probably shouldn't while traveling with another man.

His smile grew bigger when he saw her take out her phone and snap a picture of his contact info. *Tony Yankovic, accordionist and rigger*. He worked up front and backstage. Interesting.

She slipped out the door on the opposite side of the room to continue her sojourn through the museum. She wanted to text him and ask him out. The disloyalty stuck in her craw. She already had enough boyfriends, didn't she? She couldn't add another. Even a cute Canadian who played a mean accordion and got her humor.

She wished she had already had a conversation with Ross and Adam about each other and about exclusivity.

It was already three o'clock by the time she finished at the museum.

Adam's rehearsal ended at four, right when the accordion player was getting off his shift. She wondered if he ever made it to the west coast of the US. Maybe she should stick around and ask him.

Or maybe she should focus on the two guys she was already dating instead of adding a third.

Maybe.

Chapter 30

Alex walked back across the concourse to the rehearsal hall. She had learned long ago that if you confidently said, "I'm with the band," you could get in most places. It was especially effective when carrying a bass.

She went for honesty instead this time. If she couldn't get in, she could always head to a café nearby. "I'm picking up a friend from the T3BO rehearsal. May I wait inside?"

The security guard looked her up and down and waved her inside.

"Merci." She nodded at him as she walked into the hushed interior of the performance hall entryway. Towering wood walls led to three sets of double doors. She slowly and quietly tried each one until one opened silently on well-oiled hinges.

It was dark inside. She waited for her eyes to adjust. It took her a moment to realize she was looking at the back of a wall with a walkway around the side. She followed it and the performance hall opened up into a huge expanse with red seats and tan carpet. She could smell the wood and the fabric refresher they used on the velvet seats.

The conductor was asking for more sound from the bass section. Alex laughed to herself that usually bass sections were told to play more quietly.

She folded down the flip-up seat and quietly settled into the chair. It was a large orchestra. She counted fourteen first violins, twelve seconds, ten violas, and twelve cellos, but only six basses. There would usually be eight in an orchestra this size. No wonder Maestro Touati wanted more low-end.

Alex enjoyed listening to the last hour of the rehearsal. The conductor was delightfully easy to follow and kept asking the orchestra to dial up the drama. She liked it dramatic and emotional - right up to, but not crossing the line – into schmaltzy. She was Alex's kind of conductor!

When they wrapped up, Alex approached the stage. She was sure the conductor had heard it a million times before, but Alex wanted to tell her that her style really spoke to Alex and congratulate her on conducting this group.

"Maestro?"

The conductor turned to her, smiling. "Please, call me Nkechi. Did you need something?" Her voice held laughter.

"I was sitting in the audience for part of this rehearsal. It is a joy to watch you conduct." Alex pressed her hands together. "I played for you in college. I was impressed then, and I'm impressed now. You're so clear and I love the sound you get out of this group. They're lucky to have you."

"Why thank you. I'm lucky to have them." She smirked. "I take that back. I worked hard to get here. Maybe some was skills."

They both laughed.

"I'll let you get back to it." Alex started to back away.

"But if there's anything you need, I'm here with a friend in the orchestra and will be around."

"Unless you have a bass player in your pocket, I don't need anything."

"Wait, what?"

"Two players are down with Covid. They're holed up in an apartment unable to perform."

"I'm a bass player." Alex pointed at her sternum. "I play in a bunch of groups in the US. I have a degree in bass performance."

"Do you now? If we could arrange to get one of the instruments here, would you play an audition for me?"

"In a heartbeat! But…" Alex pointed to her face. "Look at me. My grandfather was Native American, but I don't really fit in with this group."

"Hmm." Nkechi looked thoughtful. "I'm changing the name to T4BO." At Alex's puzzled look, Nkechi explained. "The Black, Brown, Beige, and Bassist Orchestra."

They both laughed again.

"I could borrow a bass right now and whip through the opening of the fourth movement and the witches dance if you like."

"You know the Berlioz?"

"I basically have it memorized."

"Okay, then. I have a feeling about you. Let's skip the audition. I'll get it arranged. Welcome to T4BO, um…?"

"Alex. Alex Taylor."

"Welcome, Alex."

She couldn't believe it.

"WELL THAT'S one way to get into the orchestra!" Adam sounded happy for her when he joined her after packing up his oboe.

"The orchestra manager gave me the phone number for one of the sick bass players and I had a quick WhatsApp chat with her. Turns out we know a few players in common, so she trusts me to use her bass. I'm going to head to the apartment where she's staying tomorrow morning, and she'll send the bass down in the elevator so we can do a contactless exchange. That'll let me get one rehearsal and the dress rehearsal in before the concert. Amazing."

"And I've learned to always travel with a bass player." He took her hand as they walked outside into the plaza. "Let's grab a drink before dinner."

Alex couldn't help but look for the accordion player as they left the area.

———

ALEX WAS UP EARLY SO she could check in on work before heading to the seventh arrondissement to pick up the bass she would be using. Rehearsal started at ten, so she had plenty of time. After braving the Turkish toilet, she popped open her laptop and quickly scanned her messages for anything urgent.

Yes, she was on vacation, but she had learned it was expected that people were still available for urgent items. She answered questions, pointed people to documents, and reminded others she was out of the office and would get back to them next week on their requests.

Mischief managed, she got dressed and pulled her hair back into a ponytail. Adam hadn't stirred from the bedroom yet. She'd slept on the couch. Adam was pretty tipsy after they shared two carafes of wine at dinner the night before, so it was just easier that way.

Alex left a note and quietly shut the door behind her.

She would see him at rehearsal. At rehearsal! She could hardly contain her excitement. Performing the Berlioz and the Ellington in Paris! At L'Opéra!

If only she could feel this wonderful about anything at LampLight that generated revenue. She couldn't have it both ways. Either she loved what she was doing and was broke or she trudged through bureaucratic administrivia and had money.

She had to choose, and for now, she chose wealth. If she hadn't had her job at LampLight, she couldn't have paid for her own ticket to Paris and she wouldn't be playing with T3BO – T4BO, she corrected herself with a giggle. She was glad all over again that she played the relatively unpopular instrument. It opened so many doors.

And so did money. Cash certainly had its advantages, and she enjoyed getting used to them.

She hopped on the Métro to get to the bass player's apartment. One good thing about living in New York City was that public transportation made sense. In the Paris Métro, you just had to know which direction you wanted to go, and the rest was easy.

She made her two transfers, stopping to put a euro into each busker's suitcase as they played on the subway platforms or in the stations. Each of them gave her a smile or a nod as she dropped the coins. Musicians had to stick together everywhere around the world.

With the help of her phone, she found the building near the stop for Place D'Italie and rang the buzzer. An answering buzz let her in. She found a modern-looking entranceway. So much for the charming French architecture. It was almost like they had removed everything behind the nineteenth century façade and it was a new building behind it.

Three minutes later, the elevator opened to reveal a

bass propped in the corner. She retrieved it and stepped out of the elevator.

She sent a WhatsApp message to Diana, the owner of the instrument, with a promise to take good care of it and have it back after the concert on Saturday night. She added a note that if Diana felt better before the concert and tested negative for Covid that she would happily return the bass and bow out of the concert.

She humped the strap onto her shoulder, adjusted her backpack purse out of the way and headed back to the Métro station. Luckily, it was a straight shot up the orange line to the rehearsal with no transfers.

She could have gotten a cab, but it was so hard to find one big enough for a bass. She had gotten used to carrying her instrument around cities. It was only about thirty-five pounds with the case – it was hollow after all.

At the Porte de Pantin station, she found the handicapped exit and zipped up the stairs. She knew just where to go since she had dropped Adam off the previous day.

She arrived at the rehearsal and started unpacking. She had to make friends with the instrument. Each bass was basically the same, but they came in different sizes. She was delighted to find that this one, like hers at home, was a three-quarter sized bass with an E flat neck. She had played full sized basses before, but the notes were a little too far apart for her to play comfortably.

She took a place at the end of the section. She didn't know what position Diana was playing, but no reason to make a thing out of it. She sat at the end and was happy to be there. She started searching the pocket in the case for a tuning fork.

"Polka Varieties." She stopped rooting around in the pocket and looked up.

"Mr. Yankovic." Alex felt the jolt of surprise at seeing him again. She smiled warmly.

"You're in this group?"

"Nah, I just lug the instrument around for one of the guys in the section." *Feisty*, she thought.

"You're joking, right?"

"Yes." She stole a glance at Adam, but he was chatting with another oboist.

Alex slanted her eyes trying to figure out why he was there. "Obviously, you aren't playing in the group because you were at the museum during the last rehearsal."

"I'm a stagehand here. I do the lights. I freelance all over the city. You weren't at rehearsal yesterday either." He pointed at her with a questioning look.

"I was too busy flirting with you." She blinked her eyes at him in fake innocence. "It's actually a long story of how I got here."

"Maybe you could tell me about it later."

"That would be great. I have your contact info."

"See that you use it." He looked at her with a pointed expression.

"Excuse me." A tall man with ebony skin and black glasses handed her a stack of music. "You must be Alex. I'm Bryce. Here are the parts. The bowings are marked. Thanks for helping out."

"I am so delighted to be here. This is Tony. He works here at the hall."

"Nice to meet you." Bryce turned back to Alex. "I hear you're Adam the oboist's girlfriend. Lucky for us you traveled with him." She bristled at the term girlfriend. When she turned to explain to Tony, he was gone. Maybe she could track him down later. Had he heard Bryce's comment or had he already moved away?

Alex smiled at Bryce and started to rosin her bow. She

used long strokes in the same direction to keep the hair on the bow aligned and unbroken. Gliding the sticky substance down the bow hair helped it grip the strings better and, importantly to Alex, make more sound.

"Where did you study?" Bryce looked just slightly down his nose at her. No wonder. He had to audition for this gig, and it was just handed to her. She had to play the credential game. It was one of her least favorite parts of being a musician, but where you studied and who you studied with made a difference.

"New York City."

Alex was happy that Adam picked that moment to come and say hello, so she didn't have to say anything more. "Missed you this morning." He came in for a kiss.

Were they those people? It was nice to feel wanted, but it was a little off-putting that it felt like he was trying to put his mark on her in this rehearsal.

She looked around for Tony. "Hope I didn't wake you up. I wanted to pick up the bass and get up here in time."

"No. All good." He looked at Bryce like he was sizing him up, a potential rival. Alex didn't know how to casually let Adam know there was no issue there. If he was going to be jealous, he should find Tony.

Or maybe she should. Based on the punch she felt at seeing him again, it was definitely something to explore.

"Talk to you at the break." Alex went back to rosining her bow and warming up. She didn't want to risk an injury, and the strings were a little farther from the fingerboard than she was used to. She would have to compensate for the high action and do some extra warm-ups to avoid tendonitis.

Promptly at ten, Nkechi called on Adam to play an A so the orchestra could tune. They were starting with *Black, Brown and Beige*. The timpani player looked ready to go.

Alex heard the driving rhythm in her head before the piece even started. Nkechi gave the downbeat. Alex reveled in the sound that surrounded her.

This.

Not the weak sound of a community orchestra, but the rich tapestry of the parts perfectly weaving together under a conductor who knew how to lead.

She let the sound envelop her, like a warm blanket, and readied to play her part.

She was home.

Chapter 31

The four-hour rehearsal whizzed past, leaving Alex in a high-energy good mood.

"Where to now?" Adam asked her as they opened the doors and breathed in the fresh Parisian air.

"I need to put this somewhere safe. How about a quick trip back to the apartment to drop off our instruments, and then a nice dinner somewhere? The guys in the bass section mentioned a place called Le Cav on Île Saint-Louis that's really good. Want to go there? My treat as a thank you for bringing me here."

"Sounds like a plan. Maybe we can start with a drink. I have to take care of these lips."

Alex knew he meant for the oboe, but the look he gave her suggested he fully meant the double entendre. She was feeling so great after the rehearsal, she just might give him another shot.

Back on the Métro after dropping their instruments off at their tiny apartment and having an aperitif at a nearby bar, Alex and Adam strolled up Rue des Fleurs just next to

Notre Dame. Le Cav sat on a tiny slice of the Parisian sidewalk, a simple sign in block letters announcing its presence.

It was only seven, so it was empty. Parisians didn't eat until eight or later. She thought that would help them get a table.

"Deux pour ce soir?" Alex held up her thumb and index finger indicating two people.

She was greeted with rapid fire French. Seeing her stunned look, the maître d' switched to English. "I am sorry, mademoiselle, but we are full this evening."

"We have a reservation. It's under Pierre-Louis."

"Ah yes, right you are, sir. This way."

He led them down a set of stairs into what looked like an old wine cellar, stone walls painted white with dark beams on the ceiling. They took their seats. The maître d' handed them their menus. "Bon appetit." He snaked his way around the crowded tables and back up the stairs.

"Thanks for making a reservation." Alex was delighted.

"You mentioned the name, so I took care of it. I haven't had a lot of luck just walking into restaurants."

It felt nice to be taken care of. Alex wasn't used to that anymore.

Adam handed her his phone. "Here. I took a picture of the menu. This cool app I got translated it." She looked into his kind eyes.

"Thanks again. You're an excellent travel companion."

"I'd certainly like to be more than just a travel companion." Alex blushed at Adam's comment.

They were both quiet while they reviewed the menu.

When she set the menu down, Adam was looking straight at her. "Have you played in Paris before?" he asked.

"Actually, yes. In college, I traveled here with the conservatory jazz band. After the final gig, a few of us went to a bar and were thrilled to find a jazz trio playing in the corner. My friend spoke good French and struck up a conversation with them. He came back to the table and told us that the guys in the trio didn't believe I played the bass because I was a girl."

"Kind of a dick move, isn't it?"

"There still aren't enough female bass players out there and there are a lot of sexist players. Also, this was 2008."

"What did you do?"

"I asked them if I could sit in."

"Nice."

"This is actually the funny part. They asked me what I wanted to play. I picked one of my favorite jazz tunes. 'All the Things You Are' I said to them. They looked at me blankly. My friend translated that into French and said "tout ce que vous êtes?' Still nothing. I had one more idea. 'Ull zhe sings you ahhr' I said and looked at them with great meaning."

"You just said the name with a strong French accent?"

"Yep. And it totally worked. They recognized it and counted off."

Adam laughed but kept it down in the tranquil space of the restaurant. "That's hilarious. I'm not sure I would have thought of that."

"I did three songs with them. They asked me to come back the next night, but we were leaving the next day. That's one of my favorite musical stories."

"And you taught them that chicks could play bass, too."

"Exactly."

After dinner, they decided to walk back to the apartment. Their map app said it was about a forty-minute walk. After the boeuf bourguignon, salad, cheese course, and Gran Marnier souffle, she needed the walk.

"How's the woodwind section? They sound great from across the stage."

"We're learning how to play better together. The first flute on the Berlioz does this weird breathing thing that's distracting, but oh well. It's nice to play in an orchestra where there are more than two black people."

"Yeah, I feel like I stand out. I don't mind though. I got used to being the only white-looking person at Madou's house. It was eye-opening to be the minority. Unsettling, but in my case, not scary."

She nodded at another couple as they strolled by. "It's nice to see so many biracial couples here. It's like it's not a thing."

"Please, girl. The English Horn player told me that when she was here a few years ago, she got stopped in a fish market and asked for her papers."

"Papers?"

"Yeah, showing that she was a citizen. You think that happened to the blonde she was with? Every country has its history."

"That sounds really frightening."

"You get used to that shit. I always carry my passport with me. I've been pulled over or had neighbors report me for looking suspicious, even in Seattle. It's all getting worse in the current political climate in the US. Glad I live in a big city. It's better, but still there."

Alex thought about the racial dynamics of their relationship. She had dated several black guys in college, not because she had a thing for black dudes, but because she had a thing for talented musicians, many of whom happened to be black.

"Speaking of the English Horn player, she really nailed the call and response with you in the third movement. You two sound amazing together."

Alex thought back to the music. There was a famous duet between the oboe and English Horn played as a call and response like two shepherds in a field. The oboe player sneaks off stage before the movement starts and plays from backstage.

"I held my breath when you came back on stage. It's so easy to bump into something."

"What can I say, I'm graceful."

The English Horn repeats the solo at the end but is only answered by timpani, indicating thunder and danger.

Chapter 32

"My feet hurt," Alex said as she plopped on the sofa when they got back. It groaned under her weight. She took off her shoes and started rubbing her feet.

"Let me help you with that." Adam sat on the other side of the sofa and patted his legs like she should put her feet up. She obliged.

"A foot rub? I don't think I've ever had one outside of Thailand."

"You're in for a treat. It's one of my specialties."

Alex couldn't quite stifle her moan when he ran his fingers up the center of her foot and started kneading the ball. "You like that?" he asked, his voice gruff.

"Yeah. I had no idea feet could feel so good." Alex was getting additional ideas about what else might feel good. When she opened her eyes and saw the look on Adam's face, she could tell his thoughts were running in the same direction.

She pulled her feet off his lap and straddled him on the couch. It dipped under their weight. "Think this thing can hold us?"

"We'll find out," Adam said, taking her face in his hands. He pulled her down to him and kissed her softly on the lips. His tongue started to explore. Woodwind players were always good with their tongues.

Adam's movements were slow and gentle. Not fast and reckless like Cameron's. It was nice. Alex melted against him and continued her exploration.

He reached behind her to unclasp her bra and brought his hands up under her shirt to cup her unencumbered breasts. She sat up to pull her shirt over her head.

The sagging sofa aligned her torso with his mouth, and he used the opportunity to suck on her taut nipple.

Her breath caught in her throat as he tasted her. The sofa made an unhappy clunking sound at their movement.

"Why don't we take this to the bedroom?" Alex asked.

"Yeah, wouldn't want to have to pay for couch damages."

She laughed and untangled herself from his lap. The couch looked even saggier than before on the side they vacated. "Oops." Alex giggled and placed her fingers over her mouth.

"Let's hope the bed is sturdier."

Alex followed him into the bedroom, careful not to trip over his open luggage.

She lay down on the bed. Adam stripped off his shirt and joined her. She enjoyed the feel of the skin-on-skin contact.

He kissed her tenderly and cupped her breast. His hand trailed downwards towards her waistline. She was wearing travel pants with an elastic waistband which made it easy for him to fit his hand inside.

His hand continued down, down, down.

"Is this okay?" he asked as he toyed with the top of her panties.

"Yes."

He traced the line a few times, exciting her for what would come next. He slowly reached under the elastic and found her center. He made lazy circles with his fingers, gently teasing her.

Her head fell back as she enjoyed the sensation. She spread her legs wider to give him more access.

Continuing his slow caresses, he dipped one finger into her and kissed her neck. She started slowly moving with his rhythm, pulsing into his hand.

It was like having sex in slow motion. Everything was stretched out in time.

She reached for his belt buckle, undid his pants and pushed his jeans down his hips. She took him in her hands, wishing she had a little lube to keep this slow dance going. She squeezed gently, happy with what she found.

"Any chance you brought a condom?" he asked.

"No, sorry."

"Me neither. I wasn't sure we would be doing this."

"We can stop at the store tomorrow," Alex said feeling slightly disappointed.

"I'm not ready to give up just yet. I'll be right back."

Alex lay on the bed listening to him rummage around in the apartment. She had no idea what he was doing.

Adam came back with almond oil and a feather. Alex was confused.

"I use this to oil my oboe, but maybe we can have some fun with these since we don't have a condom."

Alex was impressed with his creativity. "I would hate to ruin your feather. But give me that almond oil, please."

Adam set the feather on the nightstand, handed her the small bottle of oil, and rejoined her on the bed. She poured some oil into her right palm and lay back down with him.

"Now, where were we." She took his hand with her left and placed it between her open thighs. "Let's pick it up at letter C," she said, making a music joke.

Adam obliged by returning his fingers to the job. She also returned to her task, taking him in her nicely lubed hand and stroking his length. She took it slowly to match his pace. Up and down.

His breathing grew heavy as she increased her pace. Soon, he lost focus on what he was doing, and she let him. He started to tremble, and she increased the speed.

He groaned one last time and shot his load onto her chest. She took a moment to appreciate how far it went. She continued to stroke him as he came down from his orgasm, gradually slowing to a stop.

"Mmmm. That was nice." He sounded very relaxed. "Your turn."

It took a little while to get her going at this slow pace, but she tried to stay in the moment, thinking of it like the long exposition section of a symphonic movement.

It felt like he was massaging her from the inside, relaxation filling her body.

While she was enjoying it, she didn't think she was going to have an orgasm like this. Her mind started to wander.

She wasn't sure what to do. Should she take over and finish herself off?

This was the first time they were together like this, so it might seem kind of bossy to jump in.

Should she fake it? Do a few thrusts, groan a little, and thank him?

She was too old for that shit.

She went for honesty. "Adam, this is really nice, and it feels good, but I don't think I'm going to get there this way."

"Oh, you only like the dick, huh?"

"Not exactly, it's just kind of slow…" she tapered off.

"So you're good? Is that what you're saying?" He sounded annoyed.

That's not what she was saying. She wanted him to go down on her. But she didn't want to make a thing out of it if he didn't suggest it. She'd had her share of guys pushing her head toward their junk hoping for a blowie. "Sure. We can stop and cuddle for a bit."

"I'd like that."

She was glad Adam didn't see the look on her face.

He started snoring in about two minutes.

Should she stay or go? They may have broken the couch already. Better safe than sorry. She pulled the covers up and tried to sleep.

Why couldn't she have musicianship *and* skills in bed in one guy?

Chapter 33

Alex was back at work in her home office. She was still buzzing from the energy of Paris. The city. The concert. Playing at L'Opéra. Everything.

Well, everything except the lukewarm sex.

It was tough to get back into the swing of things and be remotely excited about the sales strategy. The sales methodology documentation was complete, and they were now in execution mode, developing the training materials and conducting landing meetings. It was all so repetitive.

Usually, repetitive didn't bother her. She was a bass player, after all, and bass players had to get used to playing the same thing over and over behind a tune. Even her favorite symphony had an entire page of the same run over and over.

But this was repetitive without a point. It wasn't building to some dramatic conclusion with audience applause. It was just churning out documentation and videos for a training site.

She rolled her shoulders and stretched her arms overhead.

She needed a break. She needed a release.

Sex would do the trick. Her appetite had been piqued by her time with Adam, but she wanted someone who knew what they were doing. Cameron flashed into her mind.

Maybe it was time to check in on the Lynda situation. She texted him.

Instead of responding, he called her. "Hey. I was just thinking about you."

"What were you thinking?"

"That I'd like to see you again. Lynda and I have officially called it quits."

"Do you still have feelings for her?"

"Of course, we were together for a long time. Almost sixteen years. But I'm a realist, and I know we aren't getting back together."

"That's fair."

She heard him sigh. "This whole thing with Lynda, what happened to Tom – it's reminded me that life is short, and you need to go for what you want."

"Funny, I was thinking along the same lines."

"What do you want?" he asked.

"You."

"That's convenient. When can I come over?"

"I have a few more hours of work to do. Want to meet somewhere for dinner?"

"How about I get takeout, and you meet me at my place?"

His comment sent a shiver of anticipation through Alex. "What time should I be there?"

"How about seven? I'll pick up sushi."

"Sounds great."

Alex had time to finish her work, take Sibby to the park, change into something sexy and head to Cameron's.

. . .

ALEX LOVED this time of year in Seattle. The rain was lightening up and the sun didn't set until almost ten at night. It's what made the rainy months bearable – knowing that the summer would be amazing. She stopped to let a group of cyclists pass by her before turning right into Cameron's condo complex.

Cameron opened the door. "Hello, *Alex*." He put extra emphasis on her name which made her giggle. She was glad they could laugh about what happened the last time they were together. She also liked that she could be Alex here, not Alexandra. "Sushi's in the kitchen. Hope you worked up an appetite." He worried his bottom lip.

Alex leaned in to kiss him. There was that spark again.

"This way." He led her to the kitchen. The sushi was nicely laid out on dishes. He had put some effort in.

She took a seat at the table and unfolded the cloth napkin at her place. "Why so fancy?"

"I wanted to make an effort here. Lynda and I will be officially divorced soon. We talked and talked but just couldn't get on the same page about what our future would look like. We parted as friends, but it's definitely over."

Alex took a piece of salmon sushi from the rainbow roll with her chopsticks. "What about emotionally?"

"That's going to take some time. We were together so long. It's tough to just forget about that."

"What was important about putting extra effort into tonight? We can be friends no matter what we decide physically."

"About that," he sounded thoughtful. "My divorce has taught me that I have to be honest about what I want. I want to date you. I want to have an emotional and physical relationship with you."

"I'm in." Alex took his hand. "I was having a really good time with you. I'm sorry that things didn't work out for you and Lynda, but if you're really single, then I'd love to date you." Cameron's eyes lit up. "But I want to be honest, too, so I have something kind of big to ask you."

"We're friends. You can ask me anything." Uncertainty shone in his eyes.

Alex decided to go for it. "I want to date you, but I don't want to only date you."

"Shit, you want to move in or something?" What looked like fear flashed across Cameron's face.

"No, kind of the opposite. I want to date you, sleep with you, all the things. But I don't want to be exclusive." It was Alex's turn to bite her lip as she looked at Cameron and waited for his reaction.

"Seriously? You're saying that you want to date but not be monogamous?"

"Yes, exactly. Be safe, but not exclusive."

"That's exactly what I want." She felt stunned. That was way too easy. "Hallelujah!" He grabbed her face and kissed her.

"That's an interesting reaction." Alex laughed.

"I didn't know I could ask for that. You're amazing and I'm lucky you're giving me a second chance. But, I figured you were looking for another marriage."

"No. No way. I don't want to do that again. I like having my own space."

"Amazing. How often would we go out?"

"We don't have to have a schedule or anything, we just have to be willing to share."

"Are you talking threesomes, too?"

"Maybe, but not with the other people I'm seeing on my own. If we meet people together, then maybe."

"You are the most intriguing woman."

"I try." She batted her eyelashes at him. This conversation was going way better than Alex thought it would.

"Will I get to meet these other people?"

"I can tell you about them, but we'd have to all decide if we wanted to meet. That could be weird. I think I prefer to keep everyone separate."

"That sounds great. And we practice safe sex, and we get checked frequently, and boom. We both get what we want."

"Yep."

"Can we start now?" He jokingly leered at her.

"Put the sushi in the fridge. We can always pull it out again later."

Chapter 34

Based on pressure from Adam and a little from Julia, Alex had rejoined a music group. She had wrapped up at five at work and was headed to rehearsal. She blocked out the guilt trip Michelle tried to take her on when she saw Alex pack up to leave the office.

She'd made it home to play with Sibby and give her dinner. Then she had dialed into her evening work call from the car during her commute to rehearsal and stayed on the line after she parked.

She must have looked ridiculous in her car with her headphones on and her seat pushed back so she could hold the laptop and type notes. Notes she would send after rehearsal.

She could get it all done.

As much fun as she would have playing tonight, Alex knew it wasn't as lucrative as her day job. This concert required two rehearsals and two performances. She would be paid five hundred and fifty dollars. With the commute to rehearsals, practicing her part, the rehearsals, and the concert, she would dedicate about fifteen hours to this. For fifteen hours of work at LampLight, she would make about two thousand dollars when she added her bonus and stock. And she didn't have to scrounge for gigs and students. She just got up every day, walked Sibby, and worked.

This was certainly a lot more fun, but the security her job provided balanced out the lack of fun.

ALEX GOT the nod from the piano player and pulled her bow across the string to play the first note of Schubert's *Trout Quintet* at the same time as he struck the first chord. She started off loudly and quickly lessened the pressure on the bow to soften the held note as the other musicians joined her.

It felt good to be playing again. Especially *the Trout*. It was one of the few popular pieces written for a string quartet along with piano and bass. Most quartets were just first violin, second violin, viola, and cello. But Schubert included a lovely, rich bass part in this piece and it was an absolute joy to play.

They were rehearsing in the piano player's living room. His house was like a temple to music. He even had a pipe organ from a church reassembled in the corner of the room. The chamber music concert would take place in a couple of weeks. Maybe she would invite Ross. He didn't know much about music and wanted to learn. Maybe she would invite Cameron. No, that would be weird. Adam didn't need any additional musical exposure.

"Let's take it from measure twenty-four in the Andante. I want another crack at those thirty-second notes," the piano-playing host said.

"Don't we all," the violinist joked.

"This is sounding great, folks. I think if we focus a bit more on the opening and the transition between movements at next week's rehearsal, we'll be good to go for the concert. Thanks all."

Rehearsal ended at nine. They all busied themselves packing up. "We're heading to The Fiddler." The violinist jerked his thumb at his partner. "Alex, you want to join us?"

"I'd love to, but I have to get home for my dog."

"Sibelius. Right. I love that name."

"See you all next week."

The cellist held the front door for Alex so she could navigate down the steep stairs to the street. A shoulder strap held the bass off the ground while she gripped a handle with her right hand. Her left hand carried the stool she sat on to play. It made for an interesting balancing act.

"Need some help there?"

"Nah, I'm used to it. In fact, if you tried to help me, I'd probably fall over."

"Has that ever happened?"

"I almost took a digger on the stairs in the New York City subway." Alex set her bass down at the bottom of the stairs to tell the story. "I was hoofing it up the stairs at the eighty-sixth street station and a lovely, probably seventy-year-old African American gentleman tried to help me by grabbing the end of my bass and lifting. He almost knocked me over because I wasn't expecting it."

"And wood doesn't heal very well if you smash it."

"Exactly. I knew he was just trying to help so I wasn't angry. I stopped at the top of the stairs to politely tell him I didn't need his help on the second set of steps. He asked me where I had come from. I told him I was on my way to jazz gig. He put his hands on his hips and said, 'you play jazz?' and I got all huffy with him."

"I can see why."

"So I asked him, 'you sound surprised. Is it because I'm a woman?' and he said, 'no. It's cuz yo white.'"

The cellist laughed, as Alex intended her to do.

"I laughed too and then said, 'sorry I had the wrong chip on my shoulder' and we both laughed some more."

"That's hilarious."

"Yeah, and then we stood there talking about jazz for about ten minutes before parting ways. He was a real cool cat."

BETSY HAD a family trip that Saturday and had asked if Alex could squeeze in a lesson during the week. She was exhausted but was happy to make time for Betsy on Thursday night. The moment Alex had put Sibby back in the house and made it out to her studio, there was a knock on her studio door.

Alex looked up to see Betsy's smiling face on the other side. Jeannie was right behind her with an even bigger smile.

Alex motioned them in.

Betsy was brimming with excitement. "I downloaded all the albums you mentioned on the radio show. They were awesome! The music is so great. I loved hearing Stanley Clarke. I want to make my bass sound like his does!"

"That's wonderful, Betsy. I met him once. He was so kind. A great role model as a human and a bass player."

"Alex, you have so many stories." Jeannie's energy

pulsed off her. "I bet we only heard a few in your debut. The team was abuzz after your show. Keith adored you and the audience feedback has been super positive. Congratulations!"

"That's wonderful to hear. I had a great time doing it."

"Keith wants you to be his regular substitute. Starting soon. What are you doing every other Thursday for the rest of your life?"

"How many hours are you looking at for this?"

Jeannie gave her a puzzled look. "That wasn't the response I was hoping for. You'll get out what you put in. Is this not a great time for this opportunity?"

"Sorry, Jeannie, I've been putting in a lot of hours at work and I'm pretty tired." Any extra hours Alex had she wanted to put into performing. Not a radio show.

"I get it. You need your corporate gig while you're building your audience. Local radio doesn't pay too much."

Alex surprised herself with her lukewarm reception, but that was her truth right now. "Okay, I can commit to a few shows. After that, we'll have to see."

Jeannie looked concerned.

Alex regrouped. This was actually pretty darn exciting. She changed her tone. "It's a fabulous opportunity. When would I start?"

"We'll have to get a contract in place and everything, but it would be amazing if you could start soon. I'd love to hear your ideas for how you would expand the show. Keith won't be around forever, and a younger, female voice who knows so much about jazz and can bring in personal stories of performances is a unique blend. We're all still laughing about your story about Doctor Billy Taylor. Imagine having one of the most famous jazz piano players alive at the time giving your all-white suburban band coaching that just didn't work. Hilarious. And you didn't even rehearse that. There's magic there."

The excitement began to bubble. Even though this was performance-adjacent, she would still be in the music scene. Alex was a bit ashamed about her first reaction.

Who was she becoming at LampLight?

Chapter 35

Adam didn't need to be at his gig Friday night until seven, so she met him for happy hour. She wanted to celebrate her radio show offer. She invited him to a French restaurant Julia had recommended. It would give them an opportunity to relive some great memories of Paris.

They drove separately since they would be going different places after dinner – he to his gig, and she on a double date with Kate, James, and Ross.

At some point, she had to tell Adam about still dating other people.

"How's my favorite bass player?" Adam leaned down to kiss her before taking a seat next to her at the bar.

"Good. I have some crazy news to share."

"Is it that you're madly in love with me and I have ruined you for all other men?"

Alex smiled. She certainly enjoyed his company, but he was pretty far off the mark. "Feedback on my guest spot on Thursday Jazz Jams has been super positive. They offered me a recurring spot."

"That's amazing! You know I missed it live because of

rehearsals, but I listened to it on their website. You were funny and engaging while giving Keith some good-natured ribbing. You were great."

"Thanks. It felt good. I did some radio shows back in college and really liked it, but then I was so busy performing I couldn't figure out a way to do both. I put it aside to focus on gigs. Now, I might be able to dust those skills off and use them again."

"Why do you say 'might'? What's holding you back?"

"You're right. I should have made that a statement. I will be dusting them off."

"That's better. Will you be Keith's sidekick or do something else?"

"I'm not sure. It sounds like he might want to be phasing himself out of the program. Please keep that to yourself. Jeannie, that's Betsy's mother who got me the gig, said there's opportunity for expansion in a few months if things go well."

"My lips are sealed." Adam drank some of his cocktail. "How will you make sure you get that shot at expansion?"

"That's what I'm struggling with. My job is very demanding, and the hours are long. And I'd rather be performing in the limited time I have left over. I don't know if I could do my day job, a radio show, teaching, and performing."

"Alex, do you hear that sound?"

"What sound?"

Adam knocked three times on the table. "That's opportunity knocking. And it might not come around again if you don't answer the door."

"I know," Alex wailed. "I'm screwed. I want to do this, but I can't do it all. I can't jeopardize my career and lose my health benefits for a lark."

"Alex. There is no money in local radio. You have to

get picked up nationally to have any chance. If you invest your time now, maybe you can turn it into something big. National syndication. You've been stuck in the corporate grind long enough. This is your chance!"

Alex knew he was right, but she had to figure out a way to do it without killing herself in the process.

"I have a lot of ideas." Alex pressed her lips together and sighed.

"I'm all ears. Hit me."

"This just happened yesterday evening, so I haven't been able to give it too much thought because of my packed day at work, but my experience with you in T3BO reminded me I should use my voice to help black, brown, and beige women get heard. I could start with my network of kick-ass female musicians and then branch out as word gets out. I could feature friends and help musicians continue the healing process after the pandemic. I could even start my own big band and feature rotating soloists on the show. T3BO really opened my eyes, and I want to say thank you again."

"You're welcome. Glad I sparked some possibilities." Adam picked up his menu. "I want to keep brainstorming this with you. But right now, I have to get something to eat so I don't pass out on stage later."

Alex and Adam kept going on ideas after placing their order. "That's a hole I haven't seen plugged anywhere. Kind of like a variety show where it's part interview, part marketing, and part music-making with an inclusive twist. What would you call it?"

Alex thought about it. "There could certainly be some play on black, indigenous, and people of color, like BIPOC Bebop or something like that. I need to give it more thought. Hard bop from the sixties is my favorite kind of jazz. I'd love to honor that."

"Who's your favorite black bass player?"

"You mean other than all of them? Charles Mingus, Stanley Clarke, Victor Wooten, Meshell Ndegeocello, Rufus Reid, Esperanza Spalding, Christian McBride, Ron Carter, need I go on?"

"Yeah, too many to list. Native American?"

"I can only name two - Robert Trujillo from Metallica and Pat Vegas from Redbone. That's a great point. I could explore that angle. Pops, my grandfather, used to tell me how important music and singing were to his tribe. Interesting."

"This sounds pretty revolutionary. Edgy even. Maybe you want to play with that angle instead of putting BIPOC in the name. I mean, white people can shred, too."

"Good point. I don't want to be uninclusive in my quest to be inclusive. I like what you said about it being edgy. What if I call the show 'Take it from the Edge.'"

"Like the guitarist from U2?"

"No. I forget sometimes that you're mostly a classical musician."

"There's nothing wrong with that." He sounded defensive.

"Absolutely not. When jazz players want to start a tune over, instead of saying 'start at the beginning,' we sometimes say, 'take it from the edge' like the top edge of the page."

"I get it."

"It's a play on words because I'll be leveraging stories from the edges of jazz, focusing on marginalized people, and being controversial."

"I love that."

She didn't want to get ahead of herself, but what if she got a regular slot on the radio?

One chord at a time, she told herself.

"I have to run to my gig, but I would love to keep talking about this. Amazing!"

"Thanks Adam, break a leg."

He stopped at the door to wave goodbye like he always did. She waved back and smiled.

Alex continued to sit at the table, thinking.

She wondered how long she could limp along at Lamp-Light and not have people notice. She had dodged a bullet by not getting that new job on Tanja's team. Funny how at the end of the day, Michelle had done her a favor. If she had gotten that job, the golden handcuffs of making more money would have tightened down on her.

She was grateful to Michelle, LampLight, and Julia for helping her, but she knew it wasn't her path.

She'd been able to scale back somewhat at work but was still working about seventy hours a week. If she put in ten hours a week on her radio show and kept her students, that was still eighty-five hours a week.

She had to take good care of Sibby, no scrimping there.

Dating would have to be out. She wouldn't have time for even one guy, let alone three.

She certainly couldn't play in any orchestras or bands. Music time would be only for the radio show preparation. She'd have to give up lessons and performing, but it would be worth it to explore this opportunity.

The problem was that to really do it right, the radio show would take a lot more time than that. The research, the preparation, the rehearsals, the guest management. It would take more like forty hours a week. To execute her full plan of leading a jazz band, she would need to dedicate another ten hours a week. Maybe more.

Fifty hours a week for the radio show? But she didn't have that.

Michelle would have a shit hemorrhage if Alex only worked fifty hours a week.

But something had to give.

Her only choice was to scale back at LampLight. The radio show and her music were too important to her not to.

She would split her hours fifty/fifty and work as many hours as she could possibly manage and still have quality time for Sibby.

LampLight and the radio show.

No dating, no performing, no students. Except for Betsy.

Even as she thought about not playing anymore, she felt the piece of her soul that was just starting to bloom shrivel up and die.

Chapter 36

"Ride on the back of your motorcycle?" Alex was sure her eyebrows were meeting her hairline. She was out with Ross on their double date with James and Kate that night after her meet-up with Adam.

Three beaming faces looked at her. "I could use some more girl power on the trip," Kate added. "If you come, maybe Julia will ride with Rob." Alex still hadn't answered.

"Yeah, it would be fun." Ross continued without missing a beat. "We're going to do a ride in Northern California to help James do some exploring for his motorcycle tour company." Ross was brimming with excitement. "James and Kate will ride their own bikes, and you can ride on the back of mine."

The idea made Alex's blood zing. "But I've never even been on a motorcycle before. I don't know how to be on the back."

Kate jumped in. "It's dead simple. You just sit there like a sack of potatoes. If you try to do anything else, you could throw off the balance of the bike." Alex could sit like a sack of potatoes. "Then you just enjoy the ride," Kate continued. "And if you don't like it, you'll be near wine country and can spend a few days there instead."

It sounded like a great opportunity. "When are you thinking?"

"We're targeting the second weekend of July, just a long weekend trip. It'll be hot inland, but we'll spend a lot of it near the coast. We'd only miss one day of work. That's important to everyone except Kate who gets to set her own schedule." Ross stuck his tongue out at Kate playfully.

"I just might be able to do that!" Alex's mind was swirling. Could she take a little more time off? It was just a day, after all. But Michelle had been so annoying about the time off for Paris and leaving early that Alex was letting most of her vacation time expire at the end of the month.

She didn't want to do that again in fiscal year 2025.

All of her work for the fiscal year end would be done since the new year would have already started by then. It would be up to the execution teams to land it all at that point. She felt rebellious agreeing without Michelle's permission, but she went for it. "I'm in."

"That's great. And one more thing. We're going to use Kate and James' house as a home base to keep costs down. There will be one night in a hotel, but since we're traveling together and I'm already getting a room, you could just stay with me."

"Okay," Alex nodded. Perhaps she'd have to take him for a test run to make sure that was a good idea.

She had a lot to think about. She was going to have to tell Adam and Ross about each other. At least Cameron knew now. But how? And when?

Kate cleared her throat. "Now that we're settled on the trip front, what's the latest on your condo, Rossypoo?"

"What's going on with your condo?" Alex asked.

"I got a notice that a recent inspection revealed a termite infestation, an issue with the roof, and a crumbling foundation, all of which need to be repaired. All four renters need to be out of our units for three weeks.

"Oh, that sucks." James took a swig of his beer.

"I thought my renter's insurance would pay for a place to stay through the 'loss of use' clause, but they've refused saying the termite abatement company should pay for it since their regular termite treatments didn't work."

"Shouldn't the HOA cover it then?" Kate sounded confused.

"In a perfect world, yes, but they're holding out for their insurance company to cover it and they're balking, too. Meanwhile, the longer we hold out waiting to get the cost resolved, the longer it'll be to get the repairs done and get us back into the building."

"With James and I both having office space at home, our guest room is now his office."

"See? I told you we should have gotten a bigger place after you became a successful author." James quipped.

"You've never said that." Kate shook her head at him.

"I know. I just like any excuse to say you're a successful author."

"Aww, that's so sweet," Ross said as he tipped back the last of his drink.

"It would be sweeter if we could offer you a place to stay."

"True that."

Alex had a guest room. Should she offer it to Ross? Or would that complicate things too much? Lots of boundary issues to work out.

"When do they want you out?" Alex asked.

"Now. The other three tenants have places lined up already. I'm the last hold-out."

"Let's talk about it. Maybe you could stay with me."

"Really? We could take this torrid affair to the next level. And I cook. And I'm housebroken. Mostly. There was that one incident in 2022, but there were extenuating circumstances."

"I can vouch for that. I was there. Ross was part of our Covid Pod. There's a reason I call him Rossypoo." Kate laughed and smirked at Ross.

"I don't think I want the rest of that story." Alex scrunched up her face in mock disgust.

"Hey hey hey. Alex, there's no poop story. We're just letting the jokes flow, right?"

"Like verbal diarrhea." James shrugged.

"See the endless, punny fun you could have if I lived with you for a few weeks, Alex? And don't forget the sex. Hot sex on tap. All day, every day."

"Are you sure you're a data scientist and not in marketing? That's a hell of a pitch, Rossypoo. I'll have to think about it." Alex laughed. She wondered if it was a good idea.

"Alex, I need to talk to you about a character I'm writing in my next book. She's a musician and I want to get the details right. Mind if we drop you off after Ross so I can pick your brain?"

Kate was amazing. She knew Alex needed to process some questions about the trip and made it easy for her.

"Sure. I can walk home from your place anyway, so we could head there after we drop Ross off."

"I'm feeling left out. Can I come, too? James, we can do man stuff while the ladies talk about fictional characters." He jabbed Kate with his index finger. Alex liked the brother/sister vibe they had going.

"Okay, Rossypoo, but you need to stay out of our hair. No nookie for you tonight."

"You don't know that. James is a very attractive guy. And I'm a catch. Maybe I could turn him. Once you try Ross, you, um –

"Never have to floss?" James suggested.

"I was going to say, know who's the boss."

"Oh yeah," James nodded. "That's better." His eyes darted back and forth.

KATE AND ALEX huddled over a glass of wine at Kate's condo. The guys were in the garage discussing gear for the trip. "We kind of ambushed you out there. I got your back if you don't want to go."

"It actually sounds like a lot of fun. I just have some questions for you."

"Go for it."

"Is it really just sitting there?"

"Yeah. There are a few things they don't tell you, like it hurts your neck in the beginning because you're pushing against the wind when you're going fast, and you have to make sure you don't smack your head into the back of his helmet when he slows down. Your butt might get sore. But otherwise, yeah, it's just a ton of fun."

"Is your house big enough for all of us?"

"Yes. There are two guest rooms. Plus, I built a writing studio in the backyard that has a futon. Even if Julia and Rob head down to join us, you wouldn't have to sleep in the same room as Ross, unless you wanted to."

"We'll get back to that. What would I need to buy to go on the trip?"

"You need a helmet and a motorcycle jacket. I have extras you're welcome to borrow. Boots are a must, too. Your big feet won't fit into my extra boots. Any heeled boot would work for footwear, and you can just wear jeans."

"I have boots and jeans."

"Then you're good to go."

"James has a few extra headsets, and he can put one in your helmet. That'll allow you to talk to us while we're riding."

"I didn't know you could do that. Cool."

"And if you don't like it, the two of us can peel off and head back to Napa, Sonoma, or back to our place."

"I forgot until tonight that you ride your own bike. You're so cool."

"Thanks. I didn't love riding on the back – too many control issues, probably." Kate laughed and Alex joined her. "I had to find a short motorcycle so my little legs could touch the ground. I love it."

"Do you feel safe?"

"Safe-ish. You're hurtling down the road with no metal cage around you at sixty miles an hour. The rule is to ride like you're invisible."

"I don't get it."

"Ride like no one can see you. It makes you hyper-aware of what everyone else is doing so you stay out of trouble. Also, Ross has been riding for twenty years. We wouldn't endanger you."

"That's not the only danger. I haven't told Ross about Adam or Cameron yet. Cameron's fine with it, but I haven't had the exclusivity chat with Ross or Adam. I'd have to do that before I travel with Ross. Hell, I need to do it anyway. It's a lot to juggle – work, the radio show, and three guys." She didn't know how to break it to Kate that she would be retreating from the romantic scene to make time for the radio show.

"I hear you, but it's fun, right? And you're really living." Kate squeezed her hand. "I love this for you."

"Thanks, Kate."

"And it'll all be in a book someday," she added with a laugh.

"Now tell me what to expect on this trip."

"I will if you tell me what Ross is like in the sack."

"Kate! You sound like Gertie."

"I take that as a compliment. Let me get more wine."

"CAN I WALK YOU HOME?" Ross popped his head into the kitchen where Kate and Alex were finishing up their wine.

"I thought you went home." Kate looked stern.

"And give up the chance to hang with James a little longer? Never."

Alex appreciated the gesture. "Sure. It's just a few blocks."

"Great. I'd love to see your dog again, um…"

"Sibelius."

"Yeah, what she said."

"You'll get it."

"Will I?" Ross sounded like he was talking about sex. Alex was tempted.

"Thanks for a fun evening. Looks like I get an escort home."

"Remember to do everything I would do." James swatted Ross on the butt before closing the door behind them.

"This way." Alex pointed up the road and they started their walk.

"I heard you went to Paris and played a gig."

Maybe now was a good time to tell him about Adam, she thought.

"Yeah, it was crazy. This guy invited me to go with him

and then I wound up playing the concert instead of just attending. And it was at the opera house."

"With the Chagall paintings on the ceiling?"

"Exactly!" Alex was impressed. "You've been there."

"Yes. I love the view of the opera house from the terrace at Les Galleries Lafayette across the street."

"There's a terrace there? I thought they just sold over-priced clothes."

"Oh yeah. You go up this little staircase and boom, there's a terrace and a bar. Looks like I'll have to take you back and show you." They walked in silence for a moment. "The main thing I liked about your trip to Paris is that Sibby was at Kate's for the week, and we bonded. I've found the best way to judge a person is through their dog. And she's amazing. Jury's still out on her owner."

The moment to tell him about Adam had passed. It wasn't like she had promised either of them exclusivity. "Really. And what would the owner have to do to be as cool as her dog, speaking hypothetically, of course."

"Good question. Well, she'd have to roll over and let me scratch her belly. Kiss me every time I saw her, and most importantly… sniff my butt."

"I was with you 'til that last part."

"Oh really?" Ross spoke like an old-time movie villain. Before she could say anything, Ross grabbed Alex with both hands and laid a big, fat kiss on her. When she threw her arms around him, the kiss quickly changed from a jokey smooch to a sizzling hot make-out session. Right there in the street.

Humor had always been the key to Alex's heart. She loved to laugh. Having her face hurt from laughing so much was one of her favorite feelings. And Ross did that to her, every time they hung out.

"That's one checkbox. Are you ready to let me scratch your belly?"

He pointed to his midsection. "This belly isn't going to scratch itself."

Now Alex's sides hurt from laughing, too.

Alex matched Ross' pace as they ate up the sidewalk on the way to Alex's little house.

Chapter 37

They were almost breathless by the time they made it to her driveway. Ross grabbed her by the waist from behind while she fumbled with her key. She could feel his erection pressing on her. She stopped and pulsed against him, hoping it would drive him a little crazy.

"Alex, you need to stop doing that or we'll wind up doing it outside."

"Doing what?" she asked sweetly.

"All the things." They both laughed. She opened the door.

Alex turned around to get back to business, but Ross was already heading for Sibby who was obviously happy to see him. "Sibs!" he yelled as they wrestled on the floor. "How's the puppers?"

"I don't know if I'm ready to mop up my dog's sloppy seconds." Alex put her hands on her hips to underscore her joke.

"Sibelius. I'm sorry it had to be this way, but it's over. I only do one bitch at a time."

"Funny, that's the name of my sex tape." Alex opened her eyes wide to help land her joke. Gertie would be proud.

"Sexy and funny. I'm a goner." Ross released her dog and lunged at Alex who shrieked with delight as he picked her up and put her on the sofa. He flopped down next to her. "So, what do you like?"

Alex laughed again. She thought they had already started the foreplay section of the evening, but he was taking a break. "You sound like we're having a business meeting."

"Oh, I can go full-on data scientist if you want." He raised his eyebrows. "What are the parameters for our model this evening? Are we testing correlation or causality between how hilarious I am and how many orgasms you have? How many standard deviations would you like to calculate?"

Tears leaked from the corners of Alex's eyes while he completed his joke.

"Parameters? I just want to bone you." Alex stated in a matter-of-fact tone.

"Technically, I don't think *you* can bone *me* without assistance from equipment, but I like to keep my clients happy."

And with that, he pulled her up and planted a kiss on her that made her forget all about laughing.

He was lighting fires behind her eyes and between her legs. So hot, so fast.

"Where's the bedroom?"

Alex grabbed his hand and led him to the small main bedroom.

"I love small houses when I'm this hot. If you lived in a mansion, I might not have survived the lack of blood flow to my brain on a long walk to the west wing."

"Well then, you better lie down."

"You first."

Alex did as she was asked, and he joined her on the bed. His hands were everywhere.

"Let's get you out of these clothes, we don't want any constraints on the model."

Alex slipped out of her jeans and shirt, but she kept her underwear on in case he wanted to remove it himself. She heard a crash behind her as she turned around.

"In my rush, I forgot to take my shoes of first and almost took a digger. I was saved by your dresser."

"Need help?"

"No, I've got it," he assured her.

Injury avoided, he joined her on the bed. He had left his boxer briefs on, too.

"Now, where were we." He nuzzled against her neck, licking her earlobe and finding just the right spot. She arched against him. "I've been thinking about this a lot."

"Stop thinking and start doing." Alex was breathing heavily.

He rolled to one side and cupped her breast, rubbing his thumb back and forth over her nipple until it was a stiff peak. He traded his mouth for his hand and sucked on her through the thin fabric of her bra. His hand traveled down across her stomach to rest on her hip.

He played with the edge of her panties, tracing his finger inside the waistline and then around the leg. She opened for him, but he continued to trace the line of her panties until she was desperate for more.

The sensations swamped her, a growing need for him to touch her.

She reached for him, encircling him with her hands and freeing him from his boxer briefs. Half crazed with desire as he had teased her, she decided to return the favor. She rolled him over and peeled his underwear all the way off.

His cock was ready, tip glistening. She scooted down and licked his head. Just the tip, moving her lips around his shaft and just holding there. "Keep going," he said.

"Make me," she challenged.

He placed his hands on the back of her head and pushed her down on his cock. She gripped the base to keep from gagging and let him guide her where he wanted her. She picked up the pace, sliding him in and out of her mouth.

"Oh God."

She could tell he was getting close. After the Paris incident, she had made sure to stock her nightstand with condoms. She reached over and grabbed one from the tiny drawer. She kept stroking him with one hand while she carefully ripped open the package with her teeth. He didn't take his eyes off her.

"Not yet. I have something else in mind."

He took the condom from her hand and set it on the nightstand before scooting down on the bed next to her. When he was about halfway down, he ran his hand down the inside of her thigh and nudged it over to the other side of his face. She found herself kneeling over him.

"Now, come here." He gently took her hips and positioned her over his mouth, sitting up slightly to reach her with his tongue. He licked up her crease and settled his mouth on her clit.

She moved against him, careful not to crush him, but controlling the pressure. He reached one hand between her legs from behind, finding her opening and teasing it with two fingers as his mouth continued its dance.

Alex pulsed against him, sensations building a tight coil

in her core. She increased her speed, throwing her head back and her hands forward as she rode his mouth. He curled his fingers into her and sent her flying. She rocked and rocked as he kept fingering her until she hovered over him panting.

When she recovered her breath, she reached for the condom while he scooted up on the bed. She rolled it down his length.

They were both hot and ready.

She straddled him and took him inside of her in one fluid motion. She placed her hands and each side of his shoulders and began to ride.

He reached up to hold her breasts while she moved. She bent down to kiss his smart mouth, opening her thighs wide to create the delicious friction she craved.

Once he was positioned right where she wanted him, she increased the pace and milked a climax from him.

His bucking and pulsing hit just the right spot and she soared with him, enjoying a long orgasm she felt from head to toe. She collapsed on top of him, black hair falling all around his shoulders. They stayed like that, breathing hard, for several moments.

He broke the silence. "Are you familiar with duffle bagging?"

She laughed. "Um, no."

"It's where we sit like this, maybe with a little motion on your part to see if I can get hard again. It actually works sometimes if you're up for it."

"Wouldn't you have to be the one who's up for it?"

"Touché," he responded.

"It's not very sexy to say, but you've got a used condom on, so I'd feel better with a fresh one if you wanted to go again."

"That checks out. Good point."

She reached down to hold the condom in place while she dismounted and discreetly threw it away in the small wastebasket near the bed.

"Round two?" She blinked innocently at him.

Chapter 38

"Happy Saturday, Gram."

"Oh, Alex, thanks for calling. I needed to hear your voice." She sounded very upset, like she'd been crying.

"What's wrong? Are you okay?"

"I'm just tired, that's all. I've been losing sleep over the Recovery Center. They lost their major donor. They only have enough money to keep the doors open for two more months and they can't take in any new people."

"Oh no! That's terrible. No one can step in and take their place?"

"Afraid not. I didn't want to bug you with this since you're so busy with everything, but it's been going on for months. I've been wracking my brain for other potential donors and writing grant proposals, but there just isn't money for this sort of thing right now. We have to shut down."

"Maybe I can help."

"Oh no, sweetie. You have your own priorities. You already share what you can. You need to support your life in Seattle. I couldn't ask that of you."

"You aren't asking. I'm offering. How much do you need?" Alex had been saving. Maybe she could help.

"They own the building, and most of the staff are volunteers. We need about six thousand a month to keep it going. That's much too much to ask of you."

Gram was right. Even with her modest lifestyle, it would be hard to carve out six thousand a month after taxes.

"That's steep Gram, but I can write you a check right now for the first two months. I just don't know how long I could keep it up."

Alex thought about her approach of backing off at work and could have kicked herself. If she had kept plugging away, even with Michelle's bad treatment, she could have already had a raise or promotion.

"You can't do that, sweetheart. You need that money." She did need the money. It was her ticket out. But Gram was her family. Her rock.

"I would do it for you and Pops. You did so much for me. And I'll work on a longer-term plan. As you like to say, there's always a way." She clasped the silver charm on her necklace between her fingers for strength.

Alex truly believed that volunteering at the Recovery Center kept her grandmother alive. It gave her something to do that helped heal the hole in her heart caused by Alex's mother's choices.

If Gram and Pops hadn't stepped in, who knows where Alex would be now. Certainly not in a well-paying job in Seattle. She owed it to them to help Gram out.

"Are you sure, Little Feather? There is absolutely no pressure for you to do this."

"I'm sure, Gram."

"I had no idea you were making so much money out there. You have twelve thousand dollars you can just give the Center? You're so successful! I'm humbled by your gift and proud of your accomplishments! I'm going to have a good cry when we're off the phone. Tears of joy, mind you."

"I'm here for you, Gram. Who do I send the check to?"

NOW WHAT? Alex thought when she hung up.

What was she going to do? She had never heard her grandmother sound so worn out. This was not good for her.

Alex had to help. She just had to. It was small payback for everything her grandparents had done for her. They made sure she felt love and encouragement. While she wondered about her mother, she never lacked care and support, so in all ways that mattered, she had parents. She never had that lost feeling of wondering what it would have been like to have a mother who loved her. She had that. A great one.

This was her chance to pay it back. Not just for Gram and Pops but for all the women who got clean and all the families who were reunited.

The timing was terrible. She had just figured out how to reduce her hours at LampLight to make room for the show. But now she needed to buckle down at work.

She would figure out a way.

There was always a way, as Gram liked to say.

Chapter 39

Alex crammed a brainstorming session for her radio shows into Saturday afternoon but had to set that aside to work on a presentation Saturday evening since she had her two concerts of the *Trout Quintet* on Sunday. With all her meetings, she hadn't had time during her work day to get the presentation done.

She couldn't keep this up. She would find a way to balance her work hours with the radio show and be successful with both. If she could just add a few hours to each day so she could get some sleep.

She couldn't let Gram down.

SHE ARRIVED at the office on Monday with a renewed sense of purpose to balance work and the radio show.

"Have you heard about the engineering team?" Eugene from Michelle's team huddled over his laptop in the conference room that morning.

"No. What happened." Alex was so busy she didn't have time to read the news or participate in office gossip.

"LampLight just laid off over five thousand people. There's an article online that says it's just the beginning of the hits according to their source in HR."

"Shit, that's a ton of people." Alex felt a flare of fear lick up her spine. She couldn't lose her job right now.

"Drop in the bucket at this place, but tough for those five thousand people."

"Do you think it could impact our team?" Of course it could impact her team. *It could impact her*, she thought.

Eugene looked up at her. "LampLight doesn't lay off engineers without making similar changes in sales, marketing and operations. Usually, they go last, but it looks like they went first this time. The exec team wouldn't fire the sales org at the end of the fiscal year. But the beginning of the next one? Watch out."

Dread flooded Alex's veins. She couldn't afford to lose her job. It would ruin everything. With the money she had given to Gram and her monthly expenses, Alex was living paycheck-to-paycheck, her cushion gone. She already planned to use her next stock vest for the Recovery Center.

Michelle entered the room to start her staff meeting.

"Hey Michelle, can you comment on what the layoffs mean for us?" Eugene sounded concerned, too.

"No comment. Even if I knew something, I wouldn't be allowed to tell you." She spoke in her most corporate tone, like she had a lot of teeth. She sat down and plugged her laptop in, avoiding eye contact with the team.

Alex's feeling of foreboding grew stronger. She had a bad review and was probably first on the chopping block.

She had to do everything she could to stay employed. More hours, less time off, more effort. Anything to keep her job. The radio show would have to take a back seat.

HUNCHED over her latest presentation the next day, Alex got an incoming text from Ross.

Ross: Dinner tonight?

Alex: Sorry - working

Ross: I'll bring take-out and then head to Jate's place

Jate was Ross' nickname for James and Kate.

That actually sounded pretty good to Alex. She could get home, take Sibby to the park, get an hour of work done, have dinner and then work until bedtime. The next evening was the one rehearsal she was still planning to attend, and Thursday night was set aside for listening to Keith's show and finalizing her plan for her show the following week. This could work.

Alex: OK, does 6 work?

Ross: Yes. I'll bring Thai

She didn't have to worry about dinner. That felt nice. Then her headache reminded her of the pressure of her deadline and Alex got back to work. Michelle had plopped a new deliverable on her plate that day and a meeting the next day to review it. She had to create it tonight.

She stared at her notes. The assignment was to write a customer value proposition that explained how the internal changes they were making to the sales methodology and team structure were good for customers.

Alex knew how to write the benefits for LampLight – more money, happier customers, happy salespeople who stuck around longer. But benefits for a customer from a new sales methodology?

Shouldn't it all be opaque to the customers? Why would a customer care about LampLight's internal organizational structure? As long as the customer got what they wanted, they wouldn't give two shits about the internal structure of how LampLight achieved it.

She was very confused.

But Michelle insisted there was a customer value proposition, and she had to find it and document it.

Alex was stumped.

She created a slide and titled it "Customer Value Proposition."

After twenty minutes, she had only typed one sentence.

Customer + Value = Customer Value

She didn't know what else to do.

Alex added a graphic of a customer in the middle of the slide, showing they were the center.

What the Hell was she doing? She could be at a rehearsal right now. Or practicing for a concert. Or planning her radio show.

The pressure of the deadline pressed down on her shoulders. She started surfing other customer value propositions on the web and asked an artificial intelligence engine for help.

Fifteen minutes later, armed with lots of generic ideas, she created a slide about positive customer outcomes. And another about a vision for how LampLight wanted customers to feel at the conclusion of each step in the sales methodology. She rounded it out with a series of actions the sales team had to take to make the outcomes and positive feelings a reality.

It was all garbage.

She felt like she was playing corporate bullshit bingo.

Alex was embarrassed to show it to her team and to Michelle, but the deadline was looming. She had to have something to share the next day.

She would just do the best she could and spend the evening after Ross left adding stock photos of smiling people and scenes from "business" like a factory floor with people wearing hard hats and excitedly pointing at a laptop. A conference room full of happy people with a graphic that had an up arrow indicating positive progress.

Horrifying. Absolutely horrifying.

THEY DUG INTO THEIR FOOD.

"Thanks for doing this, Ross. I needed a break from the grind."

"But grinding is just what I had in mind after this."

"Very funny. I have about two hours of work to do before I can think about going to bed and I start tomorrow with a 6AM meeting with the team in the UK."

"It sounds exhausting. How can I help you?"

"Want to do my laundry, pick up groceries, walk the dog?" Alex was kidding.

"Actually, I could do all those things for about three weeks if you let me crash in your guest room. Have you thought about that?"

Alex had thought of it, but guilt from dating multiple guys stopped her from offering her guest room.

"Your face suggests you don't like that idea." Ross looked embarrassed he had brought it up.

"It's not that." *Now or never,* she thought. Worst case, he wouldn't be okay with it, and they would break up. He could still stay there, just platonically. And she wouldn't have to tell Adam about them. Or Cameron. Or the accordion player she was still thinking about. "We haven't had a chat about being exclusive."

"Is this when you tell me I have to give up the hookers and blow to live with you?"

"Just the blow," she shot back, trying to keep her face serious.

"But not the blow *jobs*."

"Never those. But we're getting off track, here." Alex piled more pad thai on her plate.

"Blow jobs are never off track, Alex." Ross shrugged his shoulders when he saw Alex's baleful stare. "Just saying."

She sliced her open palms through the air like two karate chops to try to channel his thoughts in a single direction. "Focus, Ross." She took a deep breath, nerves hitting her vocal cords. She cleared her throat. "Full transparency, I'm seeing someone else, too."

"Okay." He looked at her expectantly, like he was waiting for her to continue.

"That's it. I'm seeing multiple people. Are you okay with that?"

"Not really." He scratched his head, looking thoughtful. "But I like you. I don't love knowing you're seeing other people. Give me a sec here." He sipped his beer and looked contemplative. "But I get it. I stopped trying to find other dates when I met you because of my famously poor history choosing women. Would you stop if I moved in?"

"No." She wondered if that was true, but she wanted to test herself.

"Would you mind if I moved in and tried to change your mind?"

Alex thought about that. Would she change her mind? It was only for three weeks. She would have to tell Adam she had a new non-platonic roommate.

It could get complicated.

But Ross needed a place to stay, and she had an extra room. She thought of Gram and how she said there was always a way.

"Why not?"

"Really? That's amazing! I thought you'd put up more of a fight. Sounds like I have a chance."

Alex rolled her eyes but smiled to show she was amused. "When do you want to move in?"

"Soon, like really soon. I was going to crash at Jate's tonight. I have my stuff in the car."

That *was* soon. *But what the Hell*, Alex thought.

"Why don't you clear out and spend some quality time with James and Kate so I can finish my work for tonight. Come back around nine with your stuff. The guest room is ready to go."

He grabbed her face and kissed her. "Wow. This evening's working out differently than I thought it would."

"For both of us," Alex said with a smile.

Chapter 40

"Let me help you with that."

Ross was back later than evening. She took a big duffle bag from him as he wheeled a large suitcase into her small house. His backpack looked heavy. "I know it looks like a lot for three weeks, but I'll be working from home, so I have my laptop, keyboard, and a big monitor."

"I hope it all fits in your room."

"I'm not staying in your room?"

"Your stuff won't fit in my room. There's a desk in the guest room upstairs. It should be big enough for your set up."

He looked around her house. "What a great house. I love that you kept the Craftsman charm. I didn't take the time to appreciate it last time I was here. I was in a hurry."

Alex blushed as she remembered the thrill of sitting on his face and felt a tickle between her thighs. "The previous owner knocked down the wall between what was a small dining room and a small living room and made it into a medium-sized family room. I like it, but it means that it gets messy fast." She tried to telepath her desire for a neat house to Ross.

"Want to show me to my room so I don't spread myself all over the place?"

Was he referring back to that night too? That was a good sign on both fronts. She wanted a repeat, and she liked things tidy. She walked him up the narrow staircase. "Watch your head," she said as she tapped on the header across the top of the stairs. They emerged onto a small landing with a door on either side. "Here's your room."

"Let's call it the room for my stuff."

"Okay." Alex consented. She liked the idea of sex on tap. "The room for your stuff is over here. The primary bedroom is through that door."

"There's only the one bathroom downstairs?"

"Yep. Welcome to 1912 construction."

"It's adorable. I wasn't complaining, just figuring out where we're going to shower together." Alex laughed at Ross' joke, appreciating the break.

"Why don't you get settled in? I still have a little work to do."

"Cool. When you're done, I'll meet you on the couch with a glass of some of the wine I brought with me."

Alex liked the sound of that.

AFTER WRAPPING up her final round of updates to her presentation, Alex heard Ross in the kitchen. That was easy to do since her home office was a tiny room next to the action. She popped her head through the door. "Time for that wine?"

"Ready when you are. If I could just find the glasses." Ross began opening and closing cupboards. Alex pointed to the glass-front cupboard with wine glasses in it.

"Duh. I guess I was so awestruck by the sight of you that I momentarily lost the use of my eyes."

"My grandmother always tells me to look with my eyes open." They shared a laugh and a smile.

She watched him pour two glasses of dark red wine and place them in one large hand before opening the fridge and pulling out a small cutting board of cheese and crackers.

"I brought this with me, too." Ross' eyes sparkled at her. She could get used to this.

They sat down on the couch to nibble on the snack, and perhaps each other.

"Hope you like Sangiovese."

"It's red and wet and tastes like wine. That's all I need."

"Not much of a wine aficionado?"

"Nope."

"I like a low bar." He smiled his lopsided grin at her. "Especially with things that are red and wet." Alex laughed. He was doing just fine in that department. He changed the subject. "How was work today?"

"It pays the bills."

"That good, huh?"

"I'm kind of stuck right now. I'm trying to make a lot of money to help my grandmother with a project that's very important to her. But I find my mind wandering to music and my radio show a lot."

"You can't slack off at work. They'll notice and you'll get fired. It's a crazy time right now. Layoffs are happening all over the tech industry. Stay sharp."

He was right. She needed to buckle down and keep working hard. She only agreed to do one show per month to keep her effort level down and stick with Keith's format. It would only be about ten hours per show. She could create the topic lists for the next several shows on Saturday after her morning lessons. And before her happy hour with Adam before his gig.

She would fit it all in. Somehow.

She was glad she had told Ross about not being exclusive. She wondered how Adam would take it.

"You okay over there? It seemed like you went really far away."

"Just thinking about work."

"I'll distract you with a question about…" he pointed one of his index fingers and dragged it back and forth against the other one like he was trying to start a fire.

"A new sex position?" Alex was confused.

"No. I kept Rob company at a concert you played with Julia a long time ago. There was a piece with a Barry Manilow song right in the middle of it." Ross started singing the tune.

"Rachmaninoff's Second Symphony." Alex smiled. "He borrowed parts of that melody from the main theme of the third movement, but it's not the same exact notes."

"Can he do that?"

"Sure. I don't know if he ever gave Rachmaninoff credit for it, but it's pretty obvious to anyone who knows the symphony. Just like *Could It Be Magic* is really *Chopin's Prelude in C Minor*."

"You're kind of blowing my mind here. How do you know so much about Barry Manilow?"

"Little known fact about me. I was in the Barry Manilow Fan Club when I was eight. My grandmother is a big fan."

"You're a Fanilow?"

"They didn't call us that back then."

"I'm going to sing one of those songs for you at Kate's

next party. Amazing. I bow down to your superior musical knowledge and tastes."

"It happens all the time in music. The theme from *Jaws*? Just like the opening of the fourth movement of *Dvorak's New World Symphony*."

"John Williams stole that?" Ross gave her an incredulous look.

"That is a very controversial statement you just made." Alex applauded his response. "Some call it artistic license."

"You sound like such a snob. I mean, there are only so many notes and so many combinations. It's just math really. After a few hundred years of modern western music, wouldn't you have to repeat themes?"

"That just cost you a blow job or two."

Ross spluttered. "What I meant to say is that I hope every composer who's ever been copied got paid for it."

"Better," she deadpanned.

"Now, about those reinstated blow jobs…"

"Didn't you have an actual question before we sidetracked on Barry Manilow?"

"Why would I care about Barry Manilow's blow jobs?" he said with mock incredulity.

Alex gave him a baleful stare until he continued.

"Right. I was at that concert and wondered how you got everyone's arms going the same way when they play."

"What do you mean?"

Ross mimicked pulling a bow across a string.

"Oh, up bows and down bows."

"Not helping."

"They're marked in the music," she explained. "The principal string player – that's the person who sits in the first seat of each section and is typically the best player in the section – decides which direction the bow should go for each note. Sometimes, you play multiple notes in one bow stroke and sometimes you play back and forth really fast. It depends on what the composer wanted and how the principal likes to get the desired effect."

"So, it's, like, written into the music?"

"Yeah, and there can be heated arguments about what makes sense. Personally, I like upbows into crescendos, but others hate that. I just follow what the principal player says and don't argue. Well, unless it's really really stupid."

"Music is so complicated."

"Yeah, so is data science. Most things worth learning about and doing are."

"It's so sexy when you talk about complexity." He took her wine glass from her hand and leaned her back on the sofa.

She would just have to be tired at work tomorrow, she thought with a sigh as she wrapped her arms around Ross.

Chapter 41

Alex looked around the room the next afternoon. Dread filled her. She had just wrapped up her verbal presentation of the customer value proposition deck she created the night before.

Her palms were sweaty. She felt a pearl of armpit sweat run down the inside of her shirt. She shifted in her seat, the chair creaking in the silence of the room.

People started looking at her. She couldn't read their faces.

It was all crap. She knew it. Her mouth folded down in a frown as she waited for Michelle to speak.

"Alexandra, you didn't seem to understand the assignment when we talked yesterday."

"I know, and I'm sorry." Alex braced for impact.

"This is amazing work. Exactly what I wanted." She turned to the group. "See people? This is what strategy looks like."

Alex was floored. Relief flooded her. She tried not to look surprised.

Michelle turned toward her. "Since you did such a

great job with this one, could you apply that big brain to doing a similar one for the partner value proposition for us to share with the broader team tomorrow?"

"Yep. Thanks Michelle." *Oh crap*, Alex thought. She agreed to sub for the principal bass at a symphony rehearsal that evening. She hadn't committed to any new gigs since she decided to pull back and only focus on work and the radio show. But the conductor called in a favor. She couldn't bail now.

She would just have to figure out a way to do both.

Ross could take care of Sibby tonight.

One thing off her plate.

If she left right after this meeting, she could beat traffic and get a couple more hours in before the rehearsal. That would be over at ten and she could make her final changes then.

She would be tired in Thursday morning's status update with the European team, but she couldn't pull out of the group this late, and she certainly couldn't miss this deadline. Not with the dark cloud of potential layoffs hanging over her.

She was getting used to being exhausted.

▭

ALEX HADN'T GOTTEN as far as she wanted on the partner value proposition, but she didn't want to be late to rehearsal. She ate a hastily made sandwich as she drove. At least she would see Julia tonight since she was playing in the bass section. Alex wanted to run her idea for her first solo radio show past Julia.

She didn't have time to fully change the format of Keith's show and do all the work that entailed, but she wanted to do something edgy. Something female.

"Alex!" Julia exclaimed as Alex walked in, carefully maneuvering up the stage stairs. "It's so good to see you back at these rehearsals! The bass section hasn't been the same without you."

"Thanks, Julia. I'm just subbing. Since we're both a little early, I'd love to share my idea for my first solo radio show and get your feedback."

"Hit me."

Alex launched into her plan while they took their basses out of their cases. "You're a harpist. There aren't many jazz harpists out there, and I'm wondering why."

"It's because harps aren't designed to play jazz chords. The pedals move every string in the octave, so you can't play a G sharp and a G natural at the same time. But you can play an A flat and G sharp at the same time because they're different strings. Keeping track of enharmonic notes, diminished chords with a flat nine, and where your pedals are at all times just makes it unrealistic to play jazz chords."

"But a few people do it."

"Yeah. I heard Brandee Younger in Seattle last year. Dorothy Ashby put out a jazz album in 1957. My childhood harp teacher, Laura Erb, did tons of jazzy arrangements in the sixties. It's just way beyond most harpist's skills. Especially when Handel's harp concerto stays in the same key for pages at a time."

"So, I'm onto something that it's an under-represented jazz instrument."

"Yeah, but I don't know how broadly appealing it would be. I think harps are cool but even when jazz is played brilliantly on them, it still sounds like funeral or church music. It's just how harps sound."

"That's one of the reasons I want to do it. It's odd and not well-established in the jazz genre. I want to go for it. I have a friend from college, Cian, who plays jazz harp. I think I can get them to come out to Seattle to do my show. Do you know where I can rent a harp?"

"Sure, but they can also use mine. I don't take it out much since a bass is so much easier, but I can get it to the studio. They'll want to spend some time with it, but it's a standard Lyon & Healy concert harp."

"Really? I think it would be cool to highlight a youngish biracial musician trying to make it as a jazz harpist in New York City."

"Are you talking about Cian Issa by any chance?"

"Yeah, how do you know them?"

"I don't, but they're from Cleveland. Like me. Woo hoo! We studied with some of the same teachers. Of course, they are way younger than me, but harpists are a pretty small community."

"That's amazing. And my idea isn't too weird?"

"Super weird, but definitely not something others have covered. I say go for it."

The conductor called the orchestra to tune.

Alex would call her friend Cian in the morning on the way to work.

▭

AFTER CALLING CIAN, Alex called Gram before her Saturday morning lessons. "You caught me just before lunch."

"You don't sound good. How are you doing? I have so much to tell you!" Alex was bursting with all her updates for Gram.

"I'm good. I managed to catch a cold. Don't worry – I did a Covid test. It's negative and I'm keeping a low profile. Everyone delivers now so I don't even have to leave the house while I'm under the weather."

"Do you need anything? Are you and Sheryl still doing your weekend lunches?" Alex thought of sweet Sheryl who lived across the street from Gram and had for as long as Alex could remember. She had already seemed like an old lady when Alex met her as a little girl. But she was probably closer to forty-five then. She was Gram's best friend.

"Oh yes, and Sheryl and I have our signal."

"Signal?"

"When you reach a certain age, you have to do these things. Every night, we close the curtains in our front windows. Every morning we open them. If one of us doesn't open them by about ten in the morning, the other calls. If there's no answer, we walk across the street and investigate."

"That's a great strategy. I'm so glad to hear she's still there after all these years."

"We've known each other for almost thirty years now. It went by so fast."

"Has Jake been by to visit lately?" Alex thought of her first crush, Sheryl's grandson who came to visit every summer and major holiday. He had been Alex's first kiss. And several other things.

"He came by with his wife and baby a few weeks back. Cute little thing, all chubby cheeks and cute toes."

"And drool and crying and life-ruining," Alex added.

"That too." Gram tried to hide it, but she liked children about as much as Alex did. Not very much.

"Have I thanked you recently for not being one of those mothers or grandmothers who constantly ask when there's going to be a baby?"

"I respect you too much for that, Little Feather. As with all things, you have to make your own mind up. I made my choice, and I would do it again. Especially if I could inherit them at age three like I did with you. We skipped all the toilet training and the terrible twos."

"Thanks Gram."

"I'm pretty tired, and I feel about as good as I sound. I'm going to go take a nap. You take care until next weekend, okay?"

"Love you, Gram."

"Love you, Little Feather."

They hung up. She would call again in a few days to check on her. Alex had wanted to tell her grandmother all about her radio show and work, but she had sounded so sick and tired. She wanted to share the great news that Cian had jumped at the chance to join her in the studio the following week. And that Alex was able to get their plane ticket covered by the radio station and Julia was happy to let Cian stay with her. Jeannie talked to a few folks on the Seattle scene and found three gigs for Cian to play while they were in Seattle.

Gram was right. There was always a way.

Chapter 42

"The joke is that harpists spend fifty percent of their time tuning and the other fifty percent playing out of tune." Cian laughed and set their tuner down on the studio table. Cian and Alex were in the studio, ready to play some tunes and talk through the history of jazz harpists on the air. Alex had assembled about thirty minutes of recordings. They chose to play a couple of jazz standards together and then Cian would play their original composition called *Tektite*.

"How's your grandmother doing?"

"How nice of you to ask. She's doing okay. She had some tough financial news recently and has a cold, but otherwise, things are good. I talked to her yesterday. Sounds like the cold is holding on, so we didn't talk long. She asked me to give you a hug from her."

"What a sweet lady. She came to hear me in Boston a couple years ago. She brought cookies. So supportive."

"That's Gram."

"Quiet on the set," the producer called.

Alex felt the thrill of starting her first solo show. Cian

reached over and squeezed her hand, giving Alex a look that said they shared the excitement.

Alex watched the producer do her countdown.

"Welcome to Thursday Jazz Jams. I'm your guest host, Alex Taylor sitting in for Keith Keys. My guest tonight is Cian Issa, an accomplished jazz harpist from New York City. We'll be talking, playing, and reminiscing about old times in music school. Welcome, Cian."

"Darn glad to be here, Alex."

"Why don't we start with a little duet and then we can talk. You take the intro, Cian, and I'll join you on the head. This is Cian's original composition *Where the Party At* from their first solo album."

Cian played a run that sounded very churchy and then started the jazz melody. When they played the opening four chords, Alex answered with two bass hits, and they were off. After a few times through, Alex dropped out and let Cian finish with a flourish on their own.

As the final chord hung in the air, Alex turned her vocal microphone back on.

"That was a beautiful performance by Cian Issa visiting our studio from New York City. Thanks for that Cian. You sound amazing, as always."

"Thanks Alex. You play a mean bass line girl, always have."

"It's so great to be playing with you again, Cian. How long has it been?"

"Since you left New York City, what was that, like, 2014? The City still misses you, Al." She missed the City, too. The life, the vibrancy, the music scene.

Alex switched back to talk show host mode. "Cian, can you tell us how you became a harpist and when you decided to pursue jazz? It's a rather unlikely instrument for the jazz genre."

"We'll go back in time." Cian laughed. "When I was nine years old, my mother took me to hear two harpists play at a local grocery store in Cleveland. I was mesmerized and asked if I could learn to play."

Alex jumped in. "It's so important to introduce kids to music at a young age. It's great your mom was supportive."

"Let's not go overboard on the supportive mother angle until you hear the rest. She looked at me and said that I would need a leg up to get into heaven because I was such a bad kid and told me she'd pay for lessons if I practiced enough to get into heaven."

"That's hysterical. Were you that bad of a kid?"

"I didn't think so, but what did I know? I was nine and she sounded serious."

"And when did you get into jazz?"

"Way later than that. Harpists have notoriously bad rhythm because we always play by ourselves. We can slow down or speed up and it doesn't bother anyone because it's just us."

"I've played with guitarists like that," Alex quipped.

"Amen to that. I decided to play drums in my school band since I couldn't play the harp with them. That way, I could learn rhythm. I started learning about jazz, but it wasn't until I heard my first jazz harpist, Joanna Jordan's 1994 recording of *Mercy Mercy Mercy*. It blew my mind. I was busy learning Handel's Harp Concerto and Debussy's *Sacred and Profane Dances* and then *boom* here comes this chick from Canada playing really groovin' jazz. I was hooked."

"Joanna, if you're out there, thank you for inspiring this great musician!" Alex wondered if there was a chance Joanna Jordan would ever hear that tribute.

It was Cian's turn to ask a question. "Is it okay if I go off script and play a little of her version of that tune?"

"Nothing is off-script, Cian. Go for it."

Cian tipped their harp against their shoulder and started rocking a rhythmic bass line with their left hand before adding the melody with their right. Alex couldn't stop herself from jumping in on the cool bass line.

"Yeah," Cian said slowly when they finished the song. "That's how you do it."

"Let's hear another one of your tunes now, Cian. Why is this song called *Tektite*?"

"A tektite is natural glass formed when a meteorite hits the soil. Everything gets so hot, the debris that shoots up from the ground where the meteor hits turns into really cool glass formations. They're usually a mix of black, brown, and green. Like me. Half white Irish and half black Jamaican."

"Oh, the green comes from the Irish bit. I get it."

"And supposedly, when my parents got together, it created quite a lot of terrestrial, or at least familial, debris. I've always loved them. Tektites, I mean. My parents are okay, too."

They shared a laugh and started the tune.

The ethereal chords rang out from Cian's harp.

Alex waited for the sound of the final chord to dissipate. "Wow, that was beautiful. I love how you used your knuckles on the sounding board for a beat."

"Thanks. I'm proud of it."

"You mentioned New York earlier. A bass is hard enough to get around with in New York. How do you do it with a harp?"

"For trips like this, I rent or borrow a harp on location, like I did for this show. I'm playing a harp from another harpist from Cleveland. Thank you Julia if you're listening." Alex knew Julia was listening and smiled. "But in New York, I take it with me. Funny story about that. When

I graduated from college, my parents told me they were tired of storing my hard harp case in the garage. Now this thing is huge mind you. It's a wood and metal trunk used for safely shipping harps."

"I've seen them. I've even heard that Alice Chalifoux, the harpist for the Cleveland Orchestra from the nineteen thirties through the seventies used hers as a dressing room since there was no women's locker room at Severance Hall back in the day."

"True that. My girlfriend and I dragged it up the stairs to my third-floor walk-up in Manhattan and it would not go through the door. We tried everything including asking the guys across the hall to open their door so we could tip it back into their apartment to try all the angles. No deal. We couldn't leave it in the hallway because no one could get by it. We dragged it back downstairs, but my girlfriend had to go to work. I stood downstairs with it, calling music schools to see if anyone wanted it. One in midtown was interested. They said they could come and get it in an hour."

"That was fast." Alex was impressed they even answered the phone.

"Yeah, not fast enough. I really had to pee. An hour became ninety minutes, and I thought I would burst. I left it on the street and ran back up to my apartment."

"Oh no." Alex was suddenly concerned for the fate of the case. She hoped her audience was too.

"Oh yes. I'm a fast pee-er, but it was already gone when I got back down, maybe four minutes later."

"You gotta love Manhattan."

"I called the music company to tell them it was gone. They were pretty pissed, but also admitted they were still looking for a van to come and get it. Later that day, I was walking in the neighborhood and here comes my harp case. Being rolled right up First Avenue. I stopped the guy and asked where he got it. He told me it was a fruit selling stand and demonstrated all the features. It locked and it had wheels. He made quite the pitch."

Alex couldn't contain her laughter. "What did you do?"

"I told him I knew he stole it and that it was my harp case, and he said, 'no way, man, I bought it for four hundred dollars, but I'll sell it to you for two.' I realized there was nothing I could do. I didn't have a place for it and the music school wasn't coming, so I just wished him luck and walked away."

"And you never saw it again."

"No, that's the best part. I saw it all over the upper East Side for the next two years. People lived in it under the 96th Street exit on FDR Drive for months. I mean, it was perfect for that."

Tears were streaming down Alex's face from laughing. She tried to pull it together. "You can't make that stuff up," she said through her giggles.

"You don't have to when you're a harpist in New York City. That harp case had a whole second life. It might even still be there, but I moved out of that neighborhood."

"THAT WAS AMAZING, Cian. Thank you so much." Alex was almost bursting with energy after the show.

Cian held up their phone. "Look at that. My phone is blowing up. People are all over my Insta page and my booker has already received three inquiries about gigs. Incredible. You're really onto something. You need to keep going with this."

Alex agreed. She was flying high after the show and saw everything it could be with some effort on her part. Full time effort.

Maybe this was just the shove she needed to finally admit that LampLight Alexandra was slowly poisoning Musician Alex. Her mind flashed with ideas for expanding the show and making it her own.

"Let's get my friend her harp back and go out for a celebratory drink."

Chapter 43

She couldn't wait to tell Gram the good news about how the show went. She was sure Gram had listened online, but she wanted to share the experience. Alex called Gram on Friday morning on her way to the office, knowing the time change was in her favor. Alex listened to the sound of Gram's voicemail and clicked off. She texted that she hoped Gram was feeling better and reminded herself to call again later.

"Come on in." Michelle motioned Alex into her office for their one on one. "I have great news."

"I like great news. Did everyone approve the final training documents?"

"Yes, Alexandra, but that's not the news. Your work on the customer and partner value propositions was so strong. I want to reward you for getting your head screwed on straight and doing a great job." Alex felt her eyes bug out a bit, remembering how absurd those deliverables were. "I was able to get you that promotion after all." Michelle slid a piece of paper across the table to Alex. She didn't only get a promotion. It came with a twenty-thousand dollar raise.

Alex felt her eyes almost pop out of her head.

That was what she made in four months as a musician. And it was just her raise. She was also given a special stock award of forty thousand.

"I can't believe it." Alex fell back in her chair, stunned.

"These changes mean that at your next annual performance review, your target stock grant will be about one hundred thousand dollars."

Alex had to wait for stock grants to vest over four years, but still. That was the equivalent of over two years of earnings as a musician without her having to do anything but work and watch the balance grow.

"Wow, Michelle, thank you."

"You're welcome." Michelle's face looked thoughtful. "I was reminded of how important you've become to the team."

"Thanks for that, too."

"To be perfectly honest, though, I've noticed you haven't been working as hard lately. Taking that vacation to Paris, leaving early, asking for more time off for I don't know what."

Alex felt the shame of being called out. Guilt from phoning it in consumed her. She thought she was doing the best thing for herself, but her brain told her otherwise as she sat across from Michelle and her scolding. "That bad review made me reprioritize some things."

"That's behind you now." Michelle pointed her finger at Alex. "You need to put your shoulder to the wheel and help me prove to my boss that sticking my neck out for you again was the best use of my team's promotion money and stock budget." Michelle gave Alex a penetrating stare. "Don't let me down."

"I won't, Michelle. Thanks again."

Alex walked back to her office.

Is this what golden handcuffs felt like? she wondered. She had heard Tom's engineering tech friends talk about them. Now she knew what they felt like when they locked on. Mostly good.

Mostly.

Relief filled her. She thought she was on the chopping block. But now, she was doing well at work.

The exhaustion was worth it. Finishing deliverables after rehearsals was worth it. The rundown feeling that she just wanted a weekend to sleep was worth it. She was making the money Gram needed.

She would just have to wear the golden handcuffs for four years and the Recovery Center could get back on its feet. She could donate the entire special stock award and the vested stock over the next four years and cement the health of the organization. Then, they could use the interest from the endowment to pay monthly expenses. LampLight would match it dollar for dollar up to twenty-five thousand dollars per year.

This was the way to save the Recovery Center.

This was the way to pay Gram back for over thirty years of kindness.

It just required that she give up on her musical dreams.

Corporate Alexandra would kill Musician Alex.

But it would be worth it.

Alex called Gram on her way home. She had even more news to share now.

Voicemail.

Again.

Alex was getting concerned.

ROSS WAS WAITING for her when she got home from work that night.

It was so easy to hang with Ross. He was light-hearted and funny. He had a good job and was self-sufficient monetarily. She loved his confident approach to sex.

But he was driving her crazy.

She felt bad she was so annoyed with him.

He let Sibby sit on the couch with him. The only way to stop dog hair from getting everywhere was to keep her off the furniture. And now she was a regular fixture in between them watching television, Ross' hand constantly stroking… her dog.

Worse yet, he was eating chips and giving every fourth one to Sibby.

The last time Alex had vacuumed the sofa, she found the crunchy crumbs lodged between the cushions.

He always cleaned the dishes in the sink. When she asked him about it, he said it was to be helpful. Alex strongly believed that it was more efficient to wash them all at the end of the day. Less water.

They were less than two weeks in, but he had completely disrupted her routine. And he was always there. Always.

He could work at home whenever he wanted. He said it was so quiet in her house he was super productive.

Alex set up a TV tray in her studio so she could sit out there to get some alone time.

Whenever she came into the house it was like he was even more excited to see her than Sibby. He was always trying to get her to do something. It reminded her of her childhood friend Jake and his daily summer visits to her door saying "hey, want to ride bikes?"

She clenched her teeth and felt the tightness in her jaw

as she plastered on a smile before opening the door to the kitchen.

"Al! Are you done for the day? Want to go out for dinner? My treat! Sibby and I had a great day together. She's learned to keep her head out of the Zoom frame, so I can keep petting her all through my meetings. She's the smartest dog in the world."

Alex wanted to join in his exuberance over everyday things. She really did. But with these huge, life-altering decisions hanging over her, she wasn't feeling very jovial. And she was worried about Gram.

"I'm just going to have a salad. Why don't you call James? I bet he'd love a dinner out."

"Great idea!" Ross pulled out his phone.

Alex let out a heavy sigh, her shoulders dropping about three inches. Why did she let him stress her out? He just wanted to spend time with her.

It was because she had learned to value her alone time.

"James is in," Ross beamed. "Good call, Al. Can I get you anything before I head out?"

"All good, Ross, thanks."

"Want to go for a motorcycle ride on Sunday?"

"No can do, Ross. Julia's hosting brunch on Sunday."

"Then Kate's out for the ride, too. Man time!"

He was like a grown-up child. When they were hanging out previously, she found it cute and uplifting. But living with that much positivity annoyed the shit out of her.

It shouldn't, she scolded herself.

But it did. If she was going to live with someone, she needed calm energy. More like Adam's energy. But then there was the lukewarm sex issue with him.

"Are you doing anything after your Saturday lessons? I was thinking we could take a walk to go get coffee at Green Lake like our first date."

"That's when I call Gram. And then I need to work on my radio show."

"Okay after that, then. You're working so hard. I want to make sure you have time for you, too."

And then he said stuff like that, and the annoyance flashed away. "How sweet of you to think of that. It sounds great." She put her hand on his arm.

"Are you trying to delay me from leaving to meet James with your sexy caresses?"

"Uh, no, I was just being affectionate."

"But you know what that does to me. And you're wearing my second favorite outfit."

Alex looked down at her crisp business shirt and black pants. "What's your most favorite outfit? Yoga pants?"

"No. Nothing pants. No clothes. Naked. I'd love to see you in that right now. I mean, you did touch my arm and everything."

"We better hurry then. I'd hate to keep James waiting."

Maybe a little annoyance was worth the instant access to sex, she thought.

ALEX LAY in bed that night listening to Ross' light snoring.

Should she be exclusive with Ross? He was in the lead, after all, and they were already living together. She could stop the physical side of things with Adam and Cameron.

But she didn't want to. Especially not with Cameron. And she didn't want to stop her happy hours with Adam before his rehearsals and gigs. She loved talking to him.

Tough to keep dating three guys while she was living with one of them.

Maybe it was time to choose. Or maybe she should just invite all three to live with her on a rotating basis. She bet

Gertie knew the word for that kind of relationship. Polyamorous rotating cohabitation.

Polyroco?

Polycohabitating?

It could be a thing.

But no, that's not what you did. You found a partner to love, and you settled down. That's what she did with Tom. They didn't think too hard about moving in together. It was an easy financial decision when you lived in New York City. Rent was expensive and moving was easy because you only ever had a tiny apartment's worth of stuff.

Was she cut out to live with someone again?

Alex loved living with Tom. But she also cherished her alone time when he was at work during the day. She had gotten very used to it as her full-time, at-home situation in the last five years.

But like she told the Steak and Bourbon crew back in February, she was a little lonely for a built-in companion.

She couldn't have it both ways.

Chapter 44

"The guy just doesn't know how to shop." Melanie was looking harried when she arrived. Alex handed her a drink. "It was a simple trip to the grocery store."

"Uh uh," Angela said wagging her finger back and forth. "Jeremy and I never shop together."

"Perhaps now I know why. First, he went in the wrong door. Produce first, seriously. And then he headed for the freezer section because he wanted ice cream."

"The horror!" Gertie clasped her chest.

"I don't mind the ice cream, but who puts the frozen stuff in their cart first?"

"Savages, that's who." Julia pointed with her spatula.

"Savages and husbands," Lesley added.

"I hate being predictable, but that's the name of my sex tape." Gertie pointed with both fingers at the women gathered around Julia's kitchen island watching her crisp the duck for duck confit with steamed buns. Gertie made everyone laugh, as usual.

"People with fully developed pre-frontal cortexes start with non-perishables, then produce, then stuff that has to stay cold." Julia placed the crisped duck on the platter. "Then, you unload the cart onto the belt in the proper order to facilitate packing by temperature. And then you unpack in reverse order. Everyone knows that."

"Preach," Angela raised her glass to Julia and tipped it against Melanie's.

Alex watched Margaret and Brie share an uncomfortable shrug. She stayed quiet. No wonder Julia was so good at managing every detail at work and home.

"Anyway, that's why I was late today. Major fail at the grocery store."

"No worries, Melanie. Have a drink. I packed the cold champagne in the cart at the liquor store last."

Melanie sat back with her drink. "Back to the important stuff. Alex, I heard you on the radio. You sounded amazing! Cheers!" The ladies lifted their glasses at Alex.

"Thanks friends. It was so fun! I might be able to expand it into my own thing…someday."

"You go girl! That's fabulous! You deserve it!" Margaret joined in.

"What does it look like to expand it? You mean, like have your favorite friends come and sing on your show?" Angela batted her eyelashes at Alex. "Who am I kidding? I'm not good enough to sing in front of other people."

"That's not true, Angela. Your voice is gorgeous."

"I don't have any formal training. You don't just get up and sing on the radio without singing lessons. I'd rather be on stage as a back-up singer than train to be a lead. But back to you, Al."

Alex had to process that later. She wondered how she could help people like Angela get on stage. "It could mean all kinds of things. Helping launch and highlight female musicians. Adding jazz history into the program. Using it to attract a younger audience to jazz. Have my own big band for guest artists to jam with. I could do anything with it… if I had the time."

"Eeeeeerrrrrrrkkk." Lesley made a noise like car brakes. "What do you mean by that? You'd *make* time."

"Except that I won't *have* time. I'll be lucky to be able to host the show once a month in its existing format."

"Hold on, girl. What's this nonsense?" Angela grabbed her hand. "Tell mama you're joking."

"Michelle promoted me this week and slapped a set of golden handcuffs on me."

"Gold is a very soft metal. I could get through it with my teeth." Gertie motioned like she was biting the handcuffs off her wrists.

"I've told you about the Recovery Center my grandmother supports. They lost their funding, and I need to make up the gap. I'm going to turn down a bigger role on the radio show so I can make the money necessary to support my grandmother."

"The classic money or art argument." Margaret shook her head.

"Capitalism or creativity." Lesley's tone sounded sad.

"Love or duty," Kate added.

"Self or others." Julia gave Alex a pointed look.

"All those things." Alex hung her head. "I had decided to slowly decrease my hours at LampLight while I increase my focus on the radio opportunity."

"I like that idea." Angela tipped her glass toward Alex.

"I know. I did, too. But then Michelle said she realized how valuable I am to the team and threw a bunch of money and a promotion at me. How could I say no?"

"Easy. It's just like I told my college English Professor. No means no." Gertie pursed her lips.

"But I don't think I want to say no. So many of my musician friends would kill for the kind of money I'm making. They would call me a fool for walking away. And then there's my grandmother."

"I call you a fool for staying." Several people sucked in their breath at Brie's honesty. "Sorry, sweetie, but this is your chance. It's not going to come around again."

"I know, but I only have one grandmother. And she was there for me when I needed her to be."

"Did she ask you to help?" Julia asked.

"No. She would never do that. And that's one of the reasons I feel like I have to."

"Tough situation and a tough call." Melanie sounded sympathetic.

"Yeah, poor me – making more money than I ever thought I could versus a pipe dream. Kind of a first world problem."

"Don't belittle the pain and struggle." Lesley was firm. "It's real. Having choices can be just as difficult as having none."

"This is my fault." All eyes turned to Julia.

"Because you got her the job in the first place?" Akiko's brow wrinkled in confusion. "I think you're off the hook for that one, Jules."

"No. I may have had a little chat with Michelle when she blocked Alex from getting that new job."

"Julia strikes again!" Lesley laughed.

"I told her I tried to hire you but that you wanted to stay loyal to her. Then I reinforced that she better make it worth your while to stay because I was spreading the word about your positive impact on the team and that people would start headhunting you soon."

"You threatened my boss?"

"No, Alex. I just reminded her not to fuck with you." Julia's tone sounded protective.

"Or you." Gertie pointed at Julia with her fork.

"Yeah, that too."

"Julia, are you hiring?" Lesley sounded very hopeful.

"No, it was just a ploy. But it worked." Julia's lips turned down. "Apparently a little too well."

"Sponsorship. Boom." Kate made explosion noises and popped her hands open.

"What was that you were telling us about sponsorship versus advocacy?"

"Yeah, maybe I'll have to introduce a new category called 'misplaced sponsorship' to describe what I did. I had noble intentions." Julia looked at Alex, a hopeful expression on her face. "I'm sorry I complicated your life."

"You have nothing to be sorry about. You're enabling me to help my grandmother."

"She's enabling something." Brie was sticking to her guns. "I don't like this, Alex. But as you know, I'll support you in whatever decision you make."

"And I understand both sides too. Sometimes you have to make the money while you can." Kate's tone was supportive.

"Thanks friends."

AS they carefully stacked Julia's grandmother's dishes next to the sink to make room for dessert, Julia took Alex aside. "Hey there. I'd really like to help you work through this. Pros and cons, life purpose, that sort of thing."

"Nothing heavy then." Alex chuckled. "Happy to have your help. Can we meet up later this week? Right now, I have my eyes on dessert."

"Solid priorities, like always." Julia took Alex's plate.

She wondered if she had the right priorities. Brie certainly didn't think so. Kate got it. That was one of the many things Alex loved about this group. They called each other on their shit and provided different perspectives. They spoke their truth in a safe environment, always backed with love and a desire for their friends to be happy.

Alex wanted to make the best choice and was also comforted that these women, her Board of Directors, as Julia liked to call them, would be there for her.

Alex returned to the table and took a slice of apple pie.

Brie was already tucking into her gluten free chocolate torte. "Chocolate makes me almost as happy as sex."

"I'll drink to that!" Margaret raised her glass.

"Speaking of sex, how's it going on the dating scene, Alex? Are you ready to give lonely Carlos a try?" Lesley asked.

"You're still pulling for him, Les, sadly hanging out all alone in Angela's Bowl of Men."

"Yeah, or patiently waiting my turn."

Alex didn't like how much they were focusing on her in these brunches. "Can't we talk about something else?"

"Classic evasion. She has an update." Akiko wiggled her eyebrows at Alex. "Spill."

Chapter 45

"It's about Ross."

"What did he do now? Because if he messed things up, I'll kill him." At Akiko's shocked look, Kate added, "Kidding. Kidding… or am I?"

"It's not his fault."

"That usually means it's his fault." Lesley quipped.

"I'm just used to living alone."

"So you don't like him anymore?"

"The opposite. I'm really starting to care about him, even love him, but…"

"Ick." Margaret's mouth turned down in a frown. "It's always bad when there's a 'but' immediately following that statement."

"He's driving me nuts and it's only been about two weeks of co-habitation."

"That didn't take long." Angela shook her head back and forth, her locs cascading over her shoulders.

Kate jumped in. "I love the guy and love the two of you together. I know he loves living with you," Kate paused to sip her drink, "but what about what you want?"

"I want to laze around in my pajamas after taking Sibby for a walk. I want to sleep in the middle of the bed. I want to leave dishes in the sink until I feel like washing them."

"You want to be you."

"That makes it sound so simple."

"Why can't you do those things when Ross is around?" Brie asked around a forkful of chocolate torte.

"Because he's clingy as fuck."

"Because he loves you." Kate batted her eyelashes.

"Yeah, I just want him to love me from a distance."

"Well then, there you have it." Angela waved her hands.

"Have what?" Alex asked.

"Your answer. Be with him but maintain separate living spaces. Jeremy and I still have separate houses. We've been together for over fifteen years, but we've only been married for two and that's because he got sick, and I realized I didn't have the right to visit him in the hospital." Angela made it sound so easy. "I know that doesn't seem very romantic, but I think it really, really is. He has his space, and I have mine and we choose when we want to spend time together. It keeps it special."

"Preach, girl." Gertie added.

"Wait, Gertie, you live full-time with Paul." Margaret stopped with her fork in mid-air and looked confused.

"Doesn't mean she's wrong about living separately," Gertie explained.

"Wow. I thought I had to choose. You make it work as a married couple who doesn't live together."

"I didn't want to get married, but James pretty much forced me." She paused. "Okay, that's a bit harsh, but I married him for his sake. I'm not saying I wouldn't do it again, but..." She trailed off as she looked at the group. "I wouldn't do it again," she admitted with a blush. "I'm not going to divorce him or anything, but I would have been fine just living together."

After the laughter died down, Julia added her opinion. "Rob and I have stopped sleeping in the same room. He snores like a fucking banshee."

"How do you know what a banshee snores like?" Lesley asked in a thoughtful tone.

"Well, I hope for banshees everywhere, it's not as bad as how Rob snores." They stopped to clink glasses. "When one of us in in the mood, we stop in for a visit. It works for us. And I can sleep in the middle of the bed."

"Interesting. So, I guess I can have it both ways if Ross is into it."

"All ways," Gertie added.

"I'll be super honest because I know it's safe in this group. I don't want to give up Adam or Cameron either. Does that make me a slut?"

"No, you're a complex woman with lots of needs. Why do you put the pressure on one person to fulfill all of those for you?" Lesley tucked into her apple pie. "Why do you think I'm still single?"

"Let's be clear ladies, I put the pressure on *you* to give me everything Rob can't." Julia laughed.

"And we deliver!"

"Yeah, but monogamy isn't for everyone." Julia nodded. "I mean, maybe I'm just too lazy to date multiple people."

"I would argue monogamy isn't for *anyone*. It's just what society tells us to do." Gertie's words hung in the air for a few beats.

"But what other choice do I have? Somebody's going to get hurt."

"Yeah, but it shouldn't be you." Akiko made it sound so straightforward.

"What you're looking for is solo polyamory."

All eyes turned to Brie.

Alex asked the first question. "I know what a solo is, and I know what polyamory is, but I don't get how they go together."

"It's what you're describing. The solo, you in this case, is the center. The solo has three, or four, or even five people they are in an emotional and physical relationship with but chooses who to be with based on what they want in that moment."

"Isn't that just called playing the field?" Others seemed to have the same question as Margaret.

"No. It's different because you tell the other people about each other. And unlike polyamory, you don't necessarily form lasting relationships."

"I knew there would be a word for this! That's so much better than what I came up with!"

"Do-who-the-fuck-you-want-omy?" Gertie suggested.

"No. Polyamorous rotating cohabitation, or polyroco. It's the label I came up with for what I want."

"How do you spell that?" Brie asked.

"F-R-E-E-D-O-M!" Angela and Brie clapped at that joke.

"Point, set, and match to Gertie." Margaret pretended to tip her hat.

"Why do you need a label, or even a description? Just do it. Do what's best for you."

THE BRUNCH CONVERSATION rocked Alex's world. So much to process. Support for her radio show. A push to carry on at work. Deep questions about what she was doing. Insight into her relationships.

Brie's advice to do the best thing for herself.

What was the best thing?

Could she do the best thing for herself? What about Gram? Her partners? They should have a vote, too.

She needed to talk to Gram. She needed wisdom that only Gram could provide.

Gram hadn't answered the phone that morning before brunch, so she called again on her drive home from Julia's. It was only seven on the East Coast.

Voicemail.

She tried again later that evening.

No answer.

NO ANSWER ON MONDAY MORNING.

Alex knew she had to get in touch with Sheryl immediately.

But she didn't have her number. Why hadn't she asked for it?

She had an idea of where to get Sheryl's number.

Chapter 46

"Hey Jake. It's Alex Taylor." Her middle school and early high school boyfriend.

"Little Al, how are you?" He used his nickname for her from when they were twelve. Jake knew her grandfather called her Little Feather, and Jake's dad's name was Allen. He went by Al, so Alex became Little Al.

"Can I have your grandmother's phone number? I can't get hold of Gram and I'm worried.

"Sure. I'll text it to you. What's new with my favorite musician?"

"All good here and I heard about your little one. Congrats."

"Thanks!"

"Sorry to cut this short, but I'm really worried."

"Okay, sending it now. Let me know if you need anything. I'm in Boston."

"Thanks."

Alex dialed the number. Thankfully, Sheryl answered. "Oh, Alex, I'm so glad you called. We're at the hospital."

Dread lodged in Alex's chest. "What's happening?"

"Her cold has progressed to pneumonia. She's not doing well."

"I wish you had called me."

"She asked me not to – said she didn't want to worry you since there was nothing you could do from Seattle anyway."

"That sounds like Gram."

"She seemed okay when I checked on her on Saturday, but she didn't open her curtains this morning. I had to let myself into her house and she was having trouble breathing. I called the ambulance and here we are. I realized I didn't have your number when we got here, and she was too weak to give it to me."

"Can I talk to her?"

"No. She's been intubated and is breathing through a machine. She can't talk."

Alex tasted fear.

"I'll be on the first flight I can get on. Thank you so much, Sheryl."

"You're welcome, dear. She's been a great friend to me. It's hard to see her like this. Hurry."

Alex raced around her house, grabbing the basics to shove in a bag.

Ross wasn't awake yet. She felt bad disturbing him, but it was an emergency.

"Ross. My grandmother is in the hospital, and I have to leave for Boston right away. Can you take care of Sibby for the next few days? I don't know how long I'll be gone."

"What?" He rubbed the sleep from his eyes.

"Grandmother. Hospital. Leaving now. Can you take care of Sibby?"

"Of course." He bolted upright. "Go go go."

Alex ordered a ride. Two minutes out. Just enough time to pack up her computer so she could work from Boston.

She emailed Michelle so she would know not to expect to hear from Alex for a while.

TEN HOURS and a connection through Minneapolis later, Alex was on her way to the hospital. Sheryl had sent her all the details. Alex decided to go straight to the hospital. She could go back to Gram's and get things to make her more comfortable in her hospital room after she had seen her.

The pandemic was definitely behind them. Alex walked right into the hospital and to Gram's floor. She checked in at the nurse's station. "I'm here to see Annabelle Eagle. Room 402."

"Down the hall to your left."

"Thank you."

Sheryl was sitting by the bed. Her grandmother looked like a small bird, a tiny bundle in the sheets, tubes connected to an IV and the ventilator.

"Alex, you made it." Sheryl looked exhausted.

"Thank you for staying so long. Can you go home and get some rest? I'll stay here tonight with her."

"That would be very nice. I couldn't leave her alone."

"You're a good friend. Let me order a car for you, Sheryl."

"You're a dear. I'll just gather my things."

"Gram. I'm here." Alex took her grandmother's small, frail hand.

Gram's head rolled to the side, and she slowly opened her eyes. She squeezed Alex's hand. Her eyes started to focus. Gram pointed to the tube in her mouth and rolled her eyes.

Sheryl provided an update. "She can't talk, obviously.

She was too weak to talk when I got her here. She was dehydrated and had low blood oxygen. No one's been in to see her for a while. They'll probably come in at the shift change. You have my number. Please text me with any updates."

"I can't thank you enough, Sheryl."

"We'll all need that kind of help someday. Be strong, Little Feather. Hang in there, Annabelle."

Alex felt the tears well up in her eyes as she turned back to her grandmother.

Gram's eyes were closed.

But she kept hold of Alex's hand.

Alex let her sleep.

She didn't know how much time had passed when Gram stirred. An hour? Two?

"Gram, let's have a chat. I'll ask you some questions and you can squeeze my hand once for yes and twice for no. Sound good?"

Gram squeezed her hand once without opening her eyes.

"Are you in pain?"

Two squeezes. No.

"Do you have what you need?"

Two squeezes. No.

"I'm going to try to figure out what you need. Are you happy about being on the ventilator?"

Two squeezes. No.

"I asked that question badly. No one would be happy on a ventilator. I know you have a healthcare directive that says no mechanical breathing devices. Do you want to follow that?"

One squeeze. Yes.

"Even though you might need it to live?"

One squeeze. Yes.

"I'm sorry, Gram. This is so hard. You know you might not make it if they take it out."

One squeeze. Yes.

Gram's eyes opened and fixed on Alex's.

Alex felt like she was being torn in two. She wanted to honor Gram's wishes but she knew it would probably end her life.

"I'll find your doctor. She has a copy of your directive?"

One squeeze. Yes.

"I'm sorry you had to go through that. But I'm glad they did it so I could see you."

One squeeze. Yes.

Gram's eyes held Alex's gaze for several seconds, her eyes seeming to plead for help.

Alex pressed the call button on Gram's bed.

She could tell their conversation had tired Gram out and chose to sit with her in silence so Gram could sleep while they waited.

Strong, vibrant Gram. Now small and fragile in the big white bed.

The doctor arrived several minutes later. "Hi, I'm Doctor Sullivan. You must be Alexandra."

She recoiled a bit at her full name, reminded of work. "Yes, I'm Alex. Nice to meet you, doctor. My grandmother has a DNR, a living will, and a healthcare directive that all say she shouldn't be put on life saving machines."

"Yes, I have it here in her records. Retired nurses are good about doing the paperwork. Sorry they didn't check, Annabelle." Gram slowly winked at the doctor.

The doctor read Gram's blood oxygen level and her chart. "She's doing okay now, but she was at seventy-four when she came in. Her hypoxemia, that is, her low blood oxygen level, will continue to go down based on the fluid in her lungs from the pneumonia. She might make it through the night, or she might not. Stranger things have happened though. Let's hope she pulls through until tomorrow. The IV fluids should be helping her to feel better, too."

"I understand. But it's what she wants." Tears threatened as Alex spoke. She had to be strong for Gram.

"Annabelle, we're going to take the tube out. We'll replace it with a canula with oxygen, but you'll be able to talk again in a bit."

Alex sat back down next to her grandmother and took her hand. "Are you following, Gram?"

One squeeze. Yes.

"Do you like mushrooms?"

Two squeezes. No.

Alex laughed, as she knew her grandmother wanted. "She hates mushrooms," Alex told the doctor. "I was just testing her." Alex knew Gram would laugh too if she could.

"Alex, if you wouldn't mind stepping away from the bed, the nurse and I will remove it right now."

The nurse adjusted the bed to an upright position. "I'm going to clean out your mouth and untape the tube so we can remove it," she said to Gram and unhooked the ventilator.

"Okay now, deep breath and then cough." Doctor Sullivan spoke in a soothing tone.

Alex couldn't tell if Gram could follow the directions, but soon the tube was free.

The nurse placed the oxygen canula under Gram's nose and taped it in place.

"She should be able to talk in the next few hours." Alex didn't like that the doctor spoke directly to her instead of to Gram. Maybe Gram was in even worse shape than Alex feared. "Press the button if anything changes. I'll check back in a while." She looked back at Gram. "Good luck, Annabelle."

Gram's eyes didn't open.

"Thank you, both," Alex said to the doctor and nurse.

Alex resumed her position next to the bed. Her grandmother tried to say something and then weakly pointed at her throat.

"It'll take a few hours for your voice to come back. Just rest, Gram." Her head fell back on the pillow, and she seemed to be sleeping.

Alex hoped she would make it through the night or at least regain speech before the pneumonia won.

ALEX WOKE with a start around three in the morning. She forgot where she was for a moment. The beeping machines and smell of disinfectant soon reminded her. She sat up in the chair, stretching her neck and shoulders. She reached for her grandmother's hand.

Gram was looking right back at her in the semi-dark, the machines lighting up the room.

"Gram. You're awake. Can you talk? How are you feeling?"

"Like a tr-train hit me," she said weakly. Her voice was barely above a whisper, but she was talking.

"I got here as soon as I could. That was a great plan you had with Sheryl."

"You didn't have to come... busy."

"Never too busy for you. And I have good news. The radio show went well. I got a promotion. I'll be able to help the Recovery Center more."

Her grandmother's expression changed, her face crumpling like she was in pain.

"Gram, are you okay?"

"Music… money… do what's best." Gram coughed.

Alex saw the low number on the pulse oximeter taped to Gram's finger.

"Gram. Let me get the doctor." She squeezed Alex's hand twice. No.

"There's always a way," she wheezed. "It's time to go. Love… you."

"Gram! Oh Gram, I love you. Thank you for everything. Say hi to Pops for me." Alex felt one more squeeze before Gram's hand went limp.

The slow beep of the heart monitor turned to a solid signal.

The nurse rushed into the room.

"Annabelle. Annabelle. Can you hear me?"

Alex sat next to her grandmother, held her hand, and felt the last bits of life flicker out.

Alex looked up at the nurse. "She's gone."

Chapter 47

Alex made the necessary arrangements. She let Sheryl know what happened. She alerted Cameron, Adam, and Ross that it would be a couple of days before she could get back. She sent Michelle an update. The last two days had been a blur.

Alex didn't know how to contact her uncle – if he was still alive. She didn't have the energy to track him down at this point. He was the only living family she had left, but she had her friends.

Gram had left careful instructions that her body should be donated to a medical school. The hospital took care of that.

Gram left everything to Alex in her will. She also requested that Alex keep anything she wanted, sell the rest, and give the proceeds to the Recovery Center.

Gram was clear she didn't want a funeral or any fuss. Sheryl insisted on a small get-together with neighbors and some of Gram's nursing colleagues. It was nice to hear stories about Gram from her friends the previous evening.

Alex walked through Gram's quiet house. Gram had been living on her small nursing pension and proceeds from a reverse mortgage. The pension ended with her death. The bank owned her house. When she died, there hadn't been much left in the house but paperwork, mementos, and furniture. She had clearly been selling off everything that was valuable to fund her expenses or the Recovery Center.

Alex had so many precious memories of Gram and Pops, she didn't need physical things to remember them. And she wanted to get as much money for the Recovery Center as possible.

Alex had collected a few items and stashed them in her suitcase. A photo album from when she was a kid. Her grandfather's deerskin ceremonial shirt. One piece of her grandmother's costume jewelry – a little wooden bird that Gram said she wore when she was thinking of Alex. A small box of felt animal Christmas ornaments Gram and Pops hung on the tree every year.

The estate liquidator offered her two thousand dollars for the contents of the house and had removed everything of value earlier that day. Apparently, there wasn't a strong market for well-used nineteen seventies furniture, rugs, and knickknacks. A junk hauler arrived shortly afterwards to take the rest.

When Alex went to close Gram's bank accounts, she learned that all the money she had sent to Gram over the years was sitting in an account, untouched. That would cover a few months of expenses for the Recovery Center, but Alex still needed a plan for supporting it long-term since Gram's estate wouldn't be enough.

Gram. Too proud to use the money Alex sent her. Too proud to admit she needed financial help.

Tears welled up from the center of Alex's body. Big wracking sobs shook her to the core.

Gram was gone.

This was the last time she would ever stand in this house.

It still smelled like her. The scent of her childhood. Dove soap, cleaning products, and the slightly musty smell of a house built in the nineteen seventies and lived in by the same people for fifty years.

Home.

A home she never would have had if Gram and Pops hadn't welcomed her into their lives.

She stood there for a while, letting the memories flood her like the tears flooded her eyes.

Darkness was starting to settle outside. Alex was leaving on a red-eye flight.

Michelle was giving her a hard time for being away from the office the first week of the new fiscal year. After a perfunctory "sorry for your loss," Alex had received a lengthy email explaining that it was a critical time and that she had to be back as soon as possible.

Alex pulled herself together.

She had to face the music and get back to work.

"There's always a way." Gram's last words rang in Alex's head as she closed the door behind her.

▭

ALEX TRIED to get back into the swing of things by that Friday. She barely knew what time it was and had been staring at the same slide for about ten minutes. Alex threw in the towel and decided to head to the bar where she was meeting Julia even though it was a bit early. It *was* Friday after all. And it was the day after a holiday. No one else was working anyway.

She settled into the booth at Raymond's moments before Julia breezed in. The bar was close to the office and also close to the bridge Alex used to get home. Ross was at the house today and could take care of Sibby.

"We're both early," Julia said as she slipped into the booth opposite Alex.

"I had to get out of the office."

"Same. And I was concerned it would take me a while to get out. I get a lot of hallway drive-bys, so exiting quickly can be tough even when so few people are working."

"I appreciate you helping me out."

"That's what I'm here for. You've had a rough week. How are you doing?"

"Sad. Annoyed with Michelle. But I'm okay. I want to talk to you about the choice I have to make."

"About your life's work?"

Alex was glad that Julia hadn't assumed it was about men. Career first with Julia. "Yes. I'm really excited about the opportunity at the radio station, but I feel tons of pressure to support the Recovery Center since they lost their biggest donor. The most straightforward answer is to stay at LampLight, maximize my earnings, vest my stock, pay it to the Recovery Center and return to my music after that."

"Yes, that's the most straightforward answer."

"And it lets me honor my grandmother. She told me there is always a way, and I know that's what she meant. Keep working, fund the Center, and then turn back to music. I have to generate at least six thousand dollars a month to keep them going. More if they're going to get any of the improvements Gram and the team had planned with the money from their biggest donor. My new salary and stock grants will do that."

"What makes you believe you have to be the one to pay for that?"

"Because there's no one else. Gram said they tried fundraisers and cold-calling and even getting grants from the state, but nothing worked. Belts are tightening everywhere. And the people who live there are already low-income so they can't pass the costs on to the guests.

"There have to be other options, Al. I mean, look at LampLight's philanthropic team. They give away millions a year. Someone in Steak and Bourbon must know someone on that team. Maybe we can find federal grant money. Maybe we could all chip in. You don't have to do this alone." Julia gave her a penetrating stare. "You aren't alone."

"I know I'm not alone *in life*, Julia. Even with my mom, Tom, Pops, and Gram gone, I have the Steak and Bourbon crew, my music friends, Adam, Ross, and Cameron. But I'm not going to ask my friends for money. Moral support? Decision support? Mentoring? Hell yes, but never money. Period." *Too proud to ask for financial help*. Hadn't she just stood in Gram's living room feeling bad that Gram didn't ask for financial help? She refocused on Julia.

"I agree with your grandmother. There has to be a way, Alex. We just need to find it. You don't know what your grandmother was encouraging you to do. You said her last words to you were 'music and money. Do what's best.' What if she meant to do what's best *for you*? You've said how generous and supportive your grandparents were. It seems out of character for her to ask for something for herself."

Alex thought about it for a moment. It was a great point. Gram never asked for anything. To a fault. But that's exactly why Alex felt she had to save the Recovery Center. That's what she believed was best. "That's fair, Julia. I guess I don't know what she meant. It feels like she wanted me to save the Recovery Center. You don't understand how important it was to her."

Alex felt the noose of her paycheck wrapping around her neck and squeezing.

Chapter 48

"I want to reframe that for you." Julia was not letting Alex off the hook. "It was important *to your grandmother*." She pointed with each word. "What if she was telling you to do what's best one hundred percent for you? What would that look that?"

"I don't know."

Alex had no idea how to answer Julia's seemingly simple question.

She really didn't know.

Julia raised an eyebrow and looked at her with what Alex read as support. "I'm going to go out on a limb here. What if the *safe* thing to do is toe the line at work, make the money, and save the Recovery Center so you're putting what you want on hold because it might fail?"

Alex sat back in the booth. "That's a mic drop kind of moment, Julia. I need a minute." She sipped her drink and thought. Was she afraid to fail? Of course. Was she using the Recovery Center as a convenient excuse for not pursuing her dream?

A ripple of self-awareness flowed through Alex. She

did not enjoy looking in the mirror that Julia's question evoked.

Alex had fantasies about having her own show, leading a big band, playing in good orchestras, and helping launch or amplify the careers of marginalized or under-represented musicians. Talking openly about the bad shit that happened to female musicians and how to get through it. Maybe even change it.

What would she do if she could make her own choice? Her heart said to pour herself into the radio gig. Her brain said to make the money.

Julia seemed to sense the battle taking place in Alex's mind. "Let's take a step back. Have you ever considered your life's purpose?"

"That's pretty tough to figure out. I mean, that feels really big." Exhaustion threatened to take Alex under. The strain of her job, fiscal year end, the travel, Gram's death, and her career decision weighed heavily on her.

"When you go through it, you realize it's not that hard. When you create a life purpose statement, it feels right. You know it's true once you write it." Julia's face pleaded with Alex to engage on the topic.

"What's yours?" Alex asked.

"I want to advocate for people's great futures."

"Holy shit." Alex was momentarily stunned. "That's you."

"Yeah. I went through several iterations before I figured that out, but once I landed on exactly those words, it just felt right. And it made my choices easier. I was busy trying to make as much money as I could. But what really fulfills me is helping other people realize their dreams."

"And that's why you coach people, and continue to host Steak and Bourbon, and mentor so many people."

"Exactly. It helps me prioritize my time better in service to my life's purpose."

"How do you even get started?"

"It starts by figuring out your values. What motivates you? What do you hold dear? You outline a vision for where you want to go. Then you create a statement that embodies the vision and your values, and poof… life purpose."

"You make it sound so easy. I don't even know where to start."

"Here's how it worked for me – maybe it's something for you to leverage. I thought about the people in my life who I respect and admire. And then I wrote down what stood out about them. It only took about twenty minutes. And I recognized the pattern. Each of them advocated for me at an important moment in my life. Or maybe because they advocated for me it became an important moment in my life. Doesn't matter." Julia paused to sip her drink. "Think of Harry. You've heard me talk about my first business mentor. He defended me to a horrible boss – that awful woman I talked about when we were discussing female on female aggression at work. I got so used to it, I didn't see it anymore. But Harry did and told Marla to fuck right off. That taught me the value of sticking up for people. Advocating. The pattern became clear. I value that in others because it's what I want to do for people. What do you value in people?"

"I value my grandparents for giving me a home and love. And supporting my musical aspirations both financially and emotionally. If they hadn't paid for lessons, I never would have learned how to be a musician."

"Who else comes to mind?"

"Madou's family. They accepted me even though I was different. They taught me an entirely new culture."

"Who else?"

"Dr. Tjong. I mean, the dude tried to sexually assault me, but he also taught me to be confident instead of criticizing me on stage."

"Anyone else stand out?"

"Rufus Reid, the amazing bass player. He was the judge at a high school jazz band competition. My high school jazz band made fun of me because I didn't play electric bass – that's the instrument most other high schoolers played. They would write 'get a real bass' on my music. I was embarrassed. He taught me that the upright bass *was* the real bass for most of the jazz we were playing. He told the band how lucky they were that I played upright. He gave me the award for the best bass player at the festival. I got a week-long summer jazz camp out of that. He believed in me and gave me an opportunity. He made me feel like I could be successful as a musician. We're still in touch."

"That's a beautiful story, Alex. Are you seeing any themes?"

"Love." Julia waited for Alex to continue. "Acceptance. Encouragement. Teaching."

"I also hear confidence and opportunity," Julia added.

Alex flopped against the back of the booth and thought about that.

Julia held the silence until Alex looked at her.

"Your homework is to create your purpose statement and then work through which values you honor with each choice. You can't optimize for every value all the time. Just make sure you're aligning your choices to enough values to feel fulfilled, because that's what matters. There are no wrong choices. Just choices that honor different values."

"Choices that honor different values," Alex repeated, letting it sink in. "Thanks Julia. For everything. Not just for this, but for the job and the advocacy. For introducing me to the people who have become my best friends and advisors over the past few years. I owe you a lot."

"You can see I mess up sometimes, too. Ahem, intervening with Michelle."

"Yeah, but now that I know your life's purpose, I can absolutely understand your motivation. It's all coming together."

They shared a warm smile.

"So what are you going to do with all of this knowledge about yourself?" Julia's question hung in the air.

Chapter 49

"Sak pase?" Alex smiled at Adam's Haitian greeting.

"N'ap boule," she responded to let him know she was doing well. Alex was still mulling over her conversation with Julia when she met up with Adam for a happy hour before his rehearsal.

"How does it feel to be a local celebrity in the music scene?"

"I had no idea so many people would listen!"

"Are you kidding? They announced you would be guest hosting at three rehearsals I was at with different orchestras. You have a lot of friends in the music community here, Alex."

"That's so nice to hear. How many of them will come on Keith's show?"

"Don't you mean *your* show? You're not just subbing for Keith. You're making your own following."

"I can't commit to doing my own show just yet. I'm still working out the plan for the Recovery Center."

"Sorry about your grandmother. I still miss mine and it's been a while." He took her hand.

"Thanks, Adam. It's getting easier. Especially since I'm able to keep the Recovery Center going for a few more months while I figure out the long-term plan. I just need to keep my head down and keep going at LampLight."

"Really? Didn't your grandmother send you to music school so you could be a musician? Not to run in the corporate rat race."

That hit her like a slap. "But she did so much for me. I feel like I owe it to her legacy to keep the Recovery Center open. They were relying on her."

"I hear you, but those are her dreams, not yours. Didn't she want you to follow *your* dreams?"

"Ouch."

"Sorry. I shouldn't jump on that nerve so hard when your loss is still so fresh. That was insensitive of me. I'm worried you're letting this opportunity pass you by."

"I get it. You see me as a musician trapped in a corporate gig."

"Don't you see yourself the same way?"

Alex didn't know how to answer that. "I don't know who I am."

Adam met her gaze. She read sympathy for her situation in his kind eyes. "Are you sure?" He squeezed her hand. "Or are you just afraid to admit it?"

She felt the sting of tears. She got the same question from Julia. She grabbed her necklaces with her free hand. Was she just afraid? Afraid to walk away from comfort? Afraid to go for it and not support the Recovery Center the way she thought Gram wanted her to?

She was going to have to confront her discomfort and answer the question for herself.

Adam broke the mood. "I have to hit the head. Be right back." Adam leaned over and kissed her before walking to the restroom.

There it was again. A nice, comfortable kiss. An almost brotherly kiss. When Ross and Cameron kissed her, it hit her right in her center, a little buzz getting her excited about what was ahead. With Adam, it was more of an "oh, darn it" feeling. She wanted to feel more. She wanted to be as into him physically as she was mentally, but there just was no spark.

But he pushed her. Like he just had. Pushed her like Cameron and Ross never did. Made her think. She needed his musical sensibility and slightly judgy attitude in her life. It helped her find her blind spots. How could she be so in love with his mind and so lukewarm about their chemistry?

It was time to have the chat. It went pretty well with Ross, even though he was still trying to get her to commit to him. He hadn't broken up with her. And it was going just fine with Cameron, too.

She watched Adam walk across the restaurant and come back to their table. When he saw her watching him, his face broke into a wide smile.

"What are you looking at me like that for?" Adam took his seat.

"Like what?"

"Like you want to eat me for dinner. That can be arranged."

He couldn't have been more wrong.

She took his hand, her heart beating quickly in her chest. She could lose him in this moment. She chose her words carefully. "Adam, I think I'm falling in love with you."

His face lit up. "I love you, too. I've been waiting to tell you because you seem kind of withdrawn when we're together. You have a kind of funny way of showing it. I'm so relieved."

"But that's not all."

"Uh oh. This sounds bad." He pulled his hand away.

"Don't say that. We just have to talk about something I've been avoiding."

"You're married."

"No." She shook her head and laughed. "I just don't want a traditional relationship."

"A relationship between a white string player and black woodwind player is pretty untraditional. I mean, multi-ethnic…multi-sectional." He smiled.

"You're making this hard." She took a deep breath. "I want to be with multiple people."

"Like a threesome? Do I get to pick male or female?"

"No, not like that. I am so in love with your mind. I value your opinions and input and friendship. I just don't feel the chemistry like I want to. I enjoy the physical aspects of our relationship, but it won't fulfill me if I was just with you."

"You're saying I'm bad at sex? I've never heard any complaints before!"

"No." She sighed out of frustration with herself. "I'm not explaining this well. You're a good lover. That whole oil and feather thing in Paris was pretty ingenious. We never discussed or committed to being exclusive with each other. It's time to be clear about our expectations."

"I just kind of assumed…" he trailed off.

"That's why we need to talk about it now. I want to keep you in my life. I want things to continue like they are. I just want to be transparent that I am also seeing other people."

"I don't like that."

Alex took a page from Julia's book and let him process that in silence. She sipped her drink and looked around the restaurant waiting for him to speak. She tuned into the music playing in the background at the restaurant and silently started playing along with the bass line to quiet her mind as she waited.

"I *really* don't like that. How do you envision it working?" His tone was hostile.

"Just like it does now. We continue to date and fool around, whatever we like. But we aren't exclusive. It's not like I'm with ten other guys, but I am dating two others right now."

"And you're having sex with all of us?"

"Yes, safe sex." Alex meant that she always used a condom, but she inwardly laughed that it was just how she would describe sex with Adam. Not like the panty-drenching time she had with Cameron or the goofy, light-hearted but mind-blowing sex she was having with Ross.

"So, you aren't heading toward talking about moving in or getting married?"

"Absolutely not, I don't want to be married again. I like having my own space."

"What about that guy who's living with you now. I thought he was gay."

"Nope, not gay. And he's only at my place while his gets renovated." *In for a penny, in for a pound*, she thought and continued. "He's one of the other guys I mentioned."

"Alex, this is really uncomfortable, and I have to leave for rehearsal soon. Let's cut to the chase. Why would I stick around for only part of you?"

"You'd have all of me while we're together. My undivided attention. If you want to meet the other guys, we can talk about that. No secrets. I just want to keep my options open."

"Options? I'm not an option. I'm a man who loves you. My brain - and probably my ego - says hell no. I don't want to share you…or anyone I'm with."

Alex sighed. "Losing you would make me really sad because we have a good thing here."

"I feel the same way, but I have to protect myself. I don't want to be with someone I don't have a long-term chance at full commitment with. I have to say no."

"That's too bad." *Was it worth losing Adam to continue to be with other men too?* she wondered.

Um, yes, she decided.

"I have to go." He threw some bills on the table and walked out without looking back.

She didn't stop him.

She closed out the bill and headed home to finish her work.

Adam was right. Maybe not about the exclusivity conversation, but he was right that she was letting a career opportunity pass her by. An opportunity that might not come around again. With him or with the radio show. She sighed at losing her friend. The only guy she was dating who challenged her mentally. She would miss that.

She thought back to the question both he and Julia had asked her. If she truly answered it from her heart and in line with her values, she would choose music and the radio show.

She would quit her job.

Even saying that to herself made her uncomfortable.

She sat with the feeling for a while and recognized it for what emotion it actually was.

Fear.

She shook her head to clear her mind.

That's not who she was. She wasn't a scared little girl. She was descended from strong stock – Gram and Pops.

She would confront her fear of failure.

Chapter 50

"That's it, Betsy. You nailed it." She was in a lesson with her favorite student Saturday morning. "You're doing so well we can focus on some real subtleties in the music. Let me play it for you. Can you feel the difference?"

Alex played the bass line, focusing on the groove.

"It sounds so easy when you do it. I can get all the notes, but my head wants to bob back and forth when you play it."

"Great observation. I'm doing two things differently. The first is that I'm not moving my fingers very far off the fingerboard. See how they're barely moving as a play? It's even hard to see which note I'm playing when."

"Yeah, I never noticed that."

"The second is that I'm playing on the back of the beat."

"I don't understand."

Alex held up the thumb and index finger of her right hand with about four inches of space between them. Think of the space between my thumb and finger as one beat. When you play classical music, you usually play right in the center of the beat." She pointed to the center of the space with her other index finger. "In jazz, you move it around. When you want to create a more frenetic, driving pace, you play at the front of the beat. Not rushing, just playing here." Alex pointed to her index finger. "But when you want to create a chill, easy vibe, you play here." Alex pointed to her thumb.

"I think I understand the concept, but not how to do that."

"Let me demonstrate again, but this time I'll put a click track on so you can hear where the center of the beat is."

She played the bass line again, this time on the front of the beat.

"That makes me feel a little nervous, like you're going too fast."

"Exactly, Betsy. You have a great ear. Now I'm going to play it on the back of the beat."

She played it again, catching the end of each beat. She watched Betsy's face relax and her head start to bob.

"Oh my gosh. I totally hear it. Let me try."

It brought tears to Alex's eyes to hear the difference in Betsy's playing in only about four minutes through the introduction of a new concept. Betsy kept playing, looking down at her fingers with her eyes closed and her head moving back and forth. She was in the zone.

When she was done, Betsy looked up. "That felt great. And it was easy to play. I just kind of got out of my head and let the feel guide me."

"Welcome to being a jazz bass player, Betsy. That was a major concept you just mastered. And mastered quickly." Alex enjoyed giving support and encouragement to Betsy.

"I feel so light. It's like the music was coming through me instead of me making it."

"Let's call that the spirit of Mingus, one of my favorite jazz bass players."

Alex heard clapping and looked up to see Jeannie in the doorway with tears in her eyes. "Betsy, that sounded so great."

"Thanks Mom." Betsy smiled at her mother, blushing at the praise. "Alex says I'm a jazz player now."

"Alex, I wish I'd recorded that whole interaction. It was stunning to watch you get that out of my daughter. I can't wait to hear more of that on your show."

"You mean Keith's show."

"I mean your show. The Monday night gardening show is not doing well and there was a pitch meeting to suggest new ideas. I shared clips from your shows with Keith and from your solo debut with Cian. The programming director wants to interview you and hear your ideas for your own show."

Alex's mouth dropped open. "Jeannie, that's amazing."

"When do you think you'll be ready?"

"I don't know. I just got a promotion and more work at my job. The new fiscal year just started on Monday. Next weekend I have a motorcycle trip. I don't know when I'll have time."

"That's too bad, because I think you really have something here."

Alex hung her head and busied herself arranging music on the stand. She was so tired. Her bones ached with the need for sleep and recovery. The energy she felt at Betsy's success whooshed out of her body, leaving her drained.

"There's always a way," Alex said to Jeannie and smiled.

She just didn't know what that way was.

. . .

ALEX SPENT A SLEEPLESS NIGHT. And then another one.

Rejecting the safety net she'd been given during the pandemic was frightening. She owed LampLight and Michelle so much for the opportunity. But Julia, Adam, Jeannie, Madou, and everyone who loved her was right.

This was her chance, and she would take it.

Her one on one with Michelle was on Monday. She would tender her resignation.

⬛

ALEX SQUARED HER SHOULDERS. Nodded her head and walked to Michelle's office.

Her heart pounded like she was about to perform a solo for a sold-out audience. Anticipation, fear, and adrenaline mixed together making her want to jump out of her skin. Or at least throw open Michelle's door and yell "I quit!"

Michelle didn't take her eyes off her computer when Alex got to the door. "Come in, Alexandra. I need to jump right into my list today."

Alex controlled her energy burst and took a seat. Listening to Michelle would give Alex a chance to come up with the right words to use to quit. Even after a weekend of thinking about it, she was afraid of how this would go.

Michelle dove in. "There will be some changes on my team now that we're in the new fiscal year. Do you have people management experience?"

"Yes, I was the section leader in several orchestras, and I led an entire band in college." Alex wondered if that counted. She bet it didn't.

"That's great. I have a one-time opportunity to flip an individual contributor in high standing to being a manager.

Usually, there's a whole interview process, but time is tight and our fiscal 2025 goals are huge, so we have to act fast. You're doing well with the strategy work. I want to give you the job so you can take your impact to the next level. I'm delighted you have previous management experience."

It was like Michelle stopped listening after the word "yes."

"Are you interested? It would mean another promotion and more money. The strategy team would report to you."

Alex felt like a hypocrite.

She was supposed to be in here quitting.

Now she was being offered a role she wasn't even qualified for.

And it was another "favor." She didn't like how this world worked.

"I'll have to think about it."

"Well think fast. I need your answer by tomorrow. And speaking of tomorrow, I have some changes to the last deck you shared."

Michelle hammered away at her for the next forty-five minutes and then abruptly ended the meeting. Alex hadn't gotten up the nerve to quit. As she had listened to Michelle drone on, she felt the golden handcuffs get tighter.

Alex needed a way to clear her head. A walk with Sibby.

She checked her calendar and saw she had a three-hour break before her five o'clock meeting. She had enough time to drive home, walk Sibby, and still attend that meeting.

She had a lot to think about.

Chapter 51

Alex drove across the bridge to Seattle wondering what the heck was going on in the world. She thought of herself as a musician. But she had never had the success as a musician that she was having in the corporate world.

When she lived in New York, she didn't get into the New York Philharmonic. It was a top ten orchestra in the world so she didn't expect to get in. Seattle had a top twenty-five orchestra, but she hadn't gotten into that either and only very occasionally subbed when their regular subs couldn't make it. She had always been a tier two player and was happy with that.

With two promotions in two months, maybe she was a top corporate performer. Adam had called her out months ago for not being willing to put in the work and walk away from the big paycheck.

But maybe her path was to walk away from music because she was a better corporate employee than she was a musician.

But her identity was wrapped around being a musician and only temporarily playing the role of Alexandra.

But…

It would make it easier to help Gram.

Corporate work was easier. Less personal. Lower effort.

But there was nothing in the values work she did with Julia that said, "track action items" or "write slides."

This whole radio thing was just a replacement dream because she wasn't good enough to be a tier one musician.

If she was going to settle, she might as well settle with a lot of money.

Something inside her was cracking. She could feel it, a lightning bolt through her core. Was it the breaking of her soul or the flash of realization?

She didn't know.

Her pulse raced as she did a quick inventory of her body. She took a deep breath that shivered through her chest.

She was glad she was almost home. She shouldn't be driving when she felt like this.

ROSS WAS THERE when she came in the door. On the sofa. With her dog. Eating chips.

She wanted to scream.

"Mind if I borrow my dog? I need to take a walk and clear my head."

"Can I come?"

"What part of 'clear my head' suggests I want company?" She didn't mean to snap at him. She would apologize later. She was too consumed with her thoughts right now to take care of him.

He didn't seem to notice. "I'll distract you from what's obviously bugging you."

Alex didn't have the energy to push back. Maybe talking it out would help.

She clipped the leash on her excited dog, and they headed down the driveway.

Ross started to turn to the left.

"I go right first. Then, the way home is downhill."

"I like to go left for a warm-up and then come home uphill. Knowing you and a beer will be there is all the motivation I need."

Now she couldn't even pick her own walk direction? She had to do what he wanted?

Why did she always have to do what everyone else wanted?

"Fine."

She followed him down the hill, annoyed it was so easy to go that way.

"So, what's wrong at work?"

"I tried to quit today."

"Oh no. I know you've been stressed, but is it worth quitting over? What about Gram and the Recovery Center?"

It annoyed her that he called her Gram. He had never even met her. She was *her* Gram. Not his. "Yes, I've been stressed and feeling burnt out but that's not what this is about."

"Right. It's about the music thing."

"Don't call it a music thing. That's so patronizing. It could be my life's work. The next chapter for Alex the Musician."

"Who's Alex the Musician? Aren't you Alex the Lamp-Light employee and Alex the Smokin' Hot Babe too?"

"Ross. Can you maybe stop talking for a minute? I'm working through some stuff."

"You got it. I'll take the dog." He reached for the leash.

Alex gave it to him, feeling unconnected with the world once she gave it to him.

Nothing was holding her in place now.

She was floating without direction.

She focused on her footfalls. Where did she want to be on this journey?

She wanted to support the Recovery Center.

She wanted to make music and play music.

She wanted to pour herself into the radio show so she could have a chance to get national syndication.

She wanted the stability and benefits of a steady paycheck.

She wanted it all.

Even when she talked to herself about it, she still put the Recovery Center first. The duty she felt to Gram was too strong to let her feel otherwise.

Her choice was actually easy. Work as hard as she could so she could support the Recovery Center, maximize her earnings, and squirrel away as much as possible. If she did that for just two years, she could get the Center back on its feet and then focus on her dream.

That was a full two years faster than her original plan. Progress.

But what if the opportunity was gone by then?

Then she'd just have to make a new opportunity like the one in front of her right now.

She felt the heaviness of each step weighing her down.

She looked at Green Lake, peacefully rippling in front of her. She wanted to just walk around the lake, letting her stress fall away while she created her plan for not burning out. Even though she knew she had to work harder and more hours than she ever had before.

She checked her watch. She had to be back in front of her computer in twenty minutes.

"Hey Ross, I've gotten my shit together and need to

head back. Sorry for being so grouchy earlier. I shouldn't take my bad mood out of you."

"You can do whatever you want. That's the perk of having me live in your house rent free. A little abuse is a small price to pay."

"This is that bad taste in women popping up, isn't it? You shouldn't let me abuse you." The shame of her poor behavior settled on her shoulders.

"Oh honey, that's nothing." He took her hand, and she let him. "If it's your usual hour-long meeting, I can meet you back at the house with Sibby and take-out at six."

"That would be amazing, thank you."

Maybe having a live-in boyfriend wasn't such a bad thing. She wanted to strangle him when she got home, but now he was being so sweet to her and taking care of dinner.

She was tired of the flip-flopping at work and at home.

What the fuck did she really want?

Chapter 52

It was done. Finally done. A little late, but done. It was the second Tuesday of July, and the new fiscal year was underway. The documentation was complete. The training was delivered. The team was busy congratulating themselves.

Alex couldn't join in.

She was tired.

She wasn't proud of the work she had done.

They didn't know if it would work.

Yet here they all were, celebrating like they had just cured cancer.

It was just a methodology. And some slides, for fuck's sake.

She tried to talk herself into feeling better.

It's just like a performance, she told herself. Lean in and feel it.

She tried. She watched everyone wander around the room at a happy hour set up in a conference room on the LampLight campus. There were appetizers and free drinks. A musician's paradise. But even that couldn't pull her out of her slump.

Maybe she was just burnt-out. Or depressed.

She knew she wasn't happy.

Michelle interrupted her melancholy.

"Congrats on a great job, Alexandra. Where's your drink?"

"I don't feel much like celebrating."

"Why not? You did amazing work, well beyond what your experience level would indicate. You stepped up to every opportunity offered to you. This fiscal year will be a great year for you with your promotion and new role. Nothing but greatness ahead for you!" Michelle gave her an energetic thumbs up with the hand not holding a glass of red wine.

"I thought I was no good after my last review." Alex was too tired to stop before her thought came out of her mouth.

"Oh, don't be like that. I had to push you so you could see what you could do. That's how I like to be managed."

Alex didn't get it. Michelle liked to be insulted and then rewarded? Rinse and repeat? What was Alex missing here? That was a terrible way to manage people.

But, Michelle had a point. Alex was now making forty percent more than she was last year at this time. Her bank balance was going up and she could afford the monthly payment to the Recovery Center.

But at what cost?

She pushed down the anger bubbling out of her and chose a bland statement instead. "Thanks for your leadership, Michelle. I've learned a lot from you."

Michelle smiled and put her hand on Alex's arm. "That's nice to hear. I have to mingle. Again, great job, Alexandra."

Alexandra. Her corporate persona. She hated Alexandra. Alex would have fought back. Alexandra just took it.

Alex needed a break.

A break from worrying about money. Away from the pressures of her job. Away from Ross.

Away from this stupid party.

Cameron provided just the distraction she needed.

A quick text exchange showed he was happy to oblige.

THE FIRST TWO weeks of the fiscal year had been brutal. Clearly, the celebration of their "amazing" work had been premature. Teams Alex had never heard of filled her inbox and instant message queue with detailed questions about how they were supposed to execute the new strategy.

It was like no one had read anything until they had to actually implement the changes and use the new approach.

All of that effort had been for nothing. They'd been screaming into the wind after all.

She was bone-crushingly tired. She had worked from home most days because she literally didn't have time to commute to the office.

She leveraged her program management skills and added every question and answer into a long document so that people could self-serve, but still the endless questions came.

Everyone wanted to change something. Everyone had what they thought was a better idea about how to do something.

She was overwhelmed.

She found herself getting defensive when people challenged why they had to change the way they did something. She wanted to support the strategy, but in many cases, she agreed with the people asking the questions. She couldn't just say, "Yeah, I agree with you," because she had to help sell the concepts to the field.

How could she sell something she didn't believe in?

She had believed it when she created it, but she hardly recognized the convoluted over-engineered mess the rest of the team had turned her carefully crafted strategy into. Pages and pages of role descriptions and suggested actions. Ridiculous numbers of slides that should have just said, learn what our products do, listen to what customers want, and match them up.

Working from six in the morning to nine at night left her no time for anything.

She was thankful that Ross was moving out just after their motorcycle trip because the construction delays were over, and the occupancy permit was supposed to be issued on Friday.

But she was also thankful that he was there this week. She walked Sibby at five thirty each morning, but he took care of her all day. And made sure Alex had some food. As much as she wanted her space back, she really needed him that week.

She hadn't had a moment to focus on the pitch for her show. Jeannie pinged her during the week asking when she would be ready. She had only given nebulous responses. And she had to plan her next solo version of Thursday Jazz Jams, let alone her potential new show.

The pressure crushed down on her.

After four days of the constant drumbeat of angry field teams, she had never needed a break more.

She just had to get through the rest of the day, and she would have the long weekend and her California motor-cycle ride to recover.

She checked the time and realized she had to get Sibby to the kennel and finish packing. She and Ross were meeting at Kate and James' condo for a shared ride to the airport.

Alex saw an instant message pop up from Michelle while she was doing a final check of her email.

Michelle: Emergency meeting with France tomorrow at 8AM

Alex almost burst into tears. She couldn't take even one more day of this.

Alex: I'm off tomorrow.

Michelle: Not anymore. I need you on this
call - the first of many tomorrow morning

Alex began typing but stopped. Her first response had been no. Ross' voice telling her to be careful during layoff season popped into her head. Her delay obviously annoyed Michelle.

Michelle: Hello?

Alex sighed and caved to the pressure.

Alex: OK. I'll join the call. But I can only do
8-9. Then I'll be out of cell phone range.

Michelle: Fine. We'll do 4 calls with Europe
in the morning. France at 7, Spain at 7:30,
UK at 8, and Germany at 8:30. You'll be
done by 9. Please set them up.

Alex clenched her fists and growled at the screen.

Ross popped into the room. "Everything okay?"

"No! That wench of a manager just roped me into four calls tomorrow morning – that I have to schedule. I haven't packed yet or taken Sibby to the kennel. And we have to be at Kate's in forty-five minutes."

"I got you. I'll take Sibby. You schedule the meetings and finish packing. I'll be back in thirty minutes, and we'll walk over to Jate's together to clear your head before the trip to the airport. In less than five hours, you'll be sipping drinks in California."

"You're a lifesaver. Thanks Ross."

"Just trying to nudge ahead into the top spot." He grinned at her.

Top spot? she thought. He was still trying to get her to agree to exclusivity. But she couldn't think about that now. She had meetings to schedule and boots to pack.

Chapter 53

Alex strapped on her borrowed motorcycle helmet. Ross reached over to turn her headset on.

"Can you hear me?" Alex gave a thumbs up. "I'm going to get on the bike. Once I'm settled, step on the foot peg and throw your leg over. Make sure to not touch the exhaust pipes." He pointed to the chrome tube that went from front to back on the motorcycle. "It'll be hot once we've been riding for a while. Don't want my bike to bite you. That's my job."

It was easier to get on than Alex thought. She found her seat, reminding herself to be a sack of potatoes. She wrapped her arms around Ross' waist.

It felt good.

"Ready?" She heard Kate's voice in her helmet. "Good to go!" Alex was nervous, but she knew the five of them wouldn't endanger her and decided to try to enjoy it.

She was still recovering from the beating she took that morning from the teams in Europe. She had an action item list a mile long but decided to focus on the actual miles ahead of her.

James and Kate each had their own bikes. Julia rode on the back of Rob's. They had a good laugh at breakfast that morning when Rob entered the room sporting a shirt that said, "if you can read this, the bitch fell off." Julia was not amused. Rob was trying to get her to learn to ride, but she was resisting his charms.

Alex was glad they would spend a few blocks in Kate's neighborhood before heading out onto the county highway.

They could all chat with each other because of the headsets. That made it much more enjoyable for Alex.

"We're starting with the Highway 128 Scenic Wine Route. We'll leave Winters and head over the eastern part of the Coast Range, cross the Sonoma Valley, and make it to the western side in about three hours." James had his tour guide voice on for this part of the trip. "We'll stop for coffee in Geyserville where 128 hits 101 and lunch in Mendocino. If anyone wants to stop before then, just let me know. We'll stay in the little town of Westport overnight at a hotel I want to check out and then meander back to Winters on some little squiggly lines on the map tomorrow. Remember to keep the rubber side down!"

The anger and pain of her morning calls was soon erased by the thrill of being on the motorcycle. Alex's senses were heightened on a motorcycle compared to riding in a car. The feel of the wind on her face when she opened the face shield of her helmet. The changing smells of the dry landscape, then the cow pastures, then the vineyards.

The turquoise waters of Lake Berryessa stretched out below her as they rode along the two-lane road that hugged the cliffs above the lake. The landscape continued to change, and she was soon treated to gorgeous sweeping views over a valley, hillsides still green from the Spring rains.

Even the charred trees from earlier wildfires were softened by new growth and green grass on the side of the Coastal Range.

The scar from Gram's death was starting to heal, too. She would miss her surrogate mother until the day she died. But she knew a great way to honor Gram was to live. Really live. Even if it was on the back of a motorcycle zipping through the California mountains.

"Okay Alex. You have an important job to do." Alex was on alert for her assignment from Ross. "You need to give a downward-facing peace sign when other motorcycles pass us by."

"What does it mean and why do I have to point it down? Is it insulting to point up?"

"It just means 'have a great ride,' and real motorcyclists make the peace sign instead of waving because opening your whole hand increases drag."

"It makes that much of a difference?" Alex was surprised.

"No, but it's the pageantry. You're showing that you might not be going super-fast, but you know how and care about aerodynamics."

"Oh, macho shit."

"No – Kate'll do it too." Ross sounded wounded.

"Like I said, macho shit. Kate is more macho than half the guys I know." Alex quipped.

"Thank you," Kate sang into the helmet microphone.

"Good point."

"There's another reason I do it." Julia jumped into the conversation. "I point my two fingers down to make sure they can see both fingers and don't think I'm flipping them off."

They kept up the good-natured banter for the whole ride.

"IF THIS IS the 128 Scenic Wine Route, how come we're buzzing right by the wineries without stopping?" Alex asked as if a winery perched on the side of a cliff blurred past them.

"Julia's got us covered later," Rob explained. "No drinking and riding."

"Yeah. Eight hours bottle to throttle." James laughed in Alex's ear.

"Makes sense." Alex knew they were right. She and Julia were the only ones on the back, so it wouldn't be very fair if just the two of them tasted wine while the others watched.

"It's about another hour to our planned coffee stop in Geyserville. Everyone good for that?"

Alex's butt hurt a little and her right hip was talking to her. She wasn't used to being on a bike, but she was loving this ride. The freedom, the tastes, the smells, the friends. She could do this all day.

"All good," Alex said around her smile. "Thanks again, guys."

"Another biker is born!" Kate said into the helmet microphone.

They passed through Saint Helena and Calistoga and tons of wineries. Even a few Alex had heard of before. Up and over mountains and down into valleys, lush and green.

Geyserville had a cute downtown of brick buildings. It felt good to get off the motorcycle for a bit. The coffee shop had a musical theme that Alex appreciated.

The sun was shining, as it so often did in California.

Alex let the energy from the light fill her as she breathed in the dry air.

She needed to recharge, and this was a great way to do it, with friends on the back of a motorcycle, far away from work. Speaking of work…

Alex unlocked her phone to check in. But she just wasn't motivated to open her email. Instead, she opened the webcam at the dog kennel to check on Sibby.

There she was, romping around in a huge indoor play space with fifteen of her furry friends. Alex and her friends were kind of doing the same thing.

"Let's roll, people." Kate hopped on her bike and the others followed suit.

"It'll be about an hour and a half until our next stop," James explained.

They rode in silence for a while, the only conversation about the road.

"Gravel near the center line."

"Cop at two o'clock."

"Sit. Stay." James pointed at a white sedan pulling out of a side street.

"It's so gorgeous here." Alex didn't know she had said it out loud.

"Right? This is the Navarro River Redwoods State Park," James explained. "It's closed a lot in the winter, so we have to take tours on alternate routes. I like to come through here when we can."

"I can see why," Alex answered.

They drove through a twisty section of road with towering redwoods on each side. It was almost dark from the thick canopy of branches overhead even though she knew the sun still shone above them. The air was damp and cool, much cooler than where they stopped for coffee. It smelled of wet earth with a hint of salt.

"This smell makes me want to create a cocktail," Ross said.

"Every smell makes you want to create a cocktail," James shot back.

"Fair. It's like whiskey but with a salt rim," Alex observed.

"Yeah, that's the right vibe, but ewww." She bet Julia's face was wrinkled up in Melanie's "rude" face.

Alex inhaled deeply, filling her lungs with the refreshing air. She felt the oxygen all the way to her gloved fingertips as they wrapped around Ross on the motorcycle.

Suddenly, the trees ended, and they were at a stop sign looking over the road at the breathtaking expanse of the Pacific Ocean a hundred feet below.

The sun danced on the waves as they crashed on the beach up the coast.

"You okay back there, Alex?" Ross asked her.

"Yes, definitely."

"I thought I heard you gasp."

"You did. It's amazing to see the ocean just jump out at you like that. I wasn't expecting it."

Alex looked out at the ocean in front of her, positioning her head to one side to see around Ross's helmet as they waited for traffic to pass by before turning north.

It was just so huge. The coastline stretched as far as she could see in both directions. Endless. Miraculous. Gorgeous. Awe-inspiring.

She took it all in, the beauty coursing through her body, chasing out the fatigue and filling her with energy.

She was almost vibrating with it when Ross hit the throttle and made the turn.

"Can we stop?" Alex asked.

"Way ahead of you."

She looked straight ahead and saw Rob's blinker on to pull into a small parking lot at a look-out.

Alex hopped off and walked to the edge. She heard rustling behind her but was so engaged in the ocean she didn't look to see what was going on.

"Here." Ross handed her the sandals he advised her to pack and placed near the top of their saddle bags for easy access.

"Thanks." She smiled at him, understanding why he was insistent about the sandals being on top.

They shucked their heavy motorcycle boots, slipped on the sandals, and headed down to the water. Alex watched the waves come toward her, leaving an edge of white foam where they stopped.

The ocean didn't care about action items or money. It just kept coming and going. In and out. Sometimes peaceful, sometimes turbulent. But unrelenting.

Like she needed to be.

Unrelenting in her dreams.

She tuned into the waves, feeling the energy of the water.

Her grandfather spoke of his connection, and his people's connection, to water. In his case, it was the Great Lakes. But in this moment, she felt a profound connection to the waves lapping at her feet.

"I'm going in."

"It's really cold. Be careful."

She rolled up her jeans and walked in up to her knees.

The cold water stung her skin, reminding her she was alive.

She had been numb for weeks at work. Slogging through each day. Going through the motions. Doing what she thought she had to do.

In the water, she could just *be*.

She felt someone take each hand. She looked left and saw Julia. She looked right and saw Kate.

They were in the water with her.

"You okay, Alex?" Julia asked, holding her hand.

Kate squeezed Alex's other hand. "You look like you're going through something."

"Yes, and yes." Alex kept looking straight ahead.

They stood together, holding hands in the water.

Silent.

The water lapping around their legs and the calls of seagulls were the only sounds.

Alex pulled strength from her friends' hands, feeling their support as she worked through her deepest thoughts.

She was Alex the musician. The teacher. The supporter. The storyteller. The Partawatomi, as Pops said.

Pops always told her that a Native person's identity came from how they expressed themselves in music and dance and what they created through it.

This.

This is what Gram meant.

Everything led her here.

Her grandfather's lessons about fire and song and their importance in culture.

The musical ability.

The radio voice.

The project management skills.

She pulled the words out of the values work she did with Julia, visualizing each one as it came to her in big red letters.

Love

Acceptance

Encouragement

Confidence

Teaching

Opportunity

She could combine all of her skills and values and pursue her dream.

She would figure out the money angle over time.

She called out to the ocean, tears streaming down her smiling face. "I know the way, Gram."

The waves grabbed her words and pulled them out to sea.

Chapter 54

The hotel in Westport was modest. James already knew about expensive places and was doing research for cheaper options. The hotel was right on the coast. It was dated but clean.

And the best part was the hot tub with a view of the ocean. Alex was glad Julia told her to bring a bathing suit. She was saddle-sore after several hours on the back seat of the bike.

"Ow, my butt hurts," Alex moaned as she sank into the warm water.

"You'll get used to it. For me, it's the hands. Someday, I'll be cool and get cruise control on my bike. My right hand is glad to be off the throttle." Kate rubbed her hand under the water.

"Limber up, Katiebug. I have plans for that hand later." James wiggled his eyebrows at his wife.

Alex took a moment to appreciate her friends and everything that had happened in her life that brought her right here, right now. Tom would have liked these people.

Julia joined them a few minutes later carrying a large bag.

"I know it was tough to ride by those wineries today, so here you go." Julia pulled out a plate of cheese and crackers and set them near the edge of the hot tub. Then she retrieved six plastic wine cups out of the bag, followed by two bottles of red wine. "These are from The Berryessa Gap Winery in Winters which was the start of our ride and the beginning of the 128 Scenic Wine Route."

"Good choice, Julia. That was the first wine I had from the Winters Highlands AVA even before it was an official AVA." Kate sounded impressed with Julia's wine choice.

"That's the lake we rode by. Cool. Remind me what an AVA is?" Alex didn't know much about wine.

"It stands for American Viticultural Area. It's used to describe a distinctive region of winemaking. You have to have something that sets the area apart. It can be geographic or geologic or even weather-related – something in the soil that affects how the grapes are grown. You'll recognize the names of some famous ones around here like Rutherford, Sonoma Valley, and Howell Mountain."

Alex didn't recognize any of them, but her friends nodded like they knew them all.

"I looked into it. Winters has its own, just granted in 2023. The break in the mountains we rode through near Lake Berryessa creates unique weather in the Winters area. It has warm days and cool nights like the Mediterranean. That's why they focus on grapes from that region. The first wine is the estate grown Petite Sirah - the very grape that helped them get their new Winters Highlands AVA designation."

"Jules, I should hire you to be one of the tour guides." James smiled at her as he accepted his glass.

Kate picked up the thread. "People keep asking me why I chose the town of Winters. Then they come to visit and taste the wine, and they get it."

"And hopefully, hire me to give them a tour," James added.

"To Yolo Moto Tours."

"Julia, does your family own the town or something since your last name is Winters and Kate has a place here? Did you introduce her to this place?"

"Weird, right? But nope. Kate found it all on her own."

Kate added to the story. "Before the pandemic, I visited a friend who lived in Winters and fell in love with the town. When James and I decided to buy a second place, I brought him to check out Winters."

James jumped in. "Sometimes, you just have to take a leap. I was already hooked, but then there was the icing on the cake, or the cork in the bottle, or whatever cliché you want to use. I love to say YOLO! You Only Live Once! And that's the name of the county Winters is in. It was fate, I tell you."

"And now we have friends who come to stay with us. Everyone wins."

Alex accepted a glass from Julia.

Fate, Alex thought, and leaned against the back of the hot tub, careful to keep her wine out of the water.

She took a sip.

The rich, jammy flavor of blackberry and blueberry was followed by a light taste that reminded her of turning wet clay when she was in art class in high school. Almost like the smell near the redwoods earlier that day. "That would be great with steak."

"With steak and bourbon," Kate added, and they all laughed.

Alex sat back and enjoyed her wine.

James had followed his dreams.

Kate had followed hers.

Julia and Ross continued to grind it out at jobs they didn't love but had figured out a way to have it support their goals and values.

It was time for Alex to do the same.

She was still flying high from the thrill of seeing the massive expanse of sparkling ocean on their ride, reminding her that the world was a huge place full of opportunities. She looked out at the ocean again, sending thanks for the inspiration.

Ross took her hand. "Having fun?"

"How could I not? Look at this view."

"Yeah, it's spectacular." When Alex looked up, he was staring right at her.

Ross held up his hands. "I'm pruning up here, so I'm going to head to bed. Alex, are you coming?"

"I'll be in soon. Probably right after you're done with your shower."

"I'm heading in, too." James kissed Kate on the top of her head and hopped out of the hot tub.

"I think that's my cue to leave as well so the three of you can talk about us." Rob followed the other guys out.

Alex, Kate, and Julia watched the three of them walk away. Ross looked back over his shoulder at Alex and smiled.

"He likes you," Kate singsonged at her.

"I like him."

"How did you like the riding today?" Alex appreciated Julia's subject change.

"It was a lot for one day, but after the first fifteen minutes, I really started to enjoy it. And there's something about being on the motorcycle with my arms around Ross all day that I found very appealing."

"Like you're going to be 'a peeling' his clothes off later?"

"Yeah, exactly like that, Julia. He's so confident on the bike and then there was all that vibration of the motor for seven hours. It got me thinking about post-ride activities."

"Look at you! We'll make a rider out of you yet!" Kate sounded gleeful.

"So, you're good for tomorrow, or do you want to stay here and have the guys and Kate pick us up on the way back after we've spent a day at the spa down the street?" Alex read Julia's face as hopeful.

"As tempting as that sounds, I'd like to continue the ride. The scenery is amazing, and we're supposed to ride the Avenue of the Giants tomorrow before turning back for Winters."

"Good choice. It's a spectacular ride."

ALEX OPENED the door quietly in case Ross was already asleep when she got back to the room.

She found Ross and James at the little table in the room reviewing GPS routes from other riders.

"Hey there. Just finalizing the route for tomorrow. We're thinking of possibly splitting up so we can explore more of the backroads."

"How does splitting up help us?"

"I don't have to listen to this guy's constant stream of puns." Ross cocked his thumb at James.

"And I don't have to listen to this guy constantly telling me how much he likes you."

Alex waited for the banter to subside to get the real answer.

"But seriously," James continued. "Pavement quality is a big part of riding. Adventure bikes can handle gravel forest roads, but cruisers have to stay on decent pavement. Sometimes the small roads that seem paved on a map are actually worse than forest service roads."

"And since James, Rob, and I are experienced riders on off-road capable bikes, we could split up and do more reconnaissance for James' business."

"That makes sense. Why aren't you including Kate?"

"Because Kate rides a cruiser. She's a good rider, but she has to stay on pavement because of her bike. And she can't switch bikes because of her adorable, short little legs." James held up his thumb and index finger to demonstrate the size of her legs. "Speaking of Kate, now that you are all out of the hot tub, I'm going to see what she's up to."

"Go get 'em, tiger." Ross swatted James on the butt as he walked out. James didn't even spare him a look.

Alex liked seeing their friendship in action.

"Shall we get ready for bed?" Ross looked at her sweetly.

"Sure."

Ross quickly got naked and turned back to her. "Ready."

"Not quite," Alex said as she looked him up and down. "I'll help you with that."

"I know you will. Ready to see some more big trees?"

They fell into bed together.

Chapter 55

Six days ago, she had stood on the coastline embracing her path forward.

Five days ago, she had called Madou to invite her out for Thursday's show. Madou jumped at the chance to help Alex.

Four days ago, she had resigned from LampLight.

Three days ago, she had prepared her radio show pitch and asked Jeannie for another chance.

Two days ago, Jeannie suggested Alex use Keith's show as her formal pitch to the network of how she would run her own show. They both thought it would be better than a conference room pitch.

One day ago, Madou had arrived.

They had stayed up way too late the previous night catching up after Alex picked her up at the airport.

And today, she and Madou were arm in arm as they walked into the studio for her show.

"You're the real deal now, Alex. Mami and Papi would be so proud of you."

"Thanks, Madou. I wouldn't have gotten here without them. Or you."

"Or Gram and Pops. Let's dedicate the show to them. I hope they're all watching from heaven together."

"Or somewhere together," Alex added. "Definitely together."

Alex took a moment to picture that. Papi's huge comforting hand on Pops' back as their heads came together over a nice glass of Scotch while Mama Rosie and Gram shared cooking tips. She took a snapshot in her mind to take out and look at again after the show. She was glad it was only radio, and she didn't have any make-up to smear with the tears that came to her eyes.

"Ready?" Alex asked Madou.

"Always."

The producer started the countdown. The On Air light flashed on.

"Welcome to Thursday Jazz Jams with a twist of Alex. We're switching it up tonight and will have stories, music, and fun. I'm your host Alex Taylor, and I'm joined by Madeleine Bélizaire our key storyteller, performer, and diva. I have no idea what we'll be talking about tonight because anything goes on this show. It could be music, politics, relationships – g-rated, of course – money. Anything."

They were off and running.

"REMEMBER that obnoxious sophomore bass player, Fred?"

"Fred. I haven't thought about him in years." Alex couldn't contain her laughter.

"Okay, Alex, you're laughing too hard, so I'll start the story. Fred was one of those pompous a – wait – gotta keep it clean here, um… jack rabbits… who thought they could intimidate women by being a sexual predator."

"A gross sexual predator," Alex added. "Let's paint the picture for our listeners. Thick black hair, squinty eyes above pudgy cheeks. Probably about five foot nine. Taller than me, but shorter than Madou."

"Nailed him. I can see him like he's right in front of me." Madou nodded.

"I was seated above him which clearly pissed him off since I was a year behind him. He looked me up and down and said, 'Alex. That's the boy's name. If you're going to be a chick, you could at least have the decency to have big boobs.'"

"I forgot those were his first words to you, Alex."

"Oh yeah. And for one of only about five times in my entire life, I had the right comeback."

Madou interjected. "I would have kicked him in the… um… f-hole."

They both laughed. "For those of you in the audience unfamiliar with the anatomy of a stringed instrument," Alex tried to control her laughter, "the f-holes are the little holes that look like the letter F next to the bridge on violins, basses and other string instruments. They help project the sound."

"Girl, he would have projected a sound if he'd said that to me."

"That makes what I said a lot less funny, which was, 'I didn't realize that breasts were required to play the bass. And that's okay, because you have enough for both of us.'"

It was Madou's turn to laugh. The rich and deep sound bounced around the studio even with the sound attenuation tiles in place.

Alex spoke over Madou's laughter. "Our audience did not tune in to listen to us giggle, so while we didn't rehearse this one, why don't we play *Freddie Freeloader* in his honor?"

"The Miles Davis version in B flat?" At Alex's nod, Madou started vamping on the two-chord opening while she filled in the walking bass line. They played a few choruses and Madou took a hot solo.

"That was Madeleine Bélizaire on the piano joining me, your host, Alex Taylor on bass on tonight's edition of Thursday Jazz Jams with a twist. That was great, Madou. It's so wonderful to play with you again."

"Yeah, it's been a while."

"Madou, as her close friends - which now includes everyone listening - call her, went to music school before jumping onto the New York City Scene in 2010. Since then, she's played on over thirty albums and leads a jazz trio called Jacmel for her mother's hometown in Haiti. You can hear them next Thursday at Birdland in midtown Manhattan. Madou, is there a recording you're most proud of?"

"I'm lucky. I've been able to pick a lot of my projects in the last five years, so I love all of them. But I do have a favorite. My very first album that made any money at all was in 2012. I called it Poppy, like the flower. But it was really a tribute to my father, Papi spelled P-A-P-I."

"Papi. I loved that man."

"And he loved you, Alex." Madou looked at Alex with tenderness. "You played on that album, remember?"

"Of course." Alex's voice sounded dreamy. "I also remember doing it for free because you're my girl and you were broke."

Madou laughed. "I had to pay the drummer though. Otherwise, he wouldn't have shown up."

"What was that cat's name?" Alex wondered aloud. "Oh yeah. Johnny. Johnny May."

"Except that we called him 'Johnny May Show Up' since he had a penchant for skipping gigs at the last minute." Madou got that right, Alex remembered.

"Yeah, but dude could shred."

"And Alex, my dear, that makes up for a lot. That was my first album that made more money than it cost to produce. Once I made back by production costs, I donated the rest of the proceeds to the Foundation Opportunité that my mother and father supported in Haiti. Their charter is to ensure that all children in Jacmel have access to education, regardless of their ability to pay."

"That's so beautiful, Madou."

"I still support that charity. You can too by visiting fondop.org. It's a great cause."

"Let's play one to honor your parents and the charter of FondOP. Now, this might seem a bit self-serving because I wrote it, but it fits. It's called *Class Is in Session*."

"Great tune, Alex. I was there when you wrote it in music school. Let's jam on that head for a while – maybe not the full almost eight-minute version like the original. I'll tell another story about our music school days together while you grab your electric."

Chapter 56

Madou was sleeping in, so Alex stayed quiet. Musicians needed sleep when they could get it. Lots of late-night gigs interrupted regular sleep patterns. She would take Madou to the airport later that morning so she could get back in time for her late Friday night gig in New York.

Filled with joy from her radio success and knowing she had an open spot on her dance card since Adam made his choice to leave, Alex went through her phone until she found what she was looking for: the contact card for Tony Yankovic. She laughed again at his name.

Kate would want her to date him just for that.

She texted him.

> Alex: Hi Tony – it's Alex the bass player, lover of Polka Varieties. Do you ever get to the States?

She hit send and put her phone away. She didn't know if she'd hear back from him, and she was fine either way.

She settled down with a cup of coffee to plan out her next few radio shows.

Technically, she should be finishing her transition plan for her role at LampLight. She would do it later. Michelle had stopped speaking to her once she gave notice anyway.

"OH, Madou. It was so great having you here. Thanks for supporting my show."

"You thanking me? Please. A trip paid for by a radio station and a chance to support and jam with my girl? I'd make that choice every damn time."

"Next time in New York."

"And you won't believe it. I sold twenty albums in the last fifteen hours." Madou held up her phone to show Alex the good news.

"That's great!"

"Yeah it is, but they were all downloads of Poppy. That album is twelve years old. I've sold maybe one a year since the next one came out in 2013. That was all you and your show. Just for shits and giggles, I checked in with FONDOP. There was a spike in donations right after the show. Over three thousand dollars in five- and ten-dollar increments. It's like people liked the show so much, they supported the causes that were important to your friends."

"No way. That's amazing."

"Because you're amazing. Next time, talk about Gram's Recovery Center and your mom. Find a guest who's recovering from addiction. That'll make a great show and help you raise money for Gram's passion project."

"Holy shit, Madou. I think you just saved my life."

"That's a bit drastic."

"That was a really big piece of the puzzle that was missing. If I can leverage my voice to amplify marginalized musicians while raising money for good causes, walking away from LampLight was a good decision. I have to be super careful with my money now that I dismantled my safety net, but I could make money for the Recovery Center and other great organizations through my show." Alex stepped back, stunned at the power of the moment.

Madou took her by the shoulders.

"Wasn't that your plan all along? I saw the dullness in your eyes when you talked about working at LampLight. I see the fire and passion when you play and talk about music. Remember Pops. Willam Flying Eagle. You are of the fire people. Be the fire. The fire that lights the way."

Julia told Alex that when she heard her life's purpose, it would feel right.

It was there all along in what Pops taught her.

The words burned into her heart.

"I am the fire that lights the way."

"Damn straight, girl." They embraced one more time before Madou headed into the airport.

Chapter 57

Alex let Sibby out when she got home to her delightfully human-free house. The dishes she and Madou left were still in the sink. There was no dog hair on the sofa. Peace.

Her phone buzzed with an incoming text. Tony.

Tony: I didn't know you were famous

Alex smiled. He must have listened to her show online. She now had the freedom to flirt and more with him.

Alex: I wasn't when I met you

Tony: And I was nothing before I met you

Alex: Ha ha

Tony: I just hooked up with Cirque du Soleil's international tour. I'll be in Seattle in October. Can we get together?

Alex: Congrats! I'd love that.

Having indulged in her break, Alex went to her home office and opened the transition plan document.

She looked at her action item tracker, feedback tracker, strategy document template, and every other deliverable she had created. She had come a long way in strategy and program management in her four and a half years at the company.

She was happy to be closing the LampLight chapter of her career but was a little sad to turn off the managerial part of her brain she had worked so hard to develop.

She would still be able to use it to manage her show. She would keep those skills fresh, knowing she might have to tap into them again if another global health disaster struck.

That was another thing that made her nervous. She'd have COBRA benefits for eighteen months, but they were still expensive, and the radio show wouldn't pay much initially. If the show could sustain the Recovery Center, she took on twelve students, and gigged every night, she'd be okay.

She kept telling herself that.

Another incoming text pulled her out of her worries.

Adam.

She hadn't heard from him in weeks, not since he told her he didn't want to share her.

Adam: Heard you on the radio last night - amazing

Alex: Thanks Adam. Nice to hear from you

Dots appeared to show he was typing and then stopped. She got back to her transition plan. She was almost done for the day and had a celebration planned with Ross.

A few minutes later, her phone buzzed again.

Adam:I miss you

Alex smiled. She had really missed their chats. She appreciated the way he pushed her and wanted him to share in her success.

Alex: Right back at you

More dots without a response. She wondered what he was struggling with. Something he wanted to say but couldn't figure out? She decided to give him a nudge.

Alex: Want to get tacos on Tuesday, regular time and place?

Adam: Yes :)

Maybe he didn't want to have a physical relationship, but he still wanted to be friends. She was good either way and was happy he was back in her life.

It was time to take Sibby for a walk and wait for Ross to pick her up.

This time, there was no guilt.

Everything was out in the open and she was free to do what she wanted. Even with two, maybe three, maybe even four men. She didn't have to settle or fantasize about taking parts of each of them to make one perfect partner.

She could pick which one she wanted based on what was happening in her life in that moment, each playing a different part.

She smiled as she reached for Sibby's leash and the dog went crazy. Alex's shoulders dropped a couple of inches as she envisioned releasing her previous stress.

It felt good.
Really good.
Like she was the fire.

361

Chapter 58

When her student Dylan left his lesson and Betsy was on her way in, Alex made a note that she had to advertise additional teaching slots. She needed to start making more money. As much as she wanted to dedicate that time to the radio program, she needed the cash.

Alex was glad to see that Jeannie was following Betsy in. Since they only did electric bass now, Betsy could handle the equipment by herself in one trip, so she saw less of Jeannie.

"Good morning, you two."

"Good morning!" Betsy was her usual ebullient self. Alex loved her energy. "I listened to you on the radio on Thursday."

"What did you think?"

"I was glad you were already my teacher so I can go on your show when I'm famous."

"Betsy, everything about that answer makes me happy."

The fire that lights the way, Alex thought.

"Me too," Jeannie added. "Before I go Alex, I wanted

to let you know a few things. The most important is that our Friday programming review meeting yesterday was buzzing with excitement about your show. Our idea to use that show as your pitch totally worked."

Alex had apparently gleaned some marketing as well as strategy skills from her time at LampLight. "I was a little nervous they would be upset I used some of the airtime to push a different charitable organization." Alex planned on broaching that subject with Jeannie as part of the conversation about next steps. Now was as good of a time as any.

"It had the opposite effect."

"I don't understand." Alex was confused.

"They want you to be our new Philanthropy Officer."

"I would know how to answer if I knew what that was." Alex was puzzled, her eyes narrowing as she tried to figure it out.

"I forget you aren't a radio person – you fit in so well with the group. Your job would be to build meaningful connections with the top donators to the station. The role requires a broad range of skills – passion for radio, interpersonal skills, a strategic mindset, attention to detail, program management, and the ability to manage lots of egos. We haven't been able to fill it because it requires such a broad skillset."

"You basically just described my role at LampLight."

"I know. And here's the best part. I know money has been holding you back from being all in with the radio program. I mean, you almost said no back in the beginning because of some mysterious financial commitment. It took me a while to put two and two together and figure out that you needed a job. You could have just asked me. This position has been open for months."

"I didn't know that was an option." *Like grandmother, like daughter*, Alex thought.

"Alex, there's always a way. You just have to ask for help sometimes. The job is a thirty-hour a week job which means it comes with benefits, but you'll still have time for your music, teaching, and the program."

Alex tried to catch up quickly, but she couldn't quite believe it. "Are you saying I would get the money for planning and doing the show plus the salary and benefits from this job? A job that I would basically volunteer to do?"

"That's exactly what I'm saying."

"That's wonderful, Jeannie. I'm speechless!"

"Let's hope you don't stay that way. We have big plans for that voice and your show. I know a whole network of people at other stations who are interested in how your program develops. I've been talking about you."

"I can't thank you enough, Jeannie. You're doing so much for me."

"You don't have to thank me. I get paid back every time I hear this one play a new bass line." She jerked her thumb at Betsy. "We have to stick together. Girl power!"

Betsy fist-bumped her mother.

Alex had a flash of inspiration at their connection. "I have an idea about a show where we interview people like you, Jeannie, who weren't able to become musicians when they were kids but started later in life. Maybe you could be a 'before and after' story where we follow you along as you turn your childhood dream of being a drummer into reality."

Jeannie's eyes welled up. "Are you serious?"

"Yeah, in addition to starting my big band, I could coach a band of adult beginners. A super safe environment to learn together." Alex thought about the culture of Steak and Bourbon. She could bring that to music.

"That sounds amazing. Ever since Betsy's father and I broke up, I've been meaning to connect more with other women and dust off some of those childhood dreams before it's too late."

"I'm part of a super-supportive group of kick-ass women. I'd love to have you join us for brunch and see if you love them as much as I do. How do you feel about steak and bourbon?"

"The food doesn't matter if there's friendship, safety, and female energy."

"You just captured the spirit of the group, Jeannie. We'd be excited to have you join."

"I'd love that. I'll get out of your hair, but I just have to say I know you have a bright future ahead of you, Alex. I can't wait to watch how famous you're going to become and the positive impact you'll have on musicians everywhere."

The fire that lights the way, Alex thought.

"You're not going to get too famous to be my teacher, are you?" Betsy sounded concerned.

"Never." It was Alex's turn to fist bump Betsy. "Girl power."

Epilogue

Six months later

"We'll all be there for your show tonight."

Alex looked around the table at her Board of Directors. "Thanks ladies. All of you played a role in getting me here. Thank you."

"A musical pun! You've been spending too much time with James." Kate winked at her.

Brie gestured to Alex with her drink. "What's your plan for tonight?"

"I'm doing what I call a full spectrum program. It'll alternate between two bands, all of whose members identify as female. The first is made up of professional musicians and is called Girl Power." Alex pumped her fist. "The second is the band I started for adult beginner musicians. It's called *Bodwadan*.

"*Bodwadan*? That's beautiful, Alex." Brie cocked her head. "What language is that?"

"It's the language of the Potawatomi tribe."

"Her grandfather's tribe," Madou added. She was sitting in at Steak and Bourbon before being featured as a special guest with the band that night.

"That's right, Madou. They were the keepers of the fire. He told me *bodwadan* means 'the fire she lights.' It's here on the necklace he gave me when I left for college." She held up her grandfather's gift. "I chose that name to honor him, my native American heritage, and the musical fire each new musician is lighting in their souls."

"Fuuuuuck. That's deep, Alex." Gertie pointed at the bumps on her arm. "I just got chills."

"I wonder if that's where Padawan comes from?" Everyone looked at Kate. "Sorry, it's the name of an apprentice Jedi."

"Then you know I wouldn't understand it." Alex smiled at her friend.

"Do the bands train together, like Jedis?" Kate was fixated on the Jedi thing.

Alex chose to humor her. "Assuming for a moment that Jedis are real…"

"Jedis are real! We have some at this table." Madou, Jeannie, Gertie, Angela, and Akiko raised their hands. "See?" Kate pointed around the group.

"Thank you, Kate. Yes. The beginners get to work with the professionals and follow the light they create with their music. I'll interview people during the show from each group about their journeys."

"And I'm one of the interviewees from the beginner band." Jeannie bounced in her chair. "She recorded one when I first started six months ago, and then last month, and the third installment will be tonight. I'll talk about how I wanted to be a drummer when I was a kid, but I didn't have support to do it. Alex came along and lit the fire in me to start."

"The fire that lights the way." Julia fell back in her seat. "Alex, that's the life purpose statement you wrote, right?"

"I didn't write it. When I looked at what motivates me and my values and what I want to do with my life, it came to me, like I recognized it, and it just fit. It was there all along. I just wasn't listening." Alex looked at Madou who smiled back at her.

Jeannie was on a roll. "And *bodwadan* is a really powerful word to say. We start each rehearsal by yelling *bodwadan!* together. We're so loud. It sounds like a war chant."

"These chicks are serious." Alex nodded.

"Makes me want to join." Margaret raised her glass at Jeannie. "Is drinking allowed during rehearsals? Do you need back-up dancers?" They all laughed.

Gertie scratched her head. "What if your grandfather was wrong, and it actually means, like, flammable pajamas. Or is it inflammable? I never know." Alex saw Angela raise an eyebrow at Gertie. It accurately reflected her response as well. "Sorry. Deep emotion makes me uncomfortable."

"Whatever it means, or whatever it might also sound like, to me it means living my life's purpose by lighting the fire that shows others the way and then letting them burn even brighter."

"We'll be burning hot tonight." Madou jumped in. "We'll begin with one of my favorite Mingus tunes, *Moanin.* It starts with a kick-ass baritone sax part that my friend Gail will lay down for us. The second tune is also called *Moanin'* but it's the Art Blakey tune with the same name. He was well known for playing with and encouraging young musicians even after he was really famous. Two versions of the same title."

"I get it. The spectrum." Lesley nodded. "Nice."

Jeannie picked up the thread. "And Art Blakey was one of the most famous drummers ever. I've always loved his music, so it's fun to have my radio debut playing one of his tunes. It's a beautiful connection, just like connecting my job at the station with performing on the station." Jeannie waved her hands at her face as her voice broke. "Sorry, I get really emotional when I talk about it."

"Music does that to you," Madou said from across the table. "Sarah Vaughn took the original instrumental and added lyrics."

"That Angela will be singing tonight." Alex added.

"I'm not exactly a beginner, but I've never sung lead for a real audience – just at Kate's karaoke parties. This group has given me the confidence to go for it." Angela's smile lit up her entire beautiful face.

Alex sat back to soak it all in. She felt the love and support from everyone at the table.

Just what she needed to bolster her confidence for that evening.

ALEX WAS at the studio getting ready. The small live studio audience was filing in. She saw some of the Steak and Bourbon ladies in the front row, and waved to Akiko, Melanie, Margaret, and Lesley. Brie and Colby were behind them.

She looked around at the professional big band she had put together. Some were friends from music school who needed the gig. Others were from the local Seattle scene. The band was tight. Her girl Catherine was on the drums. They locked into the pocket on every tune and anticipated each other's fills like they had played together for years even though it had only been months.

She had learned that about playing with more women as part of this program. Women listened to each other more. They weren't just waiting for their next solos like a lot of the guys Alex had played with. There was a cohesion in this group unlike anything she had felt in other bands.

She saw Adam come in with a woman.

She spotted Ross sitting with Kate and James.

Cameron was there, too, on the other side of the studio, with their mutual friend from Tom's former company.

She felt like Tom was there, too, cheering her on.

Alex heard the ding of an incoming text. It was the accordion player from Paris.

> Tony: Break a leg tonight, Tiger

> Alex: Thanks, babe! Looking forward to seeing you again in March

> Tony: Perhaps sooner somewhere, my love

Alex laughed out loud. He always tried to sneak in the name of a cheesy accordion tune or polka. This time it was *Somewhere My Love*.

Julia and Rob took their seats next to Gertie, Paul, and Angela's husband Jeremy.

The live broadcast was set to start in five minutes.

The producer asked for quiet on the set.

Alex flipped on her headset microphone to address the crowd.

"We all need help to make our dreams come true. There are a few people I'd like to thank before we hit the air. First, my grandparents who taught me there was always a way to follow my dreams. Second, to Madou

Bélizaire and her parents for their love and support. Madou is on keys tonight." Madou waved to the crowd.

"Next is Jeannie Newkirk who gave me the opportunity to get this journey started and is playing drums tonight." Jeannie waved her sticks from the other side of the studio.

"That's my mom!" she heard Betsy yell. The audience cheered.

When the noise died down, Alex continued. "To all my friends here tonight and around the world. She smiled at the crowd, eyes landing on Adam, Cameron, Ross, Jeremy, Colby, James, and Rob.

"To the young musicians, especially girls, out there, wondering if you can do this, too. You can." Betsy let out a whoop whoop.

"And lastly, to my Steak and Bourbon crew who encouraged me to go for it and supported me from when we first met through the death of my husband Tom, right up to this moment."

The ten women jumped to their feet and hooted and hollered, some in the audience and some on the stage. Madou and Jeannie joined them, feeling the power and support of the women of Steak and Bourbon.

"Thank you to everyone on the crew here as well as in the bands. Tommy, I know you're listening. Let's do this."

The applause died down as the producer gave the countdown.

This, Alex thought, excitement filling her with electric heat. She took three calming breaths as she watched the producer's fingers. Three, two, one.

The On Air light went on.

"Welcome to *The Edge*. I'm your host, Alex Taylor. Some like to have a battle of the bands, but we're doing it differently tonight, girl style. Two incredibly supportive bands here to inspire you and get your heads bobbing. The first is a group of professionals. The other, beginners just starting the journey with their instruments. The next time someone tells you that you do something like a girl, remember this and say thank you. Hit it ladies."

Right on cue, Gail started wailing on the first few notes. The deep rich sound of her baritone sax filled the studio. After a couple of solo measures, she started the melody of the tune with the famous three-note opening. Then the next six note figure. Alex touched her necklaces as the drummer picked up the beat. Alex leaned in and dug into the quarter note driving rhythm to support them.

She saw the audience start to move their heads with the beat.

The rest of the band joined in, each nailing their part and playing together like they were one body.

It was like lighting a match and watching the flame build into a roaring fire as the intensity of the music grew. *Bodwadan.* The fire we light.

There's always a way, Alex thought, and bathed her soul in the music they created together.

The end

About the Author

Laura Preslan worked in the technology industry for thirty years leading teams, delivering successful projects, and coaching colleagues through tough situations.

She found many of the same political and people-based issues at every company she worked at as a consultant, advisor, or employee from start-ups to Fortune 100 companies.

This experience influenced her goal to create a new genre of women's fiction written by and about powerful female executives and the unique challenges women overcome at work and at home.

When asked why this vision is important to her, Laura said, "So many of us have compelling stories to tell about terrible toxicity we have conquered at work and how we found balance at home. None of us are going through this alone. With courage, creativity, and self-awareness, we will succeed in work, life, and love. I encourage all of us to write our stories (fictionalized, of course) and support each other. The more we talk about it, the better things will be for those who come after us."

Find out more at http://www.laurapreslan.com or http://www.mysteakandbourbon.com